A Deadly Game

Joanne Griffiths

Print ISBN :978-1-912175-31-4

For my Children Loren and Hannah

Prologue

Wiping the condensation off the bathroom mirror with the sleeve of her shirt, Kate Palmer stared at her reflection for a few seconds before letting out a deep sigh. She didn't like what she saw – her eyes were puffy and bloodshot from where she had been crying and an angry-looking spot was about to erupt on her chin.

She attempted to apply a fresh coat of mascara but once again she felt the tears begin to well, spilling hot and warm down her cheeks. Taking a wad of used tissue from her pocket, she quickly dabbed at her eyes before blowing her nose on the rapidly disintegrating bundle.

'How could I have been so stupid?' she muttered to herself. It was a question that she had asked repeatedly over the last few days. In her wildest dreams, she had never expected her life to turn out like this.

Kate was a bright, talented artist, with a promising future ahead of her. She was popular amongst both her tutors and peers at the university she attended, due to her warm, friendly, easy-going nature. Despite this, Kate was often plagued by deep-seated insecurities, lacking self-confidence in both herself and her abilities. Not that anyone would have guessed, mind; she was very good at hiding her feelings from those around her.

Looking back, her insecurities had probably stemmed from a period of relentless teasing during her early teenage years – her acne, her braces, her flat chest – all considered fair game by the boys in her year. However, by the age of fifteen, she had started to blossom and her natural beauty began to shine through. Her insecurities still lingered though and Kate's last year at school was a difficult one, not helped by the breakdown of her relationship with her father.

Her father.

She thought about him for a minute.

They had what could only be described as a strained relationship and hadn't been close for some time now. Over the years they had had some pretty heated arguments as Kate tried to assert her independence whilst her father tried to assert his authority, laying down the rules he expected her to abide by. Her poor mum would often find herself stuck in the middle, trying to appease both sides, yet failing miserably.

It was not a happy time for any of them and so it was with some relief all round that Kate had chosen to move into the halls of residence at the start of her first year at university, rather than commute, as her father had originally wanted. Although he would never admit it, Kate knew it had been the right decision for all of them. Still, things change, and now all she longed for was the security of home, for the days where there was no pressure, no financial worries and no responsibilities.

Just thinking about home caused another fresh wave of tears and she let out a loud sob as the enormity of her situation played out before her. Kate knew she had messed things up this time, knew her father wouldn't be happy when he found out. She could already imagine the look of disappointment in his eyes and it hurt that she had let him down. Trying to control her sobs, Kate placed the mascara she was holding on the edge of the sink and pulled off some fresh toilet tissue to mop up the tears.

Why had it all gone so wrong?

Kate had had so many hopes when she first arrived on campus at BCU and had enjoyed her first year – making new friends, going to parties, nightclubs and the student bar. Birmingham was so different to Alvechurch, the village where she had spent most of her childhood, and she loved it. That all changed though, once she had finished her first year of study. She could no longer stay in the halls of residence, and had to look for student accommodation away from the hustle and bustle of the campus.

It would probably have been easier if Kate had taken up the offer to house share with some of her fellow students, but she was determined to have her own space. She soon found herself a small, one-bedroom flat on a run-down housing estate in Newtown, a short bus journey away from the Perry Barr campus. The flat had come fully furnished, although the furniture had clearly seen better days, and whilst the decor was not to her taste, she knew that she would soon have it feeling like home.

It was a lot harder than she had imagined. Permanent work that fitted in with her studies was hard to come by and, even though she had access to student loans, paying the rent, the utilities, buying groceries, as well as paying her university fees and buying course materials, was a struggle. Before she knew it, Kate had found herself in a situation that was spiralling out of control.

She had finally made up her mind though. Tomorrow, Kate would call her mum, tell her that she had decided to drop out of uni and wanted to come back home – at least until after Christmas – then she could figure out what to do next. She just hoped her mum would understand, or at least support her decision. It would make facing her father that bit easier, knowing her mum was on her side.

Wiping her eyes one last time, Kate picked up the mascara again and carefully applied a final layer, hoping that no one would notice she had been crying. Another quick touch of powder to her cheeks, a coat of lipstick and a final brush of her hair, then Kate was ready to leave. She would sort it all out tomorrow and, while she would never be able to tell her parents everything, right now, more than ever, she just wanted to be back home with her family.

Chapter One

Tick-tock. Tick-tock. Tick-tock.

He listened intently to the rhythmic sound of the kitchen clock, noticing how it had fallen in step with his heartbeat.

Lub-dub. Lub-dub. Tick-tock. Tick-tock.

He felt as if his heart was going to burst right out of his chest, it was racing that fast. He could feel a knot tightening in his stomach, the anticipation of what lay ahead pulsing through him. Still, he needed to calm down, needed to stay focused. Shifting in his seat, he let out a low sigh to try and suppress how he was feeling.

'Are you OK?' his wife asked, a slight quiver in her voice.

Had she noticed?

'How long until dinner?' he responded, gruffly.

'It's nearly ready. I'm just sorting Emily.'

'Well get on with it. I want to go out.'

She was about to reply but perhaps thought better of it. Instead, she turned her attention back to their daughter, scraping the last of the pureed mush from the bowl to feed her, before offering a drink and wiping the remnants from Emily's hands and face. That done, Alison carefully eased herself up from the chair and set to, busying herself at the hob.

As she began to stir whatever was simmering in the saucepan, he silently watched her from behind the newspaper he had been reading. Shoulders hunched, her left hand shifting between holding on to the countertop and pushing a stray strand of hair back behind her ear, she was clearly in pain.

It was her own fault though.

1

He had wanted a cup of tea this morning and she was meant to bring it upstairs to him but didn't, which of course made him angry. It was the excuses – Emily this, Emily that – well, what about him? Before he knew it, he had punched her hard in the fat doughy mound of her stomach, causing her to fall backwards into the corner edge of the dining table.

He knew immediately that he had hurt her, more than he had intended, judging by the way she had cried out, but she shouldn't have wound him up the way she did. He hated Alison so much, almost to the point that even being in the same room as his wife disgusted him lately. She used to be so petite, so pretty, but ever since she found out she was pregnant with their daughter she had let herself go, gaining so much weight during the pregnancy that it physically repulsed him.

After the birth, everything suddenly revolved around Emily. She was too tired to dress up for him, make any sort of effort for him, or do any of the things they used to, even down to their physical relationship. At first she had made excuses to avoid any physical contact but he soon laid down the law as far as that was concerned. Still, they no longer made love like they used to. Now she would just lie there like a beached whale while he satisfied himself, so in his mind it was hardly surprising that he went looking elsewhere. If she did what she was supposed to, he wouldn't be going out tonight.

'Ah, tonight!'

He had thought about it for so long and now that it was nearly here the excitement was beginning to overwhelm him.

Alison placed a bowl of bolognese on the table in front of her husband, and was about to turn when he grabbed her wrist. 'Put Emily in her cot,' he ordered.

She knew what that meant, knew what he wanted. Without a word, she turned to do as she was told whilst her husband began eating his dinner.

* * *

Laura's heart sank as it started to rain – a fine drizzle at first, before falling heavier and faster within a few minutes of starting. Pulling her jacket tighter against the biting wind, the young woman ran towards her usual shelter. It was not turning into a very good night; it was cold, it was wet, and she was so tired, she felt as though she could fall asleep on the spot. Laura stamped her feet to try and keep them warm and rubbed her hands together, wishing she had worn gloves and a thicker coat. She felt utterly miserable and if it wasn't for the fact that she needed some money, she would not be there.

Tears pricking at her eyes, she quickly grabbed some tissue from her bag and wiped them away. The last thing she needed right now was to start crying and so she turned to focus on the graffiti that adorned the Perspex glass of the bus shelter.

'Gizzo waz ere'

'Becca luvs M'

A brief smile flickered at the corner of her mouth.

That was better.

She wondered if M reciprocated Becca's love. Did he know that the girl loved him or was he oblivious to her feelings? Maybe it was a she – Mary? Michelle? – and Becca didn't know how to tell her. An image of a young girl in her navy blue school uniform popped into her head, causing her to smile again. There she was with her closest school friends, making their own declarations of love with permanent markers. All of them laughing and talking excitedly about what they would do at the weekend, with Laura wondering if Danny Hargreaves would finally ask her out as she drew childlike hearts around their initials.

Laura sighed at the memory of happier times. Life was so much easier back then. Of course, her younger self probably wouldn't have agreed with her but compared to how things were now, she would give anything to go back, to change the mess she had made of her life and start over.

Letting out an involuntary shiver, Laura decided to call it a night. As much as she needed the money, the rain was getting heavier and the likelihood of anyone picking her up now was pretty slim. Not only that, the stench of stale urine and discarded food from the local takeout was making her feel nauseous again, but it was the only enclosed shelter here and she didn't fancy standing out in the rain. No, she would call it a night and head for home.

'God it's cold. I'm glad I put my knickers on!'

Laura instantly recognised that thick Black Country accent and quickly turned round to see her friend standing at the entrance of the shelter. She was happy to see her and it must have shown on her face as she went over to give her a hug.

'How long have you been here?' Pat asked.

'Not long,' Laura replied, a deep sigh demonstrating how fed up she was. 'I think I'm going to call it a night though. It doesn't look like this rain will let up.'

'Are you all right, chick?'

Laura knew how much Pat worried about her and she was touched by it. They had been friends for a few months now, looking out for each other, sharing a joke or two while they waited for the next punter to drive by; had even grown to care for each other, despite having separate lives away from the streets. Neither of them intruded on the other's private life, knowing they all had their secrets, their reasons for doing what they did.

Blinking back tears, Laura dismissed her friend's concern, told her she was fine, just tired. She could see that Pat didn't buy it, but she was relieved that the woman didn't carry on probing. She had been a good friend and Laura would miss Pat – a lot – but she had made up her mind, she was turning her back on this life. As of tomorrow, Laura was going to start afresh, away from the city, where no one would ever know how she had ended up in such a mess.

'Damn it.'

He was too late.

He pulled into the lay-by and thumped hard on the steering wheel. He could feel a black cloud begin to descend.

'Damn it! Damn it! Damn it!'

He had thought about this moment all day, wondering if he would be able to go through with it, *actually do it*, and now the anticipation, the excitement which had been steadily building, had quickly been replaced with feelings of anger.

Clenching his fists so tightly that the knuckles instantly turned white, he began lashing out, hitting the door, the dashboard, the steering wheel, before letting out a low frustrated sigh and burying his head in his hands. For a few minutes, he just sat there like that, listening to the splatter of rain on the roof mingling with the sound of his breathing; short, sharp, angry breaths that caught in the back of his throat.

The disappointment he felt once he had calmed down caught him by surprise. This wasn't how he had planned his evening but if she wasn't there what else could he do?

He started the car and decided to have one more drive around the island just to make sure before heading back towards the city centre. He spotted something out of the corner of his eye – two people standing in the bus shelter. Almost instantly, he felt on edge.

Was that her?

He wasn't entirely sure, thanks to the rain pinging off the windshield preventing him from getting a clear view, but he was suddenly hopeful that maybe he wasn't too late after all.

She obviously wasn't alone though.

'Shit!'

Should he risk it?

For a split second he wasn't sure what to do.

The scenario he had played over and over in his mind didn't involve anyone else being there and the last thing he wanted was to risk being caught, but then again, he had been waiting for this moment all day; he didn't know if he could back out now.

Perhaps he should take another drive past, see if it really was her, before deciding what to do next.

Driving round the island once more, he headed towards the bus shelter, slowed the car and pulled up a short distance ahead.

The rain was finally beginning to ease off, enabling him to watch in the rear-view mirror as the women had a brief conversation before the younger one started walking towards him.

As he watched, he could feel himself starting to perspire and his heart rate increased. A nervousness was building in the pit of his stomach and he found himself gripping the steering wheel tightly with both hands, trying to calm himself down.

He lowered the passenger window as she reached the door; he knew that getting her into the car would be the easy bit. Carrying out his plans would be a bit more difficult, but he was ready and the anticipation now was electric.

Alison lifted herself gingerly out of the bath and positioned herself carefully in front of the mirror so that she could take another glance at the purple etching that had spread angrily across her lower back. Biting her lip to stop herself from crying, she felt a desperate sadness as she contemplated what her marriage had become, how her husband treated her.

They had been married for two years now and although her husband had been married before, for Alison it was the fairy tale she had always dreamed of. Despite the registry office wedding, she still wore a full bridal dress and everyone commented on how stunning she looked. She felt it too, had worked hard on maintaining her figure, knowing how much her husband-to-be admired her petite frame.

They had soon settled into married life, Alison doting on her husband. Older than her, he had always valued a traditional home so whilst he went out to work, she played house, cooking and cleaning and being there for her husband when he returned. As much as Alison adored being a wife, it didn't take long for her to start feeling broody and before she knew it, she was expecting. Alison was so excited when she first found out that she was pregnant; however, something had changed with her husband. Out of nowhere, their relationship became strained and suddenly he was hostile, distant at times. Having a baby was meant to bring them closer together and yet, for some reason that she was unaware of, the pregnancy just seemed to push them apart.

Once her daughter was born, their relationship took a dramatic turn for the worse. During the pregnancy, her husband would pick fights, say some awful things to her, particularly about the weight she was gaining, and it had hurt Alison that her once loving husband could be so cruel. After Emily was born though, his rants turned to physical violence.

Alison could still remember the first time that he had hit her; how scared she had been as he flew into a blind rage, lashing out and knocking her to the floor. He was full of remorse afterwards, swore that it would never happen again and she had believed him, had genuinely thought that it was a one off – until it happened again, and again.

Every time he hit her he would apologise and every time, Alison forgave him, did her best to make their marriage work. Found herself treading on eggshells to avoid setting him off. After this morning, though, Alison didn't know how much more she could take.

It wasn't just the physical abuse, although that was bad enough, but the emotional abuse he put her through on a daily basis, constantly putting her down, chipping away at her self-esteem, was just as hard to take. Almost daily now he would tell her how fat she was, how disgusting she was, how much she repulsed him, and the venom in his voice as he hurled those awful things at her was devastating.

The trouble was, Alison didn't even know if she had the strength to walk away. A couple of months ago, following a particularly nasty beating, she had considered going to the police, telling them what he had done, but she was scared. Scared they wouldn't believe her. Scared to raise Emily on her own. Scared of what her husband would do to her if she tried to leave. Scared that he would carry out his threat to hurt Emily if she ever tried; maybe he wouldn't but what if he did? She had to protect her daughter at all costs, even if it meant keeping quiet and doing what he wanted.

She thought back to earlier this evening. Her husband had wanted sex and she knew better than to refuse him, despite the pain she was in. Although why was anyone's guess, given how much he constantly told her how sick she made him feel. On top of that, Alison had convinced herself that he was seeing another woman, which did nothing for her self-confidence. The signs were there: more than once he had come home smelling of perfume and no doubt he was there with her now, laughing, joking and being silly, just like they used to before she found out she was pregnant.

Hearing her daughter stir, Alison grabbed her robe and tightened it carefully around her waist before going into Emily's room. She couldn't give herself time to think about what her husband was up to. She just hoped that he would be in a good mood when he came home later as she couldn't handle any more of his abuse, not tonight.

Chapter Two

Checking his reflection, he ran his fingers through his hair and straightened his tie before glancing at his watch. He was going to be late if he didn't get a move on. One last look in the mirror and he was ready. At forty-one, James 'Jim' Wardell still had a youthful sort of charm. His hair, thick and brown and slightly ruffled, added to his good looks, but it was his piercing hazel eyes that drew people in, mesmerised by their intensity. There was a sadness surrounding him lately, though. He tried to hide it, but it was there, etched on his face.

Jim had not exactly had a privileged upbringing. Born to working-class parents in Brampton, South Yorkshire, his childhood had been tough but his parents believed an education would see him through and made sure he worked hard at school, despite the difficulties they faced at home. He was never university material, but he had an uncanny way of processing information, solving puzzles and recalling data, so it came as no surprise to anyone when he announced he was going to join the police force – a decision he had never regretted.

Jim had spent the first half of his career working the beat in South Yorkshire, first in uniform and then as a detective, before moving down to Nottingham where he had joined Operation Vanguard, a task unit set up to tackle gangs, guns and drugs. He was happy in Nottingham, was good at his job, earning him a promotion to detective sergeant. Then he met the love of his life, Vanessa, and they were married within a couple of months of meeting. Despite their whirlwind romance, life was pretty good and Jim quickly settled into married life.

Happiness, however, was only short-lived. Within a year their marriage was over, as Vanessa had not only met someone else, but also moved out of the marital home. With too many memories there, Jim had applied for jobs outside Nottingham, securing a role with West Midlands Police as part of their Murder Investigation Team based in Aston. It was a challenging role but one Jim threw himself into, to try and forget about Vanessa and how much she had hurt him. She was often on his mind though and he would find himself wondering what she was doing, where she was, who she was with, if she was happy. During the long nights at home, he would torment himself by replaying over and over what she had said the last time he saw her. Accusing him of working too hard or, if he wasn't at work, then he was always talking about it, thinking about it, neglecting her in the process. The venom with which she had thrown these accusations had stung and yet he knew it wasn't true. He had adored Vanessa and didn't think he would ever get over her.

Ironically, it was his work that now helped him get through the week, especially since he'd started covering the night shift. Keeping busy gave him less time to think about his ex-wife and, although the hours were unsociable, they suited him. Picking up his phone and car keys, Jim headed towards the front door. The cold gust of wind that hit him as he went to step outside saw him reaching back in for his coat. It was going to be a cold one tonight but, with any luck, he would be spending it in the office, catching up on paperwork.

'Oh my God! Oh my God! Oh my God!'

He let go of the rope and stood up and, with trembling hands, readjusted his clothes. His eyes were fixed on the pale, lifeless body that lay on the wet grass, searching for any small sign of life. Her eyes, wide open, glazed, were staring up to the sky, and yet they were empty. He looked to her chest, watching for the rise and fall that would signal she was still alive.

Nothing!

Small beads of perspiration settled on his forehead as he realised he had finally done it. There was no going back now, she was *definitely* dead, and it gave him such a tremendous high, a feeling of euphoria that he had never experienced before. At that moment he felt strong, powerful, invincible. He knew that the image of her lying on the ground would stay with him forever and a slow, cold smile of satisfaction began to work its way across his face. This, however, was soon replaced by a sense of urgency as he realised he needed to get away before anyone spotted him.

He could feel the adrenalin begin to course through his veins now, increasing his heart rate and causing cold, clammy, damp patches of sweat to form, which spread from under his arms and trickled down his spine. He quickly bent down to scoop up the girl's panties, placed them in the pocket of his jacket, took one final look at her body, then turned and ran – almost as if his own life depended on it.

By the time he reached the car, his heart was pounding through his chest and the back of his throat burned as he gulped in the cold night air. Struggling to catch his breath, he frantically searched his pockets for the keys and a brief feeling of dread washed over him before he remembered he had left them under the driver's seat.

As he started the car, the only thing on his mind was putting as much distance as possible between himself and the park. Driving carefully to avoid attention, he made his way down the backstreets, heading towards the city centre. He was still fearful of being caught but, as he reached the other side of town, he began to relax a little.

The evening had finally worked out the way he had planned it and he felt on top of the world. Once again a smile spread across his face as he thought about what he had just done, and he knew then that he wanted more, wanted that same sense of euphoria he had just experienced and he wasn't going to let anything – or anyone – stand in his way.

* * *

By the time Jim Wardell arrived at Aston Lane Police Station, it was lashing down with rain. The wind had also picked up, causing the rain to bounce off the tarmac, soaking the bottom of his trousers. With no umbrella at his disposal, Jim was thankful that at least he had had the good sense to grab his coat when leaving the house. He draped it over his head, which afforded him some cover from the rain as he quickly walked from the car park to the staff entrance at the back of the station. It was becoming an increasingly cold and wet night and Jim hoped it would be a quiet one.

He strolled into the deserted office, hung up his coat and made a beeline for the coffee machine that sat bubbling on the opposite side of the room. Jim filled a mug with the sweet nectar, hoping it was hot enough, and added a couple of spoonfuls of sugar. No milk though, he preferred it black and strong. He took a mouthful and smiled to himself. He had his priorities in order and his routine at the start of each shift was almost second nature by now.

Coffee.

Check the rota to see who was on shift with him.

Check the in tray on his desk.

Many of the detectives assigned to the Murder Investigation Team covering Birmingham West and Central worked regular office hours, with only a skeleton staff covering anything called in overnight. The night shift was not a popular one, so it was often the same few officers working ten until eight. Glancing at the rota now, Jim was pleased to see that he would be on duty with Angela Watkins again. He liked Angie and they had got on well together over the last few months since she had transferred from uniform to plain clothes. She was still finding her feet within the MIT but she was extremely bright and willing to learn. It also meant that Jim would be the Senior Investigating Officer if they were called out to anything this evening, as he had the higher rank and would need to take control until his inspector arrived at the scene.

It wasn't the only reason he liked Angie. She had a smashing figure, a cute face and long blonde hair, natural rather than bottled, which really suited her, although she always had it tied up at work. Jim was physically attracted to his colleague, enjoyed her company, but after everything with Vanessa, he had always behaved with the utmost professionalism whenever they worked together.

'I could do with a coffee.'

Jim looked up, watching as the young woman who had just entered the room began shaking off her umbrella into the wastepaper bin before discarding it on the floor. Smiling to himself, he filled another cup, adding milk this time, no sugar.

'It's freezing out there,' she continued as she hung up her coat, then, nodding towards her desk, 'that mountain of paperwork is beginning to look very appealing.'

Jim laughed as he walked across and handed Angie her coffee. The paperwork was definitely looking appealing tonight.

Chapter Three

Just after midnight a 999 call came through to the force control centre. A woman had been found in Aston Park, believed deceased. The operator took details and a patrol car and an ambulance were directed to the scene.

By the time Jim had received the information death had already been confirmed, and, as they pulled up outside the entrance to the park, he already knew they would be dealing with a murder enquiry.

Stepping out of the car, Jim took in his surroundings. There was a grammar school situated to the left of the entrance. Would they have CCTV? he wondered. It was something he would make enquiries about later. In front of him, an iron bar blocked cars from entering the park after hours and this was still locked. To the right, a muddy pathway led into a wooded area where the body had been found. This was now cordoned off with police tape, guarded by two uniformed police officers. The ambulance was still at the scene, although there was nothing more they could do, having confirmed loss of life; a few onlookers had gathered, probably due to the flurry of flashing blues. The freezing temperatures and ungodly hour didn't seem to faze them as they stood watching what was unfolding. At least the rain had stopped.

Jim took a cursory glance at the group of onlookers to see if there was anyone they perhaps needed to pay closer attention to. He spotted the dishevelled, slightly balding middle-aged man standing a few feet away from the rest of the crowd, talking to a police officer. Was he the witness who had found the body? The officer with him was taking notes so Jim was hopeful that, whoever the man was, he would have something useful for them.

Making a mental note to speak with the police officer later, Jim turned his attention back to the crime scene. He went to the boot of his car and grabbed the protective gear he needed to wear before he could go anywhere near the body. Angie was already suited, notebook in hand, awaiting her instructions.

'Are you ready?' Jim asked. Angie nodded before following her sergeant as he made his way towards the cordon. Showing their warrant cards and confirming their names to the uniformed officer protecting the scene, they then slipped under the tape and walked over to where the woman had been found.

It was clear, as soon as he saw the body, that this was a sexually motivated crime. The woman was lying on her back, her skirt hitched up, leaving her naked from the waist down. Her shirt had been ripped open and her bra pushed up to expose her breasts. There was no other underwear in the immediate vicinity, which made Jim wonder if it had been removed by whoever had committed this crime.

Jim put on plastic gloves and squatted down next to the dead girl, then lifted her hair away from her face and examined the rope that was still loosely wrapped around her neck. There was evidence of bruising both above and below the rope and, although cause of death would have to be established by the forensic pathologist, with no other obvious signs of injury Jim surmised that she had been strangled.

'She's only young, poor kid,' Angie observed, her voice cracking with emotion. 'There are some sick bastards out there.'

'As soon as the Forensic Support Unit get here we are going to need a detailed search, hands bagged, rape kit, photographs, the works,' ordered Jim. As much as he agreed with his colleague's sentiments, emotion had no place in the investigation and he couldn't let Angie get sidetracked by it either. 'For now,' he continued, softer this time, 'just detail everything we see and don't miss anything out.'

He knew Angie was right though. The girl was only young, probably around eighteen or nineteen, and had had her whole life ahead of her. She hadn't deserved to die like this, to be exposed to whoever happened to come across her body, or the police officers who now had to deal with this crime. 'Yes, whoever had snatched this girl's life away was one sick bastard,' he thought, vehemently.

The arrival of Detective Inspector Goulding and the FSU jolted him from his thoughts. As forensic technicians began erecting the tent, Jim's inspector took a quick look at the body before addressing him.

'What have we got, James?' he asked, brusquely.

'Cat one, sir. Young girl, possible rape, cause of death most likely strangulation.'

'Have we got an ID? Witnesses?'

'Not that I'm aware. I believe there's an officer with the man who found her but I haven't got any details yet. As far as I know the body hasn't been searched. There's no immediate form of ID though, no bag or purse near the body.'

'Right. I want you to take the lead on this for tonight. Get an incident room set up, secure the contact details of the man who found the body and get FSU to scan for prints so we can try and identify her.'

'Sir.'

* * *

Waving his hand in dismissal, Inspector Goulding then made his way back towards his car. Watching him leave, Jim wasn't at all surprised that his inspector had asked him to take the lead on this tonight. The man was nearing the end of his service, and he no longer had the same level of stamina as his younger officers. At fifty-five he was probably starting to feel his age as well as looking it. His hair was receding whilst his gut expanded and he had mentioned quite a few times now, that his knees were beginning to show signs of arthritis, slowing him down – especially when it was cold. Jim imagined that he was not exactly pleased at having to attend the scene, but then a category one murder required the presence of a senior officer, so he didn't have much choice, really. Still, at least for now, the inspector had left him in charge of the investigation, so Jim would do what he could until he handed the case over to his colleagues in the morning.

Chapter Four

Sensing his wife had got out of bed, he opened one eye to look at the alarm clock.

Five thirty.

Despite the early hour, he didn't feel tired, which surprised him really, as he hadn't slept much last night, what with everything that had happened running through his mind. He still couldn't believe that he had *actually* done it, had finally carried out his plans.

In the other room he could hear Emily crying and Alison trying desperately to placate her. She knew he hated being woken up by their daughter crying. At least she slept through more often than not, now. It had been awful when she was first born. Alison had chosen to breastfeed which meant that their daughter was waking up every two hours or so during the night. After putting up with it for a few weeks, he had insisted that Emily went into her own room. Of course, his wife wasn't happy about that but she eventually saw things his way and did as she was told.

Reaching over, he went to pick up a glass of water from off the bedside table but a sudden pain just under his collarbone stopped him in his tracks. He looked down and saw three long scratches from where the bitch had tried to fight him off. Her nails had been sharp and this morning the scratches were looking red raw. A slight trickle of blood was forming at the edge of one of them where he must have just caught it, so he grabbed some tissue to stop the blood soiling the sheets, then reached down for his t-shirt from off the floor, quickly putting it on before his wife came back into the room. He couldn't risk her seeing it.

When Alison did come back in, he could tell that she was on edge.

'Has she gone back to sleep?' he asked.

'Yes. I'm sorry if ...'

'Good,' he replied, lifting the quilt up for her to get back into bed. He could tell by the tone of her voice that she was worried at how he would react, having been woken up, but he ignored it.

Alison appeared relieved that he seemed to be in a good mood and quickly got back into bed. 'I'm sorry,' she began. 'I tried to ...'

'Don't worry. I couldn't sleep anyway,' he replied, reaching across her to turn on the radio, before resting his hand on the top of her leg. He felt her flinch as his hand made contact with her bare skin, which had annoyed him and he was about to comment when the news came over the radio.

'*Body of young woman found in Birmingham park. Police treating it as suspicious. Appealing for witnessed to come forward.*'

So, they had found her.

Turning his head, he couldn't help but smile but then quickly regained his composure before his wife noticed anything.

She was talking to him again, something about a cup of tea. Tea was the last thing on his mind though. He turned back towards his wife and began stroking her thigh before leaning in to kiss her, much more passionately than he had in a long time, no doubt taking Alison completely by surprise.

Chapter Five

Thanks to modern technology – and a shoplifting charge when she was eighteen – the deceased was soon identified with the use of a fingerprint scanner and so, later that morning, Jim and Angie were making their way over to her last known address in a village called Alvechurch, roughly forty minutes to the south of Birmingham. A search of the electoral roll that morning had confirmed the house they were travelling to belonged to her parents, who had no idea of the heartache awaiting them.

Turning into the quiet cul-de-sac, Jim slowed the car until he pulled up outside number twenty-five. The front garden of the house was very well presented – a small square of lawn, a well-kept privet bordering the neighbour's garden, and a decorative block-paved driveway leading up to a front door that looked warm and inviting.

Jim didn't get out of the car straight away, just switched off the engine and sat there, knowing he was about to give two people the news that no parent should ever have to hear. Despite his shift ending a few hours ago he had volunteered to make this journey but, now they were here, he did wonder if he should have left it to someone else to break the news.

'Are you OK?' Angie asked after a few minutes.

Jim glanced across at his colleague. Wearily, he rubbed at his eyes with his hands and let out a heavy sigh before replying, 'I wish I didn't have to do this. They've no idea what's coming.'

One of the hardest jobs for any police officer was breaking the news to relatives that a loved one had passed. You could think of all the ways you might tell them but you just never knew how they would react. Would they break down, lash out, collapse?

'Come on,' he said after taking the keys out of the ignition. 'Let's get this over and done with.'

He opened the gate and they walked up the driveway. Jim had noticed the flicker of the TV through the window so at least there was someone home, and it didn't take long for the door to be opened once he'd knocked. They were greeted by a smartly dressed middle-aged woman.

'Can I help you?' she asked pleasantly, no hint that she was aware they were police officers.

Jim cleared his throat. 'Are you Mrs Palmer?'

'Er, yes,' she replied, a slight edge to her voice now. 'How can I help you?'

Jim took his warrant card out of his pocket and showed it to Janice Palmer, introduced both himself and Angela, then asked if they could step inside. Concern registered on the woman's face and she looked at him, clearly trying to process what he had just asked.

'Is your husband at home, Mrs Palmer?' Jim continued, then, taking charge of the situation, he stepped up to the door, again asking if they could go inside and guiding the woman back into the house. As they entered, a man, who Jim assumed was her husband, appeared in the hallway.

'Who's this?' he asked, his voice strong, confident.

'He said they're police officers, Brian. They want to talk to us about something but …' her voice trailed off.

Jim showed his warrant card to Mr Palmer then suggested they all go into the lounge and sit down.

Sharing concerned glances, Brian and Janice led the way into a room off the hallway. Brian switched off the TV just as the upbeat theme to *This Morning* began to play, then sat next to his wife on the sofa, waiting to hear what the officers wanted.

Whilst Angela stood just inside the door, Jim also took a seat, cleared his throat and came straight to the point.

'Mr and Mrs Palmer, I'm … I'm afraid we have some bad news. Early …'

'Bad news? What bad news?' queried Brian Palmer, interrupting Jim mid-flow.

Janice took hold of her husband's hand.

'What do you mean, bad news?' she asked, her voice breaking slightly.

'Early this morning,' Jim continued, 'a body was found in a Birmingham park and we believe it is your daughter, Kate. I'm very sorry.'

The reaction was almost instant.

'What? Kate? No! *Noo!*' Janice exclaimed, panic now echoing in her voice.

'What do you mean, you believe?' asked her husband, his voice calmer, almost as if he hadn't registered what Jim had just told him. 'So you don't know, you could be mistaken?'

'I'm sorry, sir, we checked her fingerprints against those held on file. Obviously, until a formal iden—'

Janice let out a high-pitched scream and started sobbing uncontrollably.

'No! No! No! No! No!'

The woman was inconsolable; she snatched her hands away from her husband's. Although Angie stepped forward to try and offer some comfort, there was nothing she could say that would ease the woman's pain.

In stark contrast, Brian sat staring at the fire as the flames bounced and flickered in the grate. He didn't seem to notice the loud piercing sobs coming from his wife, perhaps because he was trying to comprehend what Jim had just told him.

'There must be some sort of mistake,' he said when he finally did speak. 'Why would my daughter's fingerprints be on a file? What file? It must be someone else's daughter. Kate's fine, she has to be.'

'I'm so sorry,' Jim reiterated. He could hear the pain in Brian's voice, even if the man did doubt what he had just been told.

Through her tears, Janice demanded to know how her daughter had died.

'There's no easy way to say this,' he replied, knowing that he had to tell them before they heard it through the media or someone else, 'but, we are treating her death as suspicious. We found her …'

'*Noooo!*' she screamed again, louder this time, before slumping to the floor. 'Please God no. Not my baby.'

The emotion in the room was raw and as hard as Jim found it to deal with, a look at Angie's face told him that she was finding it even harder so he asked her to go and make the Palmers some sweet, hot tea. Tea was always good for shock and doing something practical would also give her time to compose herself again.

By the time Angie had made the drinks and brought them back into the room, Brian and Janice Palmer were both sitting back on the sofa, holding on to each other as if their own lives depended on it. The woman's uncontrollable sobs had subsided but she was still clearly grief stricken. Knowing he needed them to focus, Jim waited until they had been given their tea, then, clearing his throat, he turned his attention to the father.

'We, er, we need a recent photo of your daughter, Mr Palmer.'

'Yes. Yes of course.' The man nodded.

'Did Kate have a boyfriend? Perhaps you have a list of friends we could talk to?'

Again the man nodded, but made no effort to find the information Jim needed.

'We also need one of you to go to the morgue to identify the body.'

This last request often brought a glimmer of hope, the possibility that they had got it completely wrong, that it wasn't their daughter after all, but Jim had to impress on them that it was just a formality – there was no mistake.

Pain and sorrow hung in the air as the parents had to come to terms with the fact that their daughter had died a most horrendous death and there was nothing Jim could say that would offer any comfort. From that moment on, their lives would never be the same again.

* * *

While Jim Wardell was breaking the news to the victim's parents, Detective Inspector Goulding was standing outside the press room at West Midlands police headquarters, waiting for journalists and camera crews from the various news agencies to set up their microphones and cameras so that they could hold a press conference.

It was hot and stuffy in the building so Goulding constantly sipped at a bottle of water he had brought with him. He didn't enjoy this part of the job, even though he wouldn't be the focus of attention for long. Still, the last thing he needed was a raspy voice when everyone was ready for him to introduce his senior officer.

Detective Chief Inspector Alan Jones would officially be heading the investigation whilst deferring to Goulding, who would oversee the day-to-day running of the case as well as allocating officers to the various tasks that would hopefully enable them to solve this awful crime.

As far as the press conference went, Alan Jones was well versed in how to handle the journalists who were now impatiently waiting for information about the discovery of the body. He had taken part in many such conferences over the years and was comfortable in front of the camera, unlike Goulding.

As the press officer signalled that they were ready to begin, Goulding took one last sip of water, cleared his throat and walked into the room behind his senior officer to a flash of camera bulbs. The noise was quite deafening. He sat down and waited for everyone to settle before beginning.

'Ladies and gentlemen, first of all, thank you for attending today. I am sure you have lots of questions but I need you to be mindful of the limited information we can give at this stage. With that said, I would like to introduce you to Detective Chief Inspector Alan Jones, who will be leading the investigation.'

Immediately, focus switched to the charming, grey-haired man also seated at the table.

'Thank you all for coming,' Jones began, his voice holding an edge of authority. 'At approximately 12.05 this morning, the body of a young female was discovered within a wooded area of Aston Park. Due to the manner in which the body was found, we are treating this as a murder investigation.'

Once again, cameras began flashing; DCI Jones paused until they had settled.

'The victim has been identified,' he continued, 'but obviously, we are unable to release the name of the deceased until next of kin have been informed. We are seeking witnesses who may have seen anything near the vicinity of the park in the hours preceding and immediately after the discovery of the body and would urge them to come forward, either by calling the incident room or by calling Crimestoppers,' he gave the appropriate numbers, 'where they can speak to someone in confidence. Obviously, this is a shocking crime and we are asking for the public's help to catch whoever is responsible.'

Again he paused as a murmur went round the room, and then held up his hand to signal that he hadn't quite finished. 'We have got time for a couple of questions,' he stated once the room had quietened down, 'but due to the fact that we are still in the early stages of the investigation, I hope you understand that I may not be able to answer all of them.'

A young woman at the front of the room identified both herself and the agency she represented before asking what was on everyone's mind.

'Was this a sexually motivated crime?'

'We need to keep an open mind until the post mortem has been conducted, but the way in which the body was found would suggest that it's a strong possibility.'

'Do you have a cause of death?' asked a man seated towards the back of the room.

'We can't issue a formal cause of death until after the post mortem, I'm afraid. Can I take one more question,' he asked, pointing to a young man with his hand raised.

'Was she killed in the park?' he asked simply.

'At this stage we don't know where she was killed, and that is why I would reiterate that we are urging anyone who saw anything in the hours preceding midnight on the twenty-sixth of November to come forward. Thank you.'

With that, both officers stood up and made their way towards the door whilst another flurry of camera flashes lit up the room.

Chapter Six

Within two days of that initial press conference and following formal identification of the body, Kate Palmer's identity, as well as the preliminary cause of death, was released to the media.

On that Saturday morning, many of the national newspapers ran with the story on their front pages. A recent picture of Kate along with dramatic headlines left the reader in little doubt as to what had happened. It was such a lovely photo as well. A young girl, full of smiles, her face radiant, wearing a pale yellow off-the-shoulder bridesmaid dress. She appeared so happy, looking directly at whoever held the camera, that the image would leave a lasting effect on many people who saw it.

In Alvechurch, the Palmers always had a newspaper delivered on Saturdays. No one had thought to cancel it and now Brian was sitting at the bottom of the stairs staring at a picture of his daughter smiling back at him. It was a copy of the photo he had given to the police the other day, taken at her cousin's wedding back in August. A picture where she looked so happy, so relaxed and carefree, with the sun shining down on her. It had been a good summer, one where they were finally starting to build on their relationship again. Kate had matured a lot since starting university and was doing so well that he was hopeful they would carry on building bridges. Now, though, he had to accept that he would never see her again, that this was all very real.

Of course, he hadn't believed it at first and was sure there had been some sort of mistake, but once the family liaison officer had taken him to the morgue to identify the body, straight away he knew it was Kate lying there on the hospital gurney. He broke down, lost it completely, so much so that the next couple of hours were still a bit of a haze. Walking back into the house, seeing Janice standing there in the hallway, the hope fading from her eyes as he nodded confirmation, was just too much for him to bear and he felt unable to reach out to his wife as her world came crashing down around her.

Brian knew Janice was struggling, and he did feel guilty for not being there for her, even when she had cried late into the night last night, but he couldn't offer any comfort. In all honesty, he felt so distraught, so helpless that he had withdrawn and they hadn't spoken much at all since he had got back from the morgue. What could he say, anyway? Nothing would bring Kate back, ease Janice's pain, and so he shut himself away, leaving his wife to seek comfort from the array of visitors who had called to offer their condolences since the news broke.

At least he could hide the newspaper before his wife saw it. It was hard enough for him, seeing his daughter there, reading the reports and, as much as the family liaison officer was keeping them informed of everything that was happening, having the details of his daughter's death there in black and white hurt more than he could ever have imagined.

* * *

Over in Rubery, Emily had been fractious all morning thanks to a particularly difficult tooth trying to break through her top gum. Not wanting to disturb her husband, Alison had taken her daughter out for a walk in her stroller. It had done the trick as by the time they got back home, she was fast asleep. Leaving her daughter in the stroller, Alison settled herself at the kitchen table with a pot of tea and a newspaper she had picked up during their walk. The front page had the word 'STRANGLED!' emblazoned across the front with a picture of a pretty young girl underneath.

Alison was saddened at what she read. How could someone do that to another human being? It was such an awful thing to happen that she couldn't even begin to imagine how she would feel if that was her own daughter.

'What are you reading?'

Alison turned round and saw her husband standing in the doorway. She hoped he was in a good mood. His voice gave nothing away but he had been more caring, loving even, the past couple of days.

'About the girl who was murdered the other night. There's a picture of her in the paper this morning.'

His heartbeat suddenly increased as his wife held up the front of the paper and he felt excited by the report.

Would she notice?

'She was only twenty, had her whole life ahead of her,' Alison continued, oblivious. 'Her poor parents.'

'It's shocking,' he agreed, walking over to the table to pour himself some tea.

A small smile began to play at the corner of his mouth. She had absolutely no idea that he was responsible and it excited him, but, more than that, it was all over the news and *no one* had a clue that he was the man they were looking for.

He put his cup on the table and started whistling as he grabbed some bread and placed it in the toaster. He felt unusually upbeat this morning, which no doubt surprised Alison but she didn't question why, she was probably just relieved that they had not argued since the other night.

Watching her now, engrossed in the newspaper report, he couldn't help but wonder what she would say if she knew the truth and it was all he could do to stop himself from laughing out loud.

In Lozells, Patricia McCormack was desperate for a cup of tea so was just a little annoyed with herself that she had run out of milk. She threw a pair of trackies on over her pyjama bottoms and a thick padded jacket to protect her from the bitterly cold winds, and headed off to her local newsagents. She wasn't expecting anything out of the ordinary but, as soon as she entered the shop and saw the newspapers with their dramatic headlines, she knew something was very, very wrong.

Grabbing one of the papers off the stand, Patricia could feel her anxiety rising as she tried to process the information contained in the article.

'*No!*' she cried out, causing the newsagent to look across at her.

Instinctively her hand rose to her mouth to try and stifle the cry that had escaped, but by now the tears had started to stream down her cheeks as a wave of grief washed over her. Struggling to breathe, she needed to get out of the shop, needed to think. Dropping the newspaper to the floor, she hurried outside, ignoring the newsagent's concerned enquiries, and headed back towards the safety of her home.

Her mind was racing as she tried to make sense of it all. She had heard on the news about the girl in the park but she didn't, not for one minute, think it might have been her friend.

'Why? Why her?'

The grief she felt was threatening to overwhelm her and she was openly sobbing now, oblivious of the attention she was getting from passers-by. Not that she cared anyway, all she could focus on was getting back home.

By the time she got there her hands were shaking so much that she struggled at first to get the key in the door, but once inside she rushed to switch the TV on, hoping to catch the local news.

'There *has* to be a mistake.'

There was no mistaking the picture of the girl though. Through her tears, she heard that the police were conducting a murder inquiry, believed the victim had been sexually assaulted, was found in the early hours of Thursday morning in Aston Park. Shaking her head, the woman suddenly realised that she might have been the last person to see her friend alive. This realisation brought a fresh wave of pain and tears and guilt – guilt that she had not been there for her, had not protected her, had waved her off as she got into that car with whoever had probably killed her, and guilt that she had felt jealous of her friend that night.

What time had she got in the car?

What colour was it?

She couldn't remember.

She hadn't seen her friend after that but it was raining and she had left to go home. Why hadn't she waited?

'Anyone with any information is asked to contact the incident room at Aston Lane CID.'

That last piece of the news report jolted her from her thoughts and she quickly sat down on the sofa. A heavy sinking feeling was starting to grow in the pit of her stomach. How could she? People like her didn't go to the police – didn't trust the police – and yet she had information. Information that might catch the bastard who had killed her friend.

Chapter Seven

The Monday following Kate's death, Jim arrived at the station just after eight o'clock. It felt weird being back on day shift but this case was now a priority. The incident room they had set up was already bustling with officers working on the case. Despite this, he felt disheartened; they were still no further forward in their investigation. It had been four days since Kate's body was discovered in the park and they had no tangible leads, despite several appeals for information through the various media sources.

On Saturday, officers had gone to her flat in Newtown where they had to break in as it was fully secured, but there was nothing suspicious to report, no signs of a struggle or any evidence that she was killed at that location. Jim briefly wondered where her keys were because they hadn't been found with the body.

'What was she doing in Aston Park? Was she meeting someone? Did they have her keys? What about a bag, money, bank cards?'

He had asked himself these questions, and more, over the last couple of days, but so far there were no answers, no one who had come forward to offer an explanation.

Jim grabbed a coffee and settled himself at his desk. He picked up the one signed witness statement they did have.

George Lawrence, the man who had found the body, had willingly come into the station to be interviewed. According to Goulding, he had been very cooperative; however, Jim felt there was something about him, something he couldn't quite put his finger on. Perhaps it was because he hadn't conducted the interview himself, but there was something niggling away at him.

Reading through, he noted Lawrence's explanation as to why he was in the park that night; he said in his statement that he had been in the grounds of Aston parish church because he liked to sit among the gravestones. Apparently it was peaceful, gave him time to think, but it was also bitterly cold, had been raining, and all of Jim's intuition was telling him that it didn't make sense.

The man lived on Bevington Road so he was cutting through the park to go back home when he found the girl. Mentally running through the route Lawrence would have taken, Jim could see it was plausible, so why did he have that nagging doubt that something wasn't quite right?

He dropped the statement back on his desk, wearily rubbed at his eyes and let out such a deep sigh it raised a few glances from his fellow officers.

'You OK, Jim?' Angie asked, a look of concern on her face.

He was about to answer when Goulding walked into the room.

'You look busy, James,' he muttered sarcastically as he walked up to Jim's desk.

'Was just going through George Lawrence's statement, guv,' Jim replied. 'I want to go and see him this morning. Something doesn't sit right, not sure why exactly, call it a hunch, but there's something I can't quite put my finger on.'

'A hunch, eh? He seemed OK, quite cooperative when I interviewed him.'

'I would still like to pay him a visit, go over his statement again. Maybe we missed something.'

An awkward silence ensued whilst Goulding considered the request, but he finally gave his approval before retreating into his office, leaving the officers to continue with the investigation.

The smell of cigarette smoke hung thickly in the air, strong and pervasive, made worse by the fact that the windows had been closed and the curtains drawn since Saturday. Not that she had noticed the smoke or the lingering smell of stale sweat that clung to her clothes.

Since she had seen her friend's photo in the newspaper she had hardly slept, hadn't showered, brushed her teeth or changed her clothes. Chain-smoking and endless cups of coffee had got her through the last forty-eight hours; everything else had just seemed to stop. She recalled over and over the last time she had seen her friend, what she could have done, what she didn't do. She had felt overwhelmed with guilt and despair and sadness.

It still didn't make sense though. Her photo, the clothes she was wearing, it was all in the paper, but then ...

She kept thinking back to what she had heard on the TV. 'Anyone with any information is asked to contact Aston Lane CID.' She knew she owed it to her friend to go to the police and although it had not been an easy decision, she had finally made up her mind.

She finished her cigarette and headed for the bathroom. She couldn't go looking like this. It was bad enough that they would judge her but she was damned if she was going to give them something else to look down on. Still, no matter how hard it was, she had to tell them.

A quick phone call to the caretaker at Aston parish church before he left the station proved fruitless; there was no CCTV covering the ancient graveyard and therefore no proof that their witness was there that night, as he had claimed.

Jim had doubts over George Lawrence's witness statement. There was something about him, about his explanation for walking through the park, that didn't make sense. For that reason, he wanted to re-interview Mr Lawrence and, rather than call him into the station, Jim decided that it would be better to talk to the man in his own home, where he would feel more comfortable.

As he knocked on the door of Lawrence's flat, Jim's first thought was that the place seemed as dishevelled as their witness was. Nets hung at the windows, but they were grey and dirty and didn't sit right. Weeds had free rein in the small overgrown front garden and it was clear from the smell that cats used the area as their own personal litter tray.

Giving the door a second knock, Jim was starting to regret his decision to interview the man at home and hoped that no one was there, but he could now hear shuffling inside and someone walking towards him. Groaning inwardly, he waited while the person on the other side rattled keys into the locks and opened the door slightly, as far as the security chain would allow.

'Mr Lawrence,' said Jim brightly, holding out his warrant card and pointing it towards the crack in the door. 'I'm Detective Sergeant Wardell. I need to ask you a few questions about the other night, if that's OK. Do you mind if I come in?'

Looking at the card, the man nodded before shutting the door and removing the chain so that he could open it fully.

The smell from inside hit Jim full force as soon as he stepped up onto the threshold. There was a mix of stale rubbish, cats who also seemed to have free rein of the flat, and stagnant water from a bucket placed just behind the door that added to the stench. There were also piles and piles of old books and newspapers, precariously balanced on top of anything and everything, making Jim regret his decision to interview George Lawrence at home even more.

'I haven't had chance to tidy up yet.'

'Not to worry,' Jim replied as they walked into the sitting room. This room was even more cluttered than the hallway so Jim was pleased to find a wooden kitchen stool clear of debris and immediately asked if he could sit there, to which George agreed.

Perching on the stool, Jim declined a drink and waited for the man to settle himself, light a roll-up and take a swig of tea from a heavily stained mug before he began.

'As I said, Mr Lawrence, I just wanted to ask you a few questions, go over your witness statement with you, in case you had forgotten something about what you saw the other night.'

'Have you caught him yet?' the man asked.

'Not yet, no.'

'It didn't half give me a fright,' Lawrence continued, 'seeing her there like that. I knew she were dead right off. I could tell, see.'

'How could you tell?' asked Jim. 'Did you touch her?'

'What, no, I ...'

'To check for a pulse, I mean,' continued Jim, aware that George Lawrence was getting flustered at the question.

'Ah, right, no,' he stated, calm again. 'The way she was lying there and her skirt up ...'

Jim could sense embarrassment at this piece of information so decided to change the line of questioning before it went off course. He was determined to find out whatever it was that George Lawrence was hiding.

'OK, let's go right back to the beginning,' he said, his voice calm, pleasant. 'What were you doing in the park?'

'Like I told that other fella at the station, I was in the graveyard, looking at the gravestones.'

'How long were you there for?'

'I don't know. I can't remember. A while I s'pose.'

'It was raining that night, wasn't it?' asked Jim.

'I like the rain. Don't bother me. So I was at the graveyard, looking at the headstones.'

He was getting agitated now, fiddling with his tobacco tin, so again Jim changed track.

'Talk me through what happened after you left the graveyard.'

'The grass was wet because of the rain so I walked under the trees. I did't see her at first but then there she was, on the floor, just lying there.'

'You went over to her?' It was a question more than a statement but, for some reason, George Lawrence took it as an accusation.

'I had to check in case she was, I don't know, hurt or something,' he replied, an edge of anger to his voice.

Jim nodded, noticing the question had set George Lawrence on edge. There was nothing to link him with Kate Palmer's death, not at this stage, other than the fact that he had found the body, but he was certainly becoming a person of interest. Leading the interview, Jim continued. 'And you never touched the body?'

'No!' the man exclaimed, his voice slightly raised. He stood up, clearly finished with Jim's questioning. 'We done now?'

'Yes, of course, for now,' Jim responded. 'Just one more thing, did you see anyone else in the park, before you found the body?'

'No one,' George Lawrence replied as he headed towards the door. It was clear he no longer wanted to talk to Jim and was eager to get him out of the house.

Once they were back on the doorstep, Jim turned to the man, still trying to keep the conversation friendly. 'Well, thank you for your time, Mr Lawrence. I will be in touch if we have anything further.'

'I told you what I know,' was the response, before the door slammed shut and Jim was left on his own outside. The fresh air was a welcome relief after the time spent in George Lawrence's flat and he breathed it in. Jim was even more convinced now that their witness was hiding something, but what?

Would Lawrence submit to a DNA test? He wondered.

As he opened his car door he looked back at the flat and could see the outline of George Lawrence in the window, watching him. Jim decided that it would be prudent to do a thorough background check to see if the man had a record of any sort.

Inside the flat, George Lawrence stood at the window waiting for his visitor to drive off. He didn't like the way he'd been questioned, and in his own home too. He wondered if they knew and that's why the detective came, but then surely he would have mentioned it? Either way, George was on edge. Once he was sure the car had gone, he leant behind the sideboard and pulled out the small black bag. The money had long gone but the other contents were still there – keys, ID card, a bus pass, lipstick, tissues, condoms.

He needed to get rid of them, quickly, before that detective came back again. They wouldn't believe he had simply found the bag and had just forgotten to hand it to them. No, they wouldn't believe that at all, but there was no way they were going to pin her death on him.

Chapter Eight

As he drove back into the car park at the police station following his visit with George Lawrence, Jim spotted a woman loitering outside the front entrance. Puffing nervously on a cigarette, she looked like she had been crying. He didn't pay that much attention to her – he was still thinking about the morning's visit and the niggling doubts that, if anything, had only increased since he had spoken to the man who found Kate's body.

Back in the office, Jim settled down at his desk to run a search on George Lawrence through the police database. He wasn't sure what he would find but there was something about the man he just couldn't shake off.

It didn't take long.

George Lawrence had quite a history of trouble with the law in his youth, mainly petty theft and an assault charge, but nothing following a brief spell inside during his early twenties.

'Reformed character?' Jim thought.

There was nothing in his background which would suggest George Lawrence had committed this awful crime, but Jim wasn't ready to give up on him just yet and made a note to ask his inspector if they could request a DNA sample. Hopefully Lawrence would readily agree to it but there was nothing Jim could do if he refused – they had no evidence against him.

As he jotted a few notes in his pocket book, he was interrupted by the shrill of the telephone.

Jim listened as the sergeant at the front desk informed him that a woman had come forward with some information about Kate Palmer. They had no idea what it was; she had insisted on speaking to the officer in charge of the case and no one else.

Filled with a renewed sense of hope, Jim quickly made his way downstairs to the witness lounge. The woman had apparently been very nervous as she had approached the front desk so she was shown through to the lounge rather than into a side room, which would hopefully put her at ease. It didn't seem to be helping though.

Pausing outside the door, Jim stood watching her for a few seconds through the small glass window. This was the same woman he had spotted outside the police station earlier. From her demeanour, it was obvious to Jim just how nervous she was about being there.

Briefly, he wondered how she knew Kate Palmer. All she had told the desk sergeant was that they were friends, but that was an odd match as far as Jim was concerned. He knew he was making a judgement about the woman but she had to be in her thirties at least, was slightly overweight, with poor skin, given the outbreak of angry-looking spots on her chin and forehead, and bottle-bleached hair that did not look its best. In contrast, Kate had been young, petite, well groomed.

Still, the woman was clearly upset considering how red and puffy her eyes looked and the frequency with which she took a tissue from the sleeve of her cardigan to dab at them and wipe away fresh tears. Jim knew he would need to keep an open mind and he silently chastised himself for judging the woman. He reached for the door handle and made his way into the room.

The room they had shown Pat into was not at all how she had imagined it would be. The interview rooms she had seen on the telly were stark and depressing whereas this room was light and airy, with flowers in a jug, magazines on a coffee table, and a sofa with oversized cushions. It was a pleasant room, considering where she was, and yet she still felt on edge, just by being there.

Despite chain-smoking several cigarettes before entering the building she was desperate for another; however, the 'No Smoking' sign was clear. This left her at a loss for what to do with her hands, other than to keep wiping them down the sides of her cardigan; they had suddenly become moist and clammy.

By now, her anxiety levels were through the roof and waiting for the detective in charge to come and talk to her had made her feel even more anxious, especially as he seemed to be taking forever. Pacing up and down behind the sofa, she could feel the sweat beginning to pool in her armpits and across her forehead. She caught a whiff of her body odour and wished she had brought some deodorant with her.

Trying to curtail the rising panic she felt as she waited, Pat was beginning to think that she had made a mistake in coming to the police station after all and was just contemplating walking out when she heard the door open.

'Patricia McCormack?'

Without looking up, Pat nodded.

'I'm Detective Sergeant Wardell,' the man said by way of introduction. He seemed friendly enough, although that didn't really help ease her discomfort. He was, after all, still a police officer, still the enemy.

'Thank you for coming in today,' the detective continued. 'Can I get you a drink?'

Pat didn't acknowledge him. She was desperately trying to fight the urge to rush past him and out of the door, but then the image of her friend flashed before her and she knew she couldn't let her down again.

After no more than a couple of seconds had passed – seconds which had felt like minutes, the detective took a seat in the tub chair nearest the door and motioned for Pat to sit on the sofa. Almost on automatic pilot now, Pat settled herself on the edge of the sofa, furthest away from the police officer. She looked at him briefly before dropping her eyes and focusing on a loose thread on her cardigan, instinctively picking away at it, giving her hands something to do.

'I've been told you have some information that may be helpful to us,' the detective said, breaking the awkward silence that had settled in the room.

Pat merely nodded and continued to pick at the loose thread, twisting it with her fingers as she attempted to separate it from the rest of her cardigan.

'OK,' he continued after a few more seconds, his voice still light, gentle. 'Well, I'm glad you've come in – I can see how difficult this is for you.'

For the first time since he had entered the room, Pat looked up and made eye contact with the detective, a single tear rolling down her cheek. She knew she had to tell him.

'It's about the girl,' she stated, taking a deep breath before continuing. 'The one on the news.'

'Kate Palmer?'

'Yes. No. Well, you see, her name wasn't Kate, it was Laura.'

Having spoken to Pat McCormack, Jim made his way back up to the office.

They now had a lot more information about the night leading to the discovery of the body and his hunches about George Lawrence were probably unfounded, as the last sighting they had of Kate Palmer was of her being picked up on the Lichfield Road by a regular client. It had surprised him that the girl was a prostitute – she just didn't seem the type – but their witness was adamant that it was the same girl, despite knowing her by a different name.

He was frustrated that the woman couldn't identify anything about the car that had stopped to pick Kate up, even though they had no idea at this stage if the occupant was in any way responsible for her death; however, he was certainly a person of interest, especially as he hadn't come forward himself, for whatever reason.

'This new information is going to devastate her parents though,' Jim thought, as he knocked at his inspector's door to give him the update.

'Ah, James, come in,' called Inspector Goulding. 'The post mortem is back from the Coroner's office.'

Jim took the brown folder from the inspector and glanced over it. Much of it was what he had expected regarding cause of death and sexual assault but, once again, he thought about the girl's parents and how devastated they were going to be as he read one part of the report.

'Poor kid.' He sighed and handed the folder back to his inspector.

'So, what have we got?' asked Goulding, placing the folder in his desk tray.

'A witness has come forward. She was with Kate before she died. She says a punter picked her up from her usual spot on the Lichfield Road.'

'She was a prostitute?' enquired the inspector.

'Yes, guv. She told our witness that the client was a regular so she had no hesitation getting in the car.'

'Have we got a description?'

'Unfortunately not,' Jim replied, raising an eyebrow. 'She can't even remember what colour the car was and didn't see his face. Apparently, she's short-sighted – oh, and it was dark as well.'

The sarcasm in his voice was clear, but Goulding apparently chose to ignore it. Perhaps he accepted they had more important things to deal with.

'Right then, well, you need to go to the pickup spot and canvass the area from there. Take a couple of officers with you and see what CCTV is available for the night in question. I also suggest that Watkins re-interviews your witness. See if she can get her to open up a bit more, woman to woman. She must be able to remember something else.'

With that, Jim was dismissed.

Knowing he was facing a busy afternoon, Jim got himself a mug of coffee before settling down at his desk. With any luck, they would soon have the information they needed to enable them to solve this case.

It had been a few days now since he had taken that girl to the park.

Since then, he had experienced a whole range of emotions; however, today he was feeling agitated, restless. The feelings of euphoria he had felt on the night itself when he first realised that she was dead had gone and, even though his senses had been heightened when he first heard it mentioned on the news reports and saw her picture on the front of the papers, he was now back to feeling, well … flat.

He had spent the last hour rereading reports online but they were all saying the same thing now and this was beginning to irritate him. She was no longer the leading news story either, which surprised him as it was only on Saturday that her face had been splashed across the front pages and was the first item discussed on their local evening news broadcast.

He would have to change that, he thought. 'But how?'

The man closed the lid of his laptop after wiping the search history and sat there for a while, rubbing the tops of his eyes with his hands. There was something comforting about massaging the bones just above his eye sockets, and he was soon lost in thought and didn't hear his wife come in.

'Tea?' she had asked as she entered the kitchen.

For some reason the tone of her voice irritated him.

She sounded happy.

Why did she sound so happy?

'Where have you been?' he demanded, looking at his watch. 'You said you were only going to the shops.'

'I did. I got a bit of shopping but there was a queue at the tills.'

'You're lying,' he seethed, through gritted teeth. 'You met someone, didn't you? Who was it?'

'Honestly, I just went to the shops to get a few things that we needed.'

He could hear the fear in her voice and he had briefly wondered if she was lying to him but then, who would want her anyway? Her body was that repulsive that *he* didn't even want to sleep with her half the time. It didn't stop him from feeling angry though and he stood up quickly, glaring down at her, his hands bunched into tight fists.

It would have been so easy to lash out, to teach her a lesson, but at that moment, he knew he needed to control his temper before he completely lost it. Alison wasn't helping though, wittering on about the number of people ahead of her in the shop; it was winding him up even more.

Knowing how easily her husband could turn violent, Alison did her best to convince him that she really had just gone to the shops and got caught in the queue. It annoyed her that he would think she had had some clandestine meeting with another man in those few extra minutes, but she also knew that there was no reasoning with her husband when he was like this and so she was more than a little thankful when he just picked up his car keys off the table and stormed out of the house.

The slamming of the door caused Emily to wake with a start and she immediately began to cry. Rushing to her daughter's side, Alison lifted her out of her stroller to comfort her. It wasn't easy but she was far happier dealing with a crying baby than an unpredictable husband, and at least for now she wouldn't have to worry about what his mood would lead to.

Chapter Nine

If Brian and Janice Palmer had assumed that they had faced the worst possible news they could ever imagine then, sadly, they were mistaken. The following morning, after a team briefing where all officers working on the case were brought up to speed on the new information they had, the family liaison officer who had been assigned to the Palmers phoned Brian, asking if he could call in as there had been some new developments in the investigation which he needed to make them aware of.

Perhaps the Palmers were hopeful that someone had been arrested; that would mean they would be able to focus on their daughter's funeral. They could have had no idea then that there was going to be another press appeal, nor how sensitive the information given to the press was going to be, but, for the FLO, it was vital that the parents heard this news from the police first before it was reported through any of the various media outlets.

Within the hour, the FLO was once again sitting in the Palmers' lounge, explaining what they now knew about Kate.

It was not an easy conversation to have.

Hearing that a witness had come forward with information that their daughter had been working as a prostitute and that she had possibly been picked up by the person who had most likely killed her had been devastating. Neither Brian nor Janice could understand why their daughter had chosen that lifestyle and their pain was only compounded by the fact that she had chosen not to confide in them, ask them for help if she was struggling financially. Now she was dead and Janice found this particularly hard to comprehend; she had always thought they were close, that her daughter could tell her anything.

How wrong she had been.

Knowing this information was now going to be released to the press, so that their family, their friends, would know what she had been doing, only added to their grief and Brian was ashamed to admit that he was embarrassed by what his daughter had done, angry with her, even, that she had brought this shame on her family.

The second piece of information the FLO had shared with them was the most devastating of all. The results of the post mortem had come back; at the time of her death, Kate Palmer had been approximately eight weeks pregnant. Not only had the Palmers lost their only child that night, they had also lost their grandchild and any future hopes of having grandchildren as well.

Chapter Ten

Drumming his fingers on the arm of the chair, he let out a deep, exasperated sigh as the humdrum of everyday life settled around him, leaving him feeling bored, wondering what he could do to pass the time.

He hated feeling like this.

He had tried to relive events from that night two weeks ago but his memory was becoming hazy, leaving him frustrated that he could no longer recreate those same feelings he had experienced at the time. Try as he might, it just wasn't the same as when he had actually been there. Not even the news reports could hold his attention today. He had read them so many times now they were becoming stale.

Another long sigh escaped him and he leant back and closed his eyes. To be honest, he knew why he was feeling like this, why he was suddenly on edge – Christmas was fast approaching and he was dreading it. They were going to be spending a few days in Cornwall with Alison's parents. He couldn't think of anything worse than being cooped up with his in-laws, a wife he couldn't stand the sight of and a daughter who did nothing but irritate the hell out of him lately. The child was teething as well, which meant she was constantly crying and the sound of her wails was beginning to grate on him.

No, he was not looking forward to Christmas at all and he needed something that would make the visit more enjoyable. At that moment, an idea suddenly hit him, an idea so clever that he instantly sat back up and wondered if he could pull it off. As he thought about it, he couldn't help but smile.

It would certainly generate some fresh interest, let people know that he was still out there, that they shouldn't forget what had happened to that girl. That it could happen again.

It *would* happen again.

He was sure of that.

He just needed to make sure the time was right.

For now, though, he wanted to focus on the idea that was taking shape in his mind. He quickly typed out a few words on his laptop, then read them back to himself, deleted them, then tried a few more times. Finally satisfied with what he had typed, he printed it out then headed towards the kitchen for an envelope; he placed the single sheet of paper inside. He would find the address and post the letter later today but for now he folded it up and placed it in the back pocket of his jeans, making sure it couldn't fall out. The last thing he wanted was for Alison to find it.

He hoped that the letter would generate more publicity and keep the girl's death in the spotlight. It wasn't enough to satisfy him but it would amuse him for a while until he had the chance to pick up another woman. He knew he needed to feel the way he felt that night in the park before he completely forgot what it was like. He also knew that he would have to act on it sooner, rather than later. Maybe even before he went to his in-laws. Yes, they wouldn't be so quick to forget about him then, not if another girl was found dead.

Whistling to himself now, he was finally beginning to think that perhaps Christmas wouldn't be so bad after all.

That same afternoon, Jim was also feeling frustrated.

Although they now had a clearer picture of Kate Palmer's whereabouts on the night she was murdered, thanks largely to Pat McCormack's statement, they were still no nearer to arresting anyone in connection with her death. A direct appeal, asking the man who picked her up at the bus stop to come forward, so that he could be eliminated from their enquiries, went unanswered.

Guilt, or shame, Jim wasn't sure which at this stage.

Even more frustrating for the team of officers working on the case was that despite spending hours trawling through CCTV images around the area where Kate was picked up, there was nothing of any value to the investigation, as any footage recovered had been too grainy to be of any use.

To all intents and purposes they had hit a dead end. Every lead the team followed drew a blank and even though Jim still hoped they would catch whoever was responsible, thanks to the results of DNA evidence collected from the body there was a sinking feeling in the pit of his stomach that the person responsible would remain elusive.

In the year prior to Kate Palmer's death three prostitutes had been attacked in the city centre and, although DNA from semen swabs linked all three cases, no one had ever been caught and now, worryingly for the police, whoever was responsible for those attacks had also murdered Kate. He had obviously progressed and this progression made it even more critical that the man was apprehended; there was a very real fear that he would strike again.

Unfortunately, the three women had been unable to identify their attacker because he had crept up on them. There was no description of him. He never spoke throughout their ordeals, there was no indication that they knew him, and yet Pat McCormack was certain that Kate had said she knew the man who had picked her up.

Was that why he killed her?

Through press releases, the police highlighted the dangers faced by prostitutes picking up clients on the streets and they were warned to be on their guard. Despite the obvious dangers, it wouldn't stop the women from going out there, but, at least for a couple of days, many were a lot more cautious. Of course, that didn't last long and the concern felt by these women in the days immediately following Kate's death was soon replaced with a feeling of apathy.

Three separate events, however, would soon blow the case wide open.

Shortly after Jim Wardell's visit to the man who had found Kate Palmer's body, George Lawrence had taken a short walk from his home in Bevington Road up to the clothes bank on Upper Sutton Street where he deposited the dead woman's bag and its contents. He had been desperate to get them out of his flat in case the police came sniffing round again and thought the clothes bank would be a good idea. Perhaps it would have been, as well, if he had emptied the contents out before depositing it into the metal bin. Of course, once the donated items had been collected and sent to the processing warehouse for redistribution, the worker who removed the bag from the pile of clothes knew instantly who it belonged to thanks to the university card he discovered in there, which not only gave her name, but also carried her photo ID.

Following the discovery, the police were immediately called and the bag was sent for forensic testing. Despite the urgency of the case, it would be a while before any results came back, due to the sheer volume of items in ongoing investigations being sent to the Forensic Science Lab, but fingerprints found on the bag would eventually match those of George Lawrence and Jim would finally have enough evidence to arrest the man and take DNA swabs.

The day after the discovery of the bag, a stack of letters was delivered to BTH FM, a local radio station, based in Aston. There was nothing unusual in this as the station received hundreds of letters each week, which were then sorted and sent to the relevant recipients.

Eddie Carter was one of the station's top radio personalities, thanks, in part, to the format of his *Friday Night Late* talk show where listeners either wrote to or called the station while they were on air, to discuss whatever may have been troubling them. Eddie, in his capacity of agony uncle, would either offer his own no-holds-barred advice or open the lines up to his listeners so that they too, could comment on the issues raised. Over the twelve months the show had been running, its popularity had grown so much that there was a constant stream of mail coming into the station for Eddie. Thankfully, he had an assistant who went through the mail with him, helping choose the ones he would use for his show, the ones which would need a reply, as well as the ones that went straight into the bin.

Most of the post Eddie received on this particular Friday was made up of Christmas cards sent in by listeners, wanting to wish Eddie and his team a happy Christmas. There were also a few letters detailing many of the difficulties faced at this time of year, some of which they would use that night as they had planned a discussion on debt. One of the letters, however, was different to the usual stuff he received.

'She deserved to die.

She was a whore.

I'm not done yet!'

Eddie read the few short words again, and a puzzled look settled across his face, prompting his assistant to ask if the letter was an interesting one. Eddie handed it across to his colleague, waited until the woman had read it, then passed it along to the other members of staff who were also in the room.

There was no other information on the letter, nothing else in the envelope, and, although they did not immediately connect it to the Kate Palmer investigation, everyone in the office that day agreed that it would be prudent to report it to the police rather than just dismiss it altogether.

It wasn't long before officers working on the Palmer investigation came into possession of the letter. To begin with, they had no idea whether or not it was connected to their case. There was also the possibility that whoever had sent it had done so as a joke, leading Inspector Goulding to warn everyone that they should keep an open mind, at least until they could establish its authenticity. Despite the inspector;s warning, though, there was a renewed sense of urgency amongst those working on the case, in wanting to catch whoever had been responsible for Kate's death.

Jim was quite aware that the letter sent to the radio station could turn out to be a hoax. Although he had only been a young boy at the time Peter Sutcliffe carried out his crimes in Yorkshire, so had no first-hand knowledge of the case, he had researched the investigation and, in particular, the way officers had been sidetracked by Wearside Jack's letters and tape.

He wasn't going to let that happen here.

The letter, and its envelope, were submitted into evidence and sent to the Forensic Science Lab in the hope that DNA could be recovered from either the back of the postage stamp or the gummed seal of the envelope. It was a long shot, given that the adhesive used in the gum could destroy any DNA there was, but they had to try. Fingerprint evidence was less likely to be recovered, given just how many people had touched the letter, but they were now getting desperate, especially if it *was* a genuine letter. The last line was particularly concerning; sooner or later, they could have another victim on their hands.

Ten days after Eddie Carter had received the letter, Amanda Edwards was at Zelda's, a hot new nightclub on Corporation Street, with her boyfriend, Tyrone Bailey. They were attending Amanda's works Christmas do and had been having an enjoyable evening until they got into a petty squabble over one of her male colleagues.

Amanda loved to dance and as she was now in full Christmas party mode, she was over on the dance floor strutting her stuff while Tyrone propped up the bar. He didn't mind at first – he wasn't keen on dancing given that he had two left feet and didn't feel comfortable trying to keep up with Amanda.

Watching her now, she looked gorgeous all dressed in red, with her long blonde hair swishing back and forth as she danced. Amanda had an amazing figure and Tyrone knew how lucky he was that they were together. The trouble was, as much as he thought Amanda was attractive, so did other men and, whilst the majority would back off, knowing she was in a relationship, there was always one who would push his luck. Tonight was no different, and while he watched Amanda's colleague becoming more hands on than he cared for, grabbing at her waist, moving in closer, Tyrone could feel himself getting annoyed.

He had always had a bit of a jealous streak where Amanda was concerned and – perhaps because of the amount of drink he had consumed – he was starting to feel increasingly disrespected. Downing his Jack and Coke in one, he marched over to Amanda, pushed her colleague away from her and argued with him right there in the middle of the dance floor. Of course, when Amanda tried to calm him down, he had a few choice words for her as well, which resulted in Amanda storming out of the club.

It was late and he knew he should have gone after his girlfriend, but Tyrone was annoyed with her for not telling her colleague to back off, so instead he returned to the bar and ordered another drink. He figured that he would cool off before heading home. The last thing he wanted was to get into another argument.

Amanda was annoyed with Tyrone for ruining the evening because of his unfounded jealousy. As far as she was concerned, she had done nothing wrong and had just been enjoying herself, dancing away with whoever was nearby. She would never cheat on her boyfriend, had told him so many times, and was extremely embarrassed at the way he had publicly flared up at her.

After she left the club, Amanda decided to walk back to their flat in Nechells rather than stay and put up with her boyfriend's jealousy. She probably should have called a taxi, but Tyrone was holding their money due to the lack of space in her handbag, which was only big enough to hold her phone, keys and lipstick, and she wasn't going to go back in and ask him to pay for it. She wanted nothing to do with him by then.

It was bitterly cold out by now and Amanda was dressed to party; she wasn't dressed for walking home in the early hours of the morning, so when the car approached and the man inside asked if she wanted a lift, the amount of alcohol she had consumed, coupled with how cold she was, affected her thought processes. Despite her initial reluctance, she was easily persuaded and was soon sitting in the passenger seat of the car, looking forward to getting home and getting out of her heels.

Chapter Eleven

It wasn't immediately obvious to Tyrone that Amanda had not returned home. After leaving Zelda's, he met one of his mates in the foyer of the tower block where they both lived and had gone back to his flat for a few more drinks. Truth be told, Tyrone was still annoyed with Amanda and wasn't ready to go back home just yet so the chance to carry on drinking, appealed to him.

It had gone five when he finally got through the front door. All the lights were off so he headed straight for the sofa where he collapsed and was soon in a deep sleep, thanks to the level of alcohol in his system.

At some point, he became vaguely aware of his phone ringing but it mingled with his dreams and he didn't connect that someone was actually trying to get through until around the fourth call.

Opening his eyes, he could feel the room swimming and would have preferred to shut them again but he picked his phone up off the floor to see who was calling.

His mother.

What did she want?

Wasn't she going shopping with Amanda this morning?

If she was going to give him grief over their argument last night, she could forget it. He let the phone ring off, and was about to go back to sleep when it started up again.

'What?' he asked abruptly, annoyed at his mother's intrusion.

'Tyrone,' Elsa began after a brief pause, 'I've been waiting for Amanda. She's supposed to be taking me to the market but she hasn't turned up.'

'Oh, Mum, sorry. We went out last night. I fell asleep on the sofa. Let me go see if she's left yet.'

He didn't want to tell his mum that they had rowed, so he listened to her complaining in her native Patois about how she hated to be kept waiting while he headed towards the bedroom.

Empty.

The bed had clearly not been slept in; several of Amanda's clothes still lay on top, where she had discarded them when she was undecided on what to wear last night.

Had she not come home?

Instantly, Tyrone was awake. 'She's not here, Mum. Let me call her.'

With that he hung up and immediately called Amanda.

Straight to voicemail.

Where was she?

He knew their row had been a stupid one and he should never have embarrassed her like that in front of her work colleagues – but she had annoyed him. Still, he knew he shouldn't have just let her walk out like that.

His jealousy had been a huge problem in their relationship from the very beginning. Amanda was stunning and he knew that other men fancied her, but she was with him and that should have been enough. When he saw one of her work colleagues putting his hands around her waist, though, he couldn't help but get annoyed.

Obviously, she was still angry with him. She had never let his mum down before in all the time that they had been dating, taking her to the Rag and Indoor markets every Tuesday without fail. Alison knew today was particularly important as his mum wanted to get the fish for Christmas lunch on Thursday and this would be the last chance they had to get it.

Sitting on the edge of the bed, Tyrone tried to think where she would have gone. She wouldn't be at work because she took Mondays and Tuesdays off. She had no family in Birmingham to call on, so the most likely option was that she had gone to her best friend's to cool off.

A quick call to her friend, though, proved fruitless.

It was then that Tyrone started to worry slightly. Amanda had never stayed out all night before. It was usually him who would go off if they argued.

With an edge of panic in his voice, he called his mum back and told her what had happened.

They had argued last night, or rather, he had argued and she had tried to appease him but to no avail. It seemed that, no matter what she did lately, it was never good enough. She had sensed that trouble was brewing; he had been in a foul mood for the best part of a week and last night it had come to a head.

He was due home at seven o'clock so she had tried to make sure that Emily was fed and settled and his tea was in the oven, ready for when he got back. Trouble was, Emily was teething and took longer to settle than usual, so by the time she had come back down to the kitchen, the sausages were just that little bit crisper than he liked. It didn't help that he was late home, but it was still her fault. He had thrown his plate across the kitchen, sending food and broken crockery everywhere.

He was still raging at her as she started to clean up the mess, grabbing her hair and pulling her backwards, which caused her to cut her hand on a piece of the now shattered plate. Blood dripped onto the floor, which only seemed to make him angrier, and he had slapped her, hard, straight across her face.

The look of hatred in his eyes had scared Alison and she tried her best to placate him, offering to cook something else for him to eat, but he was not going to calm down quite so easily. For over twenty minutes she listened as he ridiculed her and put her down, blaming her for what had occurred, before storming out of the house.

Thankfully, the cut was not a deep one and Alison was able to bandage it up and stop it bleeding. She also had a small cut above her lip where he had hit her and a bruise forming on her cheekbone, which upset her more than the cut on her hand. They were meant to be going to her parents' this afternoon and whilst she could have come up with an excuse for the bandage on her hand, what could she say to them about her face?

Trying to conceal the bruise with make-up, she was suddenly aware of her husband in the doorway. His mood had lightened somewhat since last night but her heart was still pounding as she waited to see whatever it was he wanted. Thankfully, he just asked how much longer she was going to be; reminding her they had a train to catch, before leaving.

Once she was alone again, Alison tried to stifle a sob that threatened to escape. Scared that her husband might have heard, she held her breath and waited. He didn't come back in the room though, which was a relief. The last thing she needed was for him to flare up again. It was going to be Emily's first Christmas and they should have been looking forward to it, excited to see how she would react to it all. Instead, Alison couldn't shake the constant feeling of dread in the pit of her stomach as she tried to work out what sort of mood he was in from one moment to the next.

Alison had no idea how they were going to get through the next few days, trying to hide their problems from her parents, and she was beginning to wish that they had not arranged to go. Still, it was too late to cancel now so she could only hope that her husband behaved himself, at least whilst they were there.

He went downstairs straight into the sitting room and switched on BBC News 24.

Nothing!

He felt a pang of dismay and was starting to think that perhaps he shouldn't have covered her up. Hopefully it wouldn't take too long though, before someone found her.

Ignoring the disappointment, his mind focused on what had transpired last night.

It had all happened by chance. He was making his way back towards the city centre when he first spotted her. Almost immediately his interest was piqued, enough for him to change plans, turn left into Aston Street, and slow the car down until he had pulled up beside her to ask if she wanted a lift.

She had hesitated briefly but he had won her over with his charm, telling her how cold it was and how he didn't mind giving her a lift to wherever it was she was headed. It did the trick and she willingly got into the car, giving him directions to her flat. At first he had followed her route, listening as the girl ranted about her boyfriend and how jealous he was.

She had clearly been drinking and, at first, she hadn't noticed when he took a wrong turn but she soon realised, as they headed down The Avenue, that they were not going the right way.

'No, wait, it's back that way,' she had said, trying to process what was going on. As he had pulled into the industrial estate, though, she must have known she was in trouble. Luckily for him, he was much stronger than the girl and it hadn't taken long before he was once again heading back home.

Chapter Twelve

Tyrone had still not heard anything from Amanda by early afternoon. Her phone constantly kept going to voicemail and even phoning her friends had been pointless – they all said they had not seen or heard from her. Of course, he did wonder if they were just covering for her while she made him sweat, but he knew Amanda, knew she wouldn't do this. Even when they had rowed before, they always made up afterwards so he couldn't shake the thought that something awful must have happened.

Not knowing what to do next, Tyrone had called his mum again and she was now sitting in his front room, having caught a taxi straight over. Elsa was also concerned for her future daughter-in-law, although she tried not to let on in front of her son. She was very close to Amanda and had often counselled her following an argument with Tyrone, as Elsa herself knew just how hot-headed her son was. Surely, if Amanda was still annoyed with her son, she would have come to Elsa to talk it through.

She didn't want to worry Tyrone any more than he already was but she persuaded him to call the hospitals, just in case Amanda had been in an accident.

No joy there, but perhaps that was a good thing – at least she hadn't been injured and unable to contact them for some reason.

Come four o'clock, though, Tyrone couldn't take anymore and decided to phone the police to report Amanda missing. If she was staying away because she was still angry with him then she could deal with the police when they found her, but he just needed his girlfriend to come home. Right now he would promise her anything if she would just come back.

With a feeling of dread growing every minute Amanda was missing, he dialled 101 to report his concerns. He didn't tell the officer that they had rowed, just that she had left the club around 1 a.m. and hadn't been seen since. The police promised to send someone round to talk to him, but there was little more Tyrone could do so he thanked the officer, hung up the phone, and waited.

Although the letter sent to the radio station had not been made public knowledge, police officers across the city were informed of the possibility that Kate Palmer's killer could strike again, so when the 101 call from Tyrone Bailey came in reporting that his girlfriend had not returned home after a night out, it didn't take long for two uniformed officers to be dispatched to his home address.

The man who opened the door to them appeared to be in an agitated state.

'Have you found her?' he demanded, before they even had chance to speak, let alone step foot inside the flat.

Shaking her head, the female officer explained that they were just there to take a statement and collect a photograph of Amanda, along with the names, addresses or phone numbers of anyone she may have gone to stay with.

It was clear the man was not happy with this. He told the officers he had already given them a description when he phoned and would rather they were looking for her instead of wasting time questioning him.

Exchanging glances with her colleague, the female officer asked if they could enter the flat then followed Tyrone into the sitting room where his mum was waiting. Motioning for him to sit down, she then sat next to his mother whilst the male officer stood at the doorway.

'Right, Mr ... er, Bailey – Tyrone,' she began, looking at her notes to confirm his name. 'We just need to go over what has happened.'

Tyrone cleared his throat then told the officers about their visit to the nightclub; about Amanda leaving to go home while he stayed at the club, arriving home drunk, and then his mother's phone calls that morning. While he was talking, the female officer made notes.

'Why did she leave the club on her own?' she asked, once he had finished.

'We had a row,' he muttered quietly, unable to maintain eye contact with the police officer as he explained. 'One of her colleagues kept putting his hands on her and I got annoyed. I'm sorry, Mum, I shouldn't have let her leave without me.'

His mother shook her head. 'That's always been your trouble, Ty. Just like your father! Always jealous.'

An awkward silence ensued.

It was clear to the officers that Tyrone was unhappy with his mother's statement and they were beginning to think that this was simply a domestic; the woman would soon be home when she had had time to cool off.

After a couple of minutes, the male officer spoke to Tyrone.

'Have you phoned any of her friends?' he asked. 'Could she have gone somewhere to calm down?'

'No!' Tyrone shouted. 'She wouldn't do that to me – and her phone is switched off too. She never switches her phone off.'

The panic was clearly recognisable in his voice but the officers needed to gather as much information as possible.

'We've phoned everyone we can think of,' Tyrone's mother interjected.

'Thank you, Mrs Bailey,' the officer replied before switching his attention back to Tyrone. 'I have to ask, Mr Bailey, did the row get physical?'

Tyrone jumped up. 'Of course not,' he screamed. 'I love Amanda. You have to find her, tell her I'm sorry.'

It was at that point that Tyrone started to cry. Sitting back down on the chair, he buried his head in his hands, sobbing loud and hard until his mother went over to him to offer some comfort.

Once again the officers exchanged glances. Perhaps it was the worry of not knowing where she was mixed with the guilt he must have been feeling over letting her leave the club on her own, that had caused the tears. Then again, it was also possible that the boyfriend had been responsible for her disappearance and this was just an act. They couldn't be sure at this point but they both knew that it was a possibility. For now though she would be recorded as a missing person.

'Try not to worry, Mr Bailey. Chances are she has stayed over at a friend's house,' said the female officer consolingly. 'We have put her description out, so officers will be aware that she is missing, but we will need a photograph of Amanda and any contact details you have for friends who she might have gone to stay with.'

Elsa Bailey picked up an envelope from the coffee table and handed it to the officer, explaining that they had already been asked to gather this information together when they had dialled 101.

There was nothing more the officers could do for now and so Elsa showed them to the front door and thanked them for their time.

'Try not to worry,' the male officer repeated, as they left the flat. 'We will go and speak to her friends. If she does contact Tyrone, can you just let us know.'

Elsa took the card the officer gave her and shut the door.

She was worried for Amanda and couldn't help the tears that silently began to flow. She knew Amanda wouldn't have stayed away by choice, that something awful must have happened to stop her from coming home.

Chapter Thirteen

Just half a mile from Tyrone and Amanda's flat, David Marshall was making his way towards the canal on Rocky Lane. Staggering from side to side, it was clear that he had been drinking. Even though he was already slightly intoxicated, he regularly took a swig from the vodka bottle he had wrapped in a brown paper bag. It was a bitterly cold day but the vodka kept the chill off, making life somewhat more bearable. Occasionally, he would beg enough money to secure a night at the Salvation Army in town, but tonight he was going down the canal to sleep in one of the arches, having spent the little bit of money he did have on his vodka.

The arches were a popular location among the city's homeless, providing shelter from the elements, and often one or other of the arches inhabitants would light a fire, giving them some warmth. Despite this, it could still get quite cold down there and so, as he walked along, David was quite pleased when he saw what he thought was a large cardboard sheet over on the waste ground. It was difficult to make out at first, as the overgrown bushes dotted around the edge of the waste ground didn't allow him a clear view, but if it was cardboard, it looked like it would be the perfect size to sleep on. David stumbled across the road and made his way towards his discovery, confirming as soon as he got closer that it was indeed a large cardboard sheet, perhaps six foot in length.

David carefully placed the bottle of vodka in his coat pocket, removed the rocks that had been placed on each corner of the cardboard and began to lift it. He was excited to find several more, slightly smaller sheets all layered on top of each other. Hoping that he could exchange these for something at the arches, maybe a bit of food or a couple of cigarettes, David started collecting them. He imagined that he must have looked a right sight as he tried to gather all the sheets of cardboard. They were awkward to hold though, given how windy it was, combined with how cumbersome they were, but he didn't care. They would be almost as valuable as money, as far as he was concerned.

The last piece of cardboard had one large rock lying in the centre of it. It was covering something but David wasn't sure what. He kicked the rock and it rolled onto the ground, allowing him to lift the final sheet. Shocked by what he saw, David fell backwards, dropping the cardboard and causing the bottle of vodka to fall out of his pocket and smash. David scrambled to his feet and hurried towards the main road, intending to stop any car that passed by. Many cars just drove past so he had little option but to stand in the middle of the road, bringing traffic to a standstill.

David tried to explain what had happened to the driver of the first car that stopped but she didn't seem to understand him, so he started banging on her bonnet. This must have scared the woman as she immediately locked her door and then he saw her reaching for her phone before screaming at him that she was phoning the police.

By now, several drivers seemed to be getting very frustrated, repeatedly honking their horns but he wasn't giving up. Still trying to get someone to listen to him, he kept pointing towards the waste ground, shouting at them, telling them what he had found but he knew he wasn't making much sense.

Thankfully, the police were soon on the scene. To allow the traffic to disperse, one of the officers moved the drunken man out of the road and patiently asked him to explain what the problem was – he could see the man was becoming more and more agitated. Eventually, although his words were slurred, the officer managed to make out that he had apparently found a body.

Cautiously, the officers walked towards the location where David was pointing, switching on their flashlights as they made their way onto the waste ground. The first thing they were drawn to was the vivid red material contrasting against pale limbs that had been awkwardly splayed on the hard concrete ground. Taking a closer look, there was no mistaking that the semi-naked woman in front of them was dead. There was also no mistaking who she was either, as the officers had only just left her boyfriend and his mother.

The female officer immediately called it in.

They had both been convinced, having spoken to Tyrone Bailey, that this was nothing more than a domestic spat, but it was clear now that it was much more than that and Amanda Edwards wouldn't be returning home any time soon.

A concerned murmur quickly spread throughout the police station after it had been radioed in that a body had been found. This was now the second woman to have been murdered in Aston in recent weeks and although officers did not want to jump to conclusions, there was a very real fear that whoever had contacted the radio station had indeed carried out his threat.

Although he was nearing the end of his shift, Jim knew he wouldn't be going home any time soon once his inspector had called to inform him that the partially clothed body of a young woman had been discovered, just a few minutes' walk away from where Kate Palmer had been picked up on the night she was murdered. The inspector wanted Jim to meet him at the crime scene, so he carefully filed away the paperwork he had just been working on before reaching for his jacket and heading for the door.

It was only a short distance between the police station and the area where the body had been found but it was also rush hour, which slowed Jim down. Roadworks on the Lichfield Road also delayed him more than he would have liked.

'This is when blue lights would have come in handy,' he thought, but he was in his own car and had to follow the rules of the road like everyone else, no matter how frustrating it was.

By the time Jim arrived, there was a flurry of activity round where the body had been discovered. A white tent had been erected on the waste ground to protect any evidence around the body as well as minimising the view of the crime scene from any members of the public who might have had a morbid curiosity. High intensity

LED lights had also been set up both inside and around the tent; it was quite dark by now and the lights would ensure they didn't miss anything of importance while they gathered their evidence.

As he retrieved his coveralls from the boot, Jim spotted Inspector Goulding making his way to the tent so he hurriedly suited up to join him. Stepping inside, the first thing he noticed were the obvious similarities between Kate Palmer and this deceased victim. They were both young, petite, with long blonde hair. This woman also had a ligature wrapped around her neck and her lower half was exposed.

A quick glance at the immediate area surrounding the body and Jim noticed a small handbag near the dead woman's left hand, but once again, no underwear.

His heart sank as he processed those similarities.

A couple of things did stand out, though.

The first was the bag.

Kate's bag had been dumped elsewhere but it looked like this woman's bag had been left with the body. Was the man worried that he had made a mistake in dumping Kate's bag in the clothes bank or had he been disturbed at this crime scene and forgot to take it with him in his rush to get away? They were still awaiting the results of forensic testing on Kate's bag and its contents, but Jim wasn't hopeful that they would find anything of use.

The other thing that stood out to him was just how open the area was compared to where Kate was found. If it was the same man, he was taking more of a risk by dumping the body here. The area ran parallel with the number 8 bus route travelling in both directions, and although there were overgrown bushes which would have provided some cover, any number of witnesses could have seen something.

Jim wondered how long the girl had been here before being discovered. The pathologist would need to establish time of death but he was pretty sure it would have occurred within the last twenty-four hours. Lividity on the body suggested that she had either been dumped at this location shortly after she was killed or she was killed here – but it seemed too open an area for that so he suspected that this was the dump site.

'James!' boomed Goulding, interrupting his thoughts. 'What do you make of this?'

Goulding had obviously been talking to him so Jim was full of apologies before continuing.

'It's not good, sir,' he replied, despondently. 'It's possible our suspect has actually carried out his threat, given the similar circumstances both victims have been found in.'

'Maybe. It would appear so,' Goulding agreed. 'Let's wait on the results of forensics first though, eh?'

Jim nodded. The possibility of a copycat was always there.

'Who found her?' he asked.

'Homeless guy. He's been taken back to the station,' Goulding replied. 'There's no way we can interview him yet though, he's as drunk as a skunk. Will need to sleep it off.'

'Any idea who she is? Has her bag been checked for ID?'

'Not yet, but responding officers had just taken a missing person report before being called to a public disturbance here. Seems it's the same girl. Went missing early this morning. I would suggest you speak to them then go and inform the family while I wait for the pathologist.'

Jim nodded.

Until the pathologist arrived they would not be able to move the body and, with Goulding overseeing this part of the investigation, there was nothing more Jim could do here. He made his way out of the tent; he would do as his inspector had asked and go and speak to the officers who called this in, find out what information they had on the deceased, before going to break the news to whoever had reported her missing.

He wished that Angie had not taken leave for the holidays, not only because he realised how much he was missing her, but also because he would have preferred her to accompany him when he spoke to the relatives. He couldn't delay it though, so would request another female officer to attend with him, once he had gathered the information he needed. It would be easier to break the news if he wasn't on his own.

Chapter Fourteen

They had originally planned to travel to Hayle on the train to Alison's parents' where they'd be staying for Christmas, as her husband didn't want to drive the four and a half hours or so it would take to get there. At the last minute though, despite having already purchased the train tickets, he changed his mind, saying that he would prefer to drive instead. Alison suspected it was because of the bruise on her face which, although she had done her best to cover it up, was still noticeable.

She didn't know what she was going to tell her mother.

At one point she thought he would cancel the trip but, after threatening her to keep her mouth shut, to which she readily agreed – she had no desire to let her parents down – they finally set off in the car a couple of hours later than anticipated.

The journey was horrendous.

A crash on the M5 meant they were stuck in traffic for a while.

Emily was still grouchy, thanks to that one tooth trying to break through. Sitting with her daughter in the back, Alison could feel the tension in the air every time Emily cried. Her husband's shoulders would stiffen and he would grip the steering wheel harder, cursing under his breath. Every now and then, he would demand that Alison shut her up, and she did try, only Emily had other ideas.

Her husband turned the radio on, presumably to try to drown out the noise in the back of the car. Unfortunately, he had turned it up louder than usual and the speakers were in the back, either side of Alison. She already had an awful headache so the added noise of the radio only served to make it much worse. She loved her parents dearly but she was beginning to wish that they had not asked her to visit for Christmas. In fact, she wished that they had not decided to retire to Cornwall in the first place. It would have been so much simpler if they had stayed in Birmingham.

It was as they neared Hayle that they heard the national news bulletin.

The body of a young woman has been found on waste ground in Aston, Birmingham, between the junction of Rocky Lane and Chester Street. Police are currently at the scene where a forensic tent has been erected, and initial reports suggest that they are treating this as a suspicious death.

This latest death follows the murder of another young woman nearly four weeks ago. Kate Palmer, a local prostitute, was found just over a mile away from tonight's scene. Police have not yet said if the two deaths are related.

We will bring further updates as we get them.

No sooner had the report finished, then her husband had switched off the radio. Emily had settled down by this point as well and the silence in the car was welcoming for a while. Alison was tired by now though and the events of the last couple of days, along with the report she had just heard, had made her emotional. She desperately tried not to show it, worried how her husband would react but he had sympathised with her; reaching for the tissues that were on the shelf under the glove box when she needed them, without being asked.

His change in demeanour had been sudden but Alison put this down to them nearing her parents' home coupled with her husband's desire to keep up appearances. He had always been the same; not wanting anyone to know that they were having problems. She just hoped it would last, at least until they were back home again. More than anything, she wanted this Christmas to be perfect – it was her daughter's first and she didn't want her husband's mood swings to spoil it.

Chapter Fifteen

Following the discovery of a second body, the investigation into the deaths of both Kate Palmer and Amanda Edwards took on a renewed sense of urgency. Despite the fact that Christmas was almost upon them, more officers had been drafted in to help deal with the influx of calls generated after Detective Chief Inspector Alan Jones led a press conference, early on Christmas Eve, asking for the public's help in finding whoever had been responsible for Amanda Edwards's death.

Tyrone Bailey's presence at the press conference, the obvious despair etched on his face, pleading for people to help, had had the desired effect and calls to the hotline were coming in steadily. Everyone had been shocked at the death of this latest victim and several officers had volunteered to come in on their days off so that the phone lines were fully manned. All they needed was that one piece of information, no matter how insignificant it seemed to the caller, to be able to identify a possible suspect.

Clearly two murders, so close to each other, were extremely worrying. However, despite the rumours, the police couldn't officially confirm that both cases were related, even though many suspected that they were and this was starting to create a sense of fear for the residents of Aston. Women going out over the Christmas period made sure that they never travelled alone. Shift workers made alternative arrangements, avoiding public transport in the early morning or late at night. Extra patrols were drafted in to cruise the area, on the lookout for anything suspicious.

Before long, though, Christmas and New Year had passed by and, once again, the investigation was no longer front page news.

Other than rehashing what was already known there was nothing new to report.

Back in the incident room, the investigation had stalled. No further contact had been made by the mysterious letter writer and any plausible tips called in after the televised appeal had been followed up without success. A couple of witnesses had seen Amanda by the old fire station but it was as if she had just vanished into thin air after that, which was immensely frustrating for the officers working on the case – surely someone must have seen something.

They knew she had not entered any of the student apartments which were now located in the former fire station as they had checked the CCTV which covered the entrance. Unfortunately, that same CCTV only covered a portion of the pavement outside so it couldn't help to determine the route Amanda had taken that night.

The question now was, did she get into a car or was she attacked on the street? How did she get from where she was last seen to where her body had been found, some 1.3 miles away? Despite canvassing the university, they had nothing concrete to work on.

The bag found next to the body was empty but her boyfriend had confirmed it was Amanda's, so what had happened to the contents? Her phone and keys were missing as well as anything else that might have been in there. Her knickers were also missing.

As with the Kate Palmer case, they were hitting a brick wall.

On the sixth of January, however, as Jim walked into the office with Angie, they were immediately greeted by Inspector Goulding waving a brown folder.

'Forensics!' he said simply, passing it across to Jim.

There were two pieces of evidence in the folder that had been returned from the Forensic Science Lab. The first had been marked a priority, and now confirmed that semen samples taken from the second victim matched those taken from Kate Palmer.

This raised a few questions.

Prior to Amanda's death, their prime suspect had only targeted prostitutes. The night Kate Palmer was murdered, she had told her friend that the car she was getting into belonged to a regular, leaving Jim to suspect that this was why she had been killed, to prevent her from identifying him.

This time, however, there was no evidence at all to suggest that Amanda was a prostitute, so was it an opportunistic attack or was he out looking for someone to pick up that night and Amanda just happened to be in the wrong place at the wrong time?

Another possibility they couldn't rule out just yet was that Amanda also knew her killer, but if that was the case, how? Tyrone Bailey had insisted that Amanda would never willingly get into a stranger's car, so how did she end up where she was found?

It was puzzling to say the least.

Jim was also curious as to why Amanda had been covered up in an apparent attempt to hide the body, whereas Kate had not. Had he been disturbed after killing Kate so didn't have time to try and hide her body? If so, why hadn't any other witnesses stepped forward?

The second sheet of paper in the folder finally confirmed what Jim had suspected all along. One set of fingerprints found on Kate Palmer's bag matched prints held on the Police National Database. Those prints belonged to George Lawrence.

'I knew it,' he exclaimed, angry at the length of time it had taken to get these results back.

'If only the tests had been carried out sooner, Amanda Edwards might still be alive,' he thought.

He knew he was being irrational. The Forensic Science Lab had a backlog of evidence they had to deal with and while each case had its own sense of urgency, there was only so much they could do at any given time. Even so, it still angered him, especially when he'd known from the start that there was something dodgy about Lawrence.

'So, are we going to arrest him now?' he asked his inspector. With any luck, they could have him back at the station and in custody within the hour.

'Who?' Angie enquired, still not aware of the contents of the folder. 'Are you going to fill me in?'

Passing the folder on to her, Jim waited for his inspector's response.

'First things first, James. I want a briefing to update everyone then you can fill us in on what we know about Lawrence *before* we go picking him up. We will also need to organise a search of his address in case there's any more evidence inside.'

'Good luck with that,' Jim responded. 'The place is a mess.'

He knew his inspector was right; everything had to be done in a timely manner. It was his own frustrations that made Jim want to arrest the man immediately. Gut instinct had been telling him that something wasn't quite right but there was nothing prior to this they could have arrested him on.

Still, at least they would be picking him up today and Jim was very interested in what he would have to say for himself.

By lunchtime, George Lawrence was safely in custody. His detention had been authorised and now the clock was ticking.

Goulding had suggested that Jim and Angie conduct the interview, which Jim was pleased about. He enjoyed working with Angie anyway, but she also had this knack of making suspects feel at ease during interviews, often getting them to open up a lot quicker than some of her colleagues. He hoped this would lead to a confession before the day was out, convinced as he was that they had now got their man.

Goulding had also stressed that everything be done by the book. He wanted to make sure Lawrence – or his solicitor on his behalf – had no reason to make any complaints about his officers' actions.

'Make sure you dot your i's and cross your t's on this one, James,' he had warned.

Not that Jim needed telling.

The interview process was nothing like it was portrayed on TV shows, with the good cop, bad cop routines screenwriters often favoured. No; during his time in custody, Lawrence would be treated with the utmost respect, irrespective of what anyone thought of him and what he was being accused of.

They had to wait a while for a duty solicitor to arrive before they could speak to their suspect, which was mildly frustrating. It was the first thing George Lawrence had asked for though, when they told him he was going to be arrested for the murders of Kate Palmer and Amanda Edwards. He had looked shocked, but had not spoken another word since. Still, it gave Jim and Angie a chance to go over their interview strategy while they waited.

Lawrence had been in custody for just over an hour by the time the duty solicitor arrived. He spent some time talking to his client before signalling that they were ready for him to be interviewed. Jim and Angie made their way down to the custody suite, informed the custody sergeant of their intention to question Lawrence so that a record of the interview could be made, then entered interview room 1.

As soon as he opened the door, a pungent smell of body odour, mingled with the stale stench of urine and old tobacco, wafted through the air, causing Jim to scrunch up his nose. It was not a pleasant smell but at least it didn't smell as bad as Lawrence's flat and he knew he would soon become accustomed to the aroma.

George Lawrence sat next to his solicitor on the far side of the table. He raised his head briefly as Jim and Angie entered the room and then appeared to show great interest in some imaginary spot on his trousers. Jim was curious about his demeanour and thought he looked even more dishevelled than he remembered.

Was this his plan to explain away what he had done? Jim wondered.

After both officers had taken a seat, Jim opened his briefcase and removed a notepad and brown manila folder which he placed on the table in front of him, one perfectly arranged on top of the other. He then took a pen from the pocket of his suit jacket, clicked the top a couple of times before placing it on top of the notepad. Pausing briefly for effect, Jim asked how George Lawrence was feeling and whether he wanted a drink.

The man didn't even look up, just shook his head.

After another slight pause, Jim busied himself with the recording equipment on the table, explaining that they were going to make both visual and audio recordings of the interview, and then asked everyone in the room to state their names clearly for the tape, which Lawrence complied with. He then read Mr Lawrence his rights and asked if he understood them.

This time George Lawrence nodded.

With formalities now out of the way, Jim was satisfied that the interview could go ahead.

'Are you ready to begin, Mr Lawrence?' he asked, keeping the tone of his voice amiable.

Again, the man nodded, whilst his solicitor took a pen from his jacket pocket and began taking notes.

'OK. Do you know why you have been arrested?'

'You said I killed that girl. The one I found, but I only found her. I didn't kill her,' he said, his voice strained.

'Do you want to tell us about that night?' asked Angie. 'How you found her.'

'I've already told *him*,' he replied, pointing at Jim. 'And that other policeman. Two times now, I've said what happened.'

Jim could see tiny droplets of perspiration settling on the man's forehead. He was clearly nervous about something.

'I know,' Angie agreed, smiling, 'but if you could go through it once more, I would appreciate it.'

George Lawrence was silent for a few seconds before going through the whole story again. Where he had been, how he found the girl, what he did then. He also added some extra commentary about how he felt he was being persecuted by the police and the injustice of it all.

Wanting to keep the interview on track, Jim opened the folder and took out a photograph, which he placed in front of Mr Lawrence.

Carefully watching his face for any reaction, Jim wasn't surprised that the man's eyes widened as he looked at the photo and he knew that George had recognised the bag. It would be interesting to see how he explained this one away.

'Have you seen that before, Mr Lawrence?' Jim asked.

The man shook his head.

'Are you sure?'

'I said no, didn't I?' Lawrence's voice was slightly raised.

'It belongs to Kate Palmer, the girl you found – it was her bag,' Jim explained.

'Well, how would *I* know that?' George spat.

George Lawrence was becoming agitated, so Jim was pleased when Angie took over the interview again, before the man shut down completely.

'The thing is, Mr Lawrence,' she said, her voice soothing, 'her bag turned up at a warehouse where they process clothes that have been deposited in clothes banks. You know those huge bins that you see in some streets. I believe you have one by where you live.'

'Yes, on Upper Sutton Street,' he agreed.

'That's right.' She smiled. 'The thing is, after we found Kate Palmer's bag, we had it tested to check for fingerprints, and what do you think we discovered?'

George Lawrence looked from Angie to Jim then back to Angie again.

'I don't know,' he whispered.

Jim knew they had him now. They had backed him into a corner.

'Look,' he said, trying to reason with him. 'Why don't you just tell us what happened.'

'I've *told* you!'

The colour had completely drained from George's face now.

'Did you kill Kate Palmer and Amanda Edwards?' asked Jim.
'No!'

'Then explain your fingerprints on Kate's bag.'

George Lawrence cleared his throat. He explained how he had seen the bag on the ground, saw that there was some money inside and had put it into his backpack. That's when he had found the body and then he had forgotten about the bag until he got home. He was ashamed then at what he had done, didn't want to admit that he had taken the bag.

Of course, after Jim had paid him a visit, he had panicked and dumped the bag in the clothes bank – scared that the police would come back and find it in his house. He was so sorry and should never have taken it to begin with, but he didn't kill the girl.

He was sobbing now and kept repeating how sorry he was. His solicitor asked for a break, which Jim readily agreed to.

Jim and Angie took Lawrence back to his cell, then went to discuss the outcome of the interview with their inspector. The interview had not worked out the way Jim had expected but he wasn't ready to give up on their suspect just yet.

The second interview, however, left Jim in little doubt that George Lawrence was not their man. He had provided them with details of his movements on the night Amanda Edwards was murdered, as well as the names of several people who could provide him with an alibi. He had also readily agreed to provide the police with a DNA sample in order to rule him out, which was not the action of a guilty man.

Even so, they were not ready to release George Lawrence just yet, not until his alibi had been confirmed and besides, they were still going to charge him with the theft of the bag so, for now, he was staying put.

He had just settled down to enjoy a quick nap when he heard something on the news which caused him to sit bolt upright, shocked at what he had just heard.

A man was arrested this morning in connection with the murders of Kate Palmer and Amanda Edwards, late last year. Police are refusing to release details of the arrest but have said that this is a significant breakthrough in their investigation.

He switched the TV off before angrily throwing the remote at the wall, causing the battery cover to break off and the batteries to roll across the floor.

Almost instantly, he could feel the rage start to build inside him – his heart was pounding, tightening in his chest, and the back of his throat felt constricted. Clenching his hands into tight balls, he had a sudden urge to lash out as a red mist started to descend.

He knew he needed to calm down.

The level of anger he was experiencing had surprised even himself, so he focused on his breathing until his heart rate had dropped again and he no longer thought that his head would explode.

After a few minutes, his breathing was more relaxed and he unclenched his fists, wiping the clammy residue on his trousers.

He needed to think.

Who had they arrested?

It didn't make sense.

He was about to switch on his laptop to find out what was going on when Alison interrupted him. She wanted to know if everything was OK – she had heard the noise the remote had made when it crashed against the wall. Although her interruption irritated him, he explained that he had simply dropped it, which seemed to satisfy her. A brief conversation ensued over trivialities. He didn't care that Emily was asleep, or that Alison was going to have a bath while she had five minutes to herself. He wanted to know why someone else had been arrested for his handiwork.

Thankfully, Alison soon made her excuses and left the room. Listening to her make her way up the stairs, he knew this would give him a little time to see what was going on. He turned on his laptop and went straight to the BBC News home page. There was the report, the first item at the top of the page. It didn't give much detail, no more than he had already heard really, just that someone had been arrested in connection with the deaths.

Closing the laptop, he sat back on the sofa and thought about the developments.

He didn't want anyone else taking credit for what he had done – but what could he do about it?

'Think! *Think!*'

Suddenly, he knew exactly what he was going to do and it would leave them in no doubt that they had arrested the wrong man.

Chapter Sixteen

On the Friday afternoon, three days after the arrest had been reported, Eddie Carter, the popular BTH FM radio host, had just arrived at the station for a meeting with his producers to run through the layout of his next show later that evening. The planned topic for that night was extra-marital affairs and everyone was in a jovial mood as they read through some of the letters they would be using to get the phone lines buzzing. It always amazed the team just how much detail listeners were prepared to go into to get on air, but that was what made the show so popular.

At one point during the meeting, Eddie's assistant came into the room and handed him that week's fan mail, which he dutifully began opening as they talked. Taking a cursory glance, he either placed the letter on the desk, where it would be dealt with later, or tossed it straight into the waste-paper basket. He wasn't paying that much attention, distracted as he was by the flow of conversation, but, as he picked up a small padded envelope from the pile, Eddie could feel that there was something solid in there. Curious as to what it could be, he quickly looked inside but was puzzled by the contents.

'What's this about?' he asked, speaking to no one in particular. Aware that he had got everyone's attention, Eddie tipped the envelope upside down and a set of keys fell onto the desk.

'Weird!' his assistant said, and then asked if there was a note in there with them.

'They sent you the key to their heart,' one of the production team, joked, causing everyone in the room to laugh.

They soon stopped laughing though, when Eddie opened up the folded sheet of paper that was also in the envelope and read the typewritten note out loud.

'They got it wrong.
Now they have blood on their hands.
I'm not done yet!'
What the hell was that all about?

'It's similar to that other letter you got,' his assistant said. 'Do you think we should contact the police again?'

After passing the letter round the room, everyone agreed that the police should be informed, and one of the producers offered to make the call. Meanwhile, everyone else tried to continue with a run-through for the night's show. The mood had changed somewhat though. They were all slightly creeped out by the letter, and the keys. What were the keys for? More importantly, whoever it was, *why* had they contacted Eddie again?

Alison replaced the receiver and sat down at the kitchen table, quickly wiping away a stray tear with the hem of her shirt.

She hated lying to her mother.

Ever since they had stayed at her parents over Christmas, her mum had suspected something was wrong. She never believed the story Alison told her about walking into the bedroom door when she had got up in the night to settle Emily down. More than once she would take her daughter aside and, in a hushed whisper, enquire if she was sure she was OK.

She had been under so much stress while they were there, trying to keep her husband happy, lying to her mum, that she couldn't wait to leave Hayle and come back home again.

It wasn't so bad when they had first arrived. In fact, her husband's mood had improved somewhat the closer they'd got to their destination, and he was as attentive as ever in front of her parents, making sure he got the cases out of the boot, settling Emily back down after she woke with a start when they lifted her out of her car seat, cracking jokes with her father.

She was glad, in a way, that he *was* keeping up appearances, but it also saddened her because that was how their relationship should have been all the time, not just in front of friends and family.

Her mother's obvious concern had not gone unnoticed by her husband and, as they were getting into bed that first night, he had grabbed hold of her wrist and warned her to keep her mouth shut.

Although Alison had told him that he was hurting her, her husband gripped harder, making sure she got the message.

How could she say anything to her mother after that?

The venom with which he had spoken to her had scared Alison and yet, within a few minutes, he had changed completely, nuzzling up to her in bed, kissing her neck and running his hands across her body.

Despite everything that had just occurred, her tiredness following their long journey, and the fact they were in her parents' house, it was easier for Alison to give in than refuse and so she just lay there, willing him to hurry up so that she could finally go to sleep.

The next day, on Christmas Eve, Alison had volunteered to cook the evening meal whilst her parents were at church with Emily. She didn't mind, it gave her something to do; however, this clearly bothered her husband and he picked an argument with her over it. He complained that she should have been giving him attention instead of spending all her time in the kitchen. She had tried reasoning with him but he wouldn't listen. He took hold of her hair and pulled her head back until she was looking up at him and she could see the rage in his eyes.

'Not here, please,' she had begged, but with his other hand he had thumped her in the stomach before letting go. Alison felt the wind had been knocked out of her and she slumped to the floor while her husband stormed out of the room. Trying to get herself together, she thanked God he had not hit her in the face again. Wiping away the tears, she picked herself up and continued with the meal, not wanting her parents to suspect anything had happened.

On Christmas Day, her sister, brother-in-law, niece and nephews arrived and the day had gone relatively well. Emily was still too young to fully appreciate the concept but she did enjoy some of her toys. At least it *had* been going well, until the men started drinking during Christmas dinner. Her husband had become argumentative, even with her dad. They stayed one more day after that before coming back home on the twenty-seventh.

Her mum had phoned her several times since then and although Alison knew she was trying to skirt the issue, today she had asked her straight out if her husband had hit her. Of course, Alison said no, that she really *had* walked into the bedroom door. She hated the fact that she had to lie, wanting more than anything to tell her mother that he had hit her just last night, giving her a black eye, but she was too scared, ashamed even, that this was what her marriage had become.

She didn't even know why he had hit her in the face again – he usually hit her where no one would see the bruises. He had been in such a foul mood over the last few days though; nothing Alison did was right.

Hearing Emily stirring through the baby monitor, Alison dried her face again before heading up the stairs to her daughter's room. She had to hold everything together, for Emily's sake. The last thing she wanted was for her marriage to break down, so she would have to do everything she could to keep her husband happy.

They had been out of the office for just under an hour, having a secret lunch up at the Barton Arms. Both Jim and Angie loved Thai food so it was the perfect place to go. It was also far enough away from the police station that, hopefully, no one would have spotted them there.

Following a rather pleasant meal, and even better company, Jim was first to arrive back to the station. Although their current investigation was a frustrating one, he was in a relaxed mood.

He started going through the paperwork on his desk and only gave a cursory glance as Angie walked into the room. Smiling to himself, Jim thought he was very lucky that Angie would be interested enough in him to go out for lunch and he hoped it was the first of many 'dates'. She was, after all, a stunning woman and fun to be with. He couldn't remember the last time he had laughed so much.

'James!'

Hearing his inspector call him, Jim felt himself blush slightly. He muttered an apology and followed Goulding back to his office.

'There's been an update,' said Goulding, sitting back in his chair. He picked up a sheet of paper off the desk and read it quickly. 'I want you and Watkins to deal with it as a matter of urgency.'

'Yes, sir. What have we got?'

Goulding had not offered Jim a seat, so he continued to stand while his inspector ran through the phone call the front desk had received from BTH FM informing them that another letter had been delivered.

'Now, until any forensics come back, we still need to be careful and not just assume this is our guy,' he warned.

Jim agreed. They were still waiting to hear back from the Forensic Science Lab, to see if there was any credible evidence that would match the DNA recovered from the two victims. It was a long shot; they had no idea if the sender had even licked the gummed seals, but it would certainly open up a whole new aspect to the case if there was a match.

'There was a set of keys with this second letter,' the inspector continued, interrupting his thoughts.

'Really?' Jim raised an eyebrow at this information. 'Kate Palmer's keys were found in her bag but Amanda's were missing. Maybe this is the confirmation we need that the letters are genuine?' he said.

'Maybe,' agreed the inspector. 'You need to go and secure them, check with the boyfriend.'

With that, Jim was dismissed.

He went straight across to Angie to fill her in and let her know they were going to BTH FM radio station to secure both the letter and the keys.

Angie was relieved when Jim came over to tell her about the latest update on the case.

When the inspector had summoned Jim into his office, her first thought was that their clandestine lunch had not been so secret after all – she kept looking up from her desk, trying to read Jim's body language to see if they had been caught out.

For a few minutes, Angie had felt like a child again with her hand caught in the cookie jar. Relationships between colleagues were not forbidden, so they had done nothing wrong, but Angie wasn't ready for anyone to know just yet. As much as she liked Jim, it was still early days and she didn't want any uncomfortable comments from work colleagues, especially as there was often a lot of ribbing in the office. They all meant well, of course, and the ribbing was just their way of letting off steam, especially on a case like this, but one or two of her colleagues didn't always know when to stop and Angie didn't want any awkwardness when she came into work, so for now, she would rather keep things between the two of them.

Now she breathed a sigh of relief. It would be interesting meeting Eddie Carter. She often listened to his radio show when she wasn't working, so she was just a little excited to be going to talk to him now. Of course, this latest update was concerning, especially as Amanda Edwards was killed shortly after the first letter had been sent to the radio station, so she would be nothing but professional, but once again, she could feel herself digging round in that cookie jar.

After arriving at the radio station, Jim and Angie only had to wait a few minutes before they were escorted up to the fourth floor by a young woman who then led them along the corridor to an office on the other side of the building. The woman knocked at the door and then opened it without waiting for a response; she showed the officers inside where they were greeted by Eddie Carter.

'Thanks for coming over,' he said, pleasantly. 'Please, take a seat. Can I get you anything – tea, coffee, perhaps?'

Angie politely declined but Jim quickly took the man up on his offer.

'A coffee would be nice, thank you,' he replied. 'Black, two sugars.'

Although they were there to collect the letter, Jim also wanted to ask Eddie Carter a few questions and a coffee would give him the opportunity to get to know more about the show and how it worked. Perhaps it would also help them figure out exactly why the letters had been sent to the radio station to begin with.

First things first, though.

'Can I have the letter you received today?' he asked.

Eddie took an envelope off the desk and handed it across to Jim.

Being careful not to touch the contents, Jim opened an evidence bag and tipped the keys straight into it. Handing this to Angie, he then took a pair of protective gloves out of his pocket and quickly put them on before removing the letter.

Straight away, Jim noticed that the last line was a repeat of the last line on the first letter.

'I'm not done yet!'

Did that mean they would soon have another victim?

It was very worrying.

What did the rest of it mean, though? Who had made a mistake? Who had blood on their hands?

The woman who had first shown Jim and Angie to Eddie Carter's office was now back in the room placing a coffee in front of Jim, interrupting his train of thought.

He would have to look at it again later.

He put the letter into a second evidence bag, and passed this to Angie, who took a cursory glance before placing both bags in the leather folder she had brought with her.

After taking a mouthful of coffee, Jim asked Eddie if he could run through the concept of the show for him. He didn't want to admit that he had never listened to it before and that the only knowledge he had of the way the show worked was from information Angie had supplied on their way over. If Eddie realised this, he didn't let on; instead he happily explained the concept, how phone numbers were recorded before anyone went live on air and how they screened their calls.

'Have there been any calls lately that have concerned you?' Jim asked.

Eddie shook his head. 'No, nothing,' he replied. 'Our listeners do try to shock us every now and then but nothing stands out other than the two letters. They seemed weird so we all agreed they needed to be reported. Do you know what they refer to?'

It was a direct question but one Jim wasn't ready to answer. They still didn't know if the letters were genuine.

'We don't know yet,' he replied, non-committal.

There was nothing more Jim could gain from this meeting. Eddie seemed to have no idea why he had been sent the letters, so Jim thanked him for his time, gave him his card and advised that, should he receive any more, he was to contact Jim directly.

'Hopefully we won't get any more, but certainly, if I do …' Eddie had agreed, placing the card in the top drawer of the desk.

They shook hands and Jim and Angie made their way back to his car, where they agreed it would be prudent to check out the keys before they headed back to the office. At least then they could confirm who they belonged to or rule that address out.

Within a few minutes, they were knocking at Tyrone Bailey's door. Jim hoped he would be at home and was pleased when he heard movement the other side. What he wasn't expecting was the sight of the man who opened the door to them.

Tyrone was a shadow of his former self. He had lost a lot of weight since Jim had last seen him, to the point where the clothes he was wearing hung loosely off his tall frame. His face looked gaunt behind an unkempt growth of beard and his eyes hollow and empty. It was clear that Amanda's death had greatly affected the man now standing before them, and Jim was shocked.

'Tyrone,' he said gently. 'I'm sorry to trouble you, but …'

'Have you caught him?' Tyrone demanded, an edge of anger clearly audible in his response.

'No. Sorry,' Jim replied, shaking his head.

'Then why are you here?' Tyrone quickly apologised; the reply had been more caustic than perhaps he had meant.

'No need to apologise,' Jim reassured him. 'We have found some keys and I wanted to see if you could identify them.'

Taking the evidence bag out of her leather folder, Angie held the bag up to Tyrone.

Almost immediately, he confirmed that the keys belonged to his girlfriend, explaining that the heart keyring was the first thing he had ever bought Amanda when they first started dating and even though it was a cheap keyring, she never wanted to part with it.

Just to be sure, Jim took the bag from Angie, placed a protective glove on one of his hands, removed the keys and tried them in the lock.

There was no doubt.

The keys were Amanda's.

Chapter Seventeen

S unday mornings were lazy mornings as far as he was concerned.

Whilst Alison got on with the household chores and kept Emily entertained, he sprawled himself across the sofa. The TV was switched on to Sky Sports, mainly for the background noise, and a mug of tea and his favourite chocolate digestives were readily to hand.

Perfect!

Sundays also meant a chance to surf the net and catch up on any news he might have missed during the week. It excited him, reading about what he had done, knowing that they didn't have a clue. This morning, though, having searched both Birmingham Police and West Midlands Police on Facebook, as well as the Birmingham Advertiser, he was now feeling puzzled – and slightly annoyed too, if he was honest.

There had been no mention of the letters he had sent to the radio station.

The first time he had put it down to no one understanding the connection, but this time he had honestly thought that the keys would have been significant, so was surprised that nothing had been reported. Did they not consider him important enough?

That wasn't all, though.

The other thing that puzzled him was that the man they had arrested earlier in the week had been released on bail.

What did that mean?

Why was the man still a suspect? Hadn't he made it clear that they had got it wrong? Surely they should have informed the press that the man was innocent?

It didn't make sense.

Closing the laptop, he wondered what else he could do for them to finally take him seriously. He hadn't been joking when he wrote that he wasn't done. It had been playing on his mind a lot lately and he knew he was getting restless, was desperate to recreate the same feelings he had experienced with the other two.

Alison didn't help.

She had been rather emotional lately, irritating him to the point where he had flared up at her for crying over something stupid, which, of course, only made her snivel even more. Between Alison and Emily, he didn't know how much more of it he could stand and this made him even more determined to strike again, to feel powerful, in control.

He sighed – a deep, heavy sigh – as he heard the vacuum getting closer to the sitting room.

Life would have been so much simpler if he had never married Alison to begin with. He should have learned his lesson after his first marriage fell apart. Maybe he should have insisted on no children – his wife had really let herself go during her pregnancy. It disappointed him that her once taut, toned body was now a flabby mess of stretch marks and cellulite.

'Urgh!' he muttered to himself.

He didn't want to think about Alison.

As he flicked the TV over to the news channel, he closed his eyes and began to focus on what he needed to do next. It didn't take long for him to start drifting off, with images of Kate and Amanda filling his mind, leading him into one of the most satisfying dreams he had had in a long time.

Chapter Eighteen

'There's every likelihood that this man *will* kill again!'

Inspector Goulding paused for effect, before continuing. 'Unless we find him. So, I want all of you to go through everything we have, re-interview witnesses, check every lead, no matter how small.'

Everyone in the briefing room on that Monday morning knew the urgency this investigation had taken on. Learning about the keys and the second letter was a worrying development and they all agreed with the inspector that, unless they found their suspect, there would be a third victim.

Since recovering the keys on Friday, Jim had already gone through the details of both cases several times, trying to find a link between the two. The cases were beginning to occupy his every waking moment, even when he wasn't on duty. Somewhere, there had to be that one witness or that one piece of evidence that would help them solve this case.

'Think!'

George Lawrence had been ruled out. His alibi for the night Amanda Edwards was murdered checked out. He was guilty of stealing Kate Palmer's bag, but that was all.

So what linked the two women?

Jim picked up his notebook and read through the comments he had made at both crime scenes. The one obvious similarity he could see was in their appearance – both petite, blonde, similar age. Kate was twenty, Amanda twenty-two. Was he targeting a specific type of woman? One who maybe couldn't fight back as easily, especially if he was well built?

Kate had not appeared worried about getting into the car. Had told her friend that it was a regular. Did the second victim know him too?

The letters puzzled Jim.

Why was he sending them and why had he chosen to send them to the radio station? The only link that he could see there was that BTH FM was also situated in Aston. He had dumped the bodies in Aston. Picked Kate Palmer up in Aston, so, local man? They could rule out any registered sex offenders living in the area as their DNA would already be on the police database – unless their crimes went back to the early 80s, but then the likelihood was they would no longer be on a register now. It would also mean they were looking for someone who, at the very least, was in their fifties.

Was that likely?

Jim couldn't rule it out.

Reported rapes linked to the deaths of the two women only surfaced around a year prior to Kate's death so maybe he had been in prison? It would have had to be a long stretch – murder conviction, perhaps? This could fit with their suspect being an older man – and why he was targeting petite girls. It was something they would need to investigate.

Why Aston though?

Once again, Jim began to wonder if he lived in the area. He certainly knew the area, knew enough to avoid any detection.

A fresh mug of coffee appearing on the table interrupted his train of thought. Looking up, he saw Angie smile at him before heading back to her own desk and he couldn't help but smile in return. Then he focused, once again, on the growing pages of notes and evidence connected to the case.

Alison was sitting on the edge of the bath, the little white stick carefully held between thumb and forefinger of both hands, almost as if it was a stick of dynamite.

She had suspected for a few days now but seeing the two blue lines rapidly make their appearance, there was no doubt at all.

She was pregnant.

She had forgotten to pack her contraceptive pills when they went to her parents over Christmas but her husband had still insisted on having intercourse – and this was the result.

Letting out a long, deep, audible breath, Alison closed her eyes and concentrated on her breathing as a wave of nausea washed over her. She didn't quite know how she felt now, especially as the pregnancy wasn't something they had planned.

One thing she did know for certain though was that her husband was not going to be very happy. He had made that perfectly clear yesterday when she told him that she had missed her period. At first, he had said nothing, just sat there at the kitchen table, playing with the cup he was holding in his hands. This in itself was disconcerting, but when he slammed his cup on the table and stormed off into the garage she had instantly felt on edge, knowing more was to come. It was just a matter of time.

She was right, of course.

After an hour or so, he came storming back into the house, ranted and raved at her, called her stupid and careless amongst other things, even accused her of deliberately trying to get herself pregnant, and then demanded that she find out for sure. It was too late to go to the chemist by then, so she'd had to wait until this morning to buy a pregnancy test.

Now, here she was, looking at the clear blue lines and her stomach was in knots. She knew how her husband would react but, if she was honest, *she* wasn't that unhappy about it. Sure, their relationship wasn't the strongest right now but they could work on that. Emily was still young so the children would be close in age and the new baby might even bring them closer again, given time.

As soon as that thought entered her head, though, Alison knew it was wishful thinking, and a stray tear began to make its way down her cheek.

It wasn't going to be easy, but she was pregnant and it was something he was going to have to get used to because there was no way she was going to get rid of it, no matter how much pressure he put on her to do as he wanted.

Chapter Nineteen

Grief, anger, guilt, despair.

Over the last three weeks he had felt all of these emotions, and more. He only had himself to blame, though. He should never have let Amanda leave the club on her own. If only he had gone after her or hadn't got so jealous in the first place, none of this would have happened and she would still be here with him now.

Instead, all he had was a few photos and memories but even the memories were twisting into nightmares of her last few minutes – punishing him, torturing him every time he closed his eyes. He couldn't sleep without hearing her screams, her voice calling him, begging him to save her, but unable to do so.

It was a constant reminder of what he had done, what he had lost, and the pain was so raw, so intense that he needed to blot it all out in the only way he knew how. He reached down and picked the bottle up off the floor; he went to pour himself another glass of scotch but was surprised to find that it was empty.

How had he managed to drink so much?

Tyrone stumbled to his feet and headed towards the kitchen to look for the cans of cider that were lurking under the sink. Alcohol was the only thing that could take the edge off his pain and, although he knew that everyone was concerned about him, he had gone past caring what anyone else thought. Without Amanda, what was the point, anyway?

Pausing at the bedroom door on his way back to the couch, Tyrone looked at Amanda's clothes, which still littered the bed, thinking back to the night she had been trying them on.

They had been so happy that night and she looked stunning in everything she had tried, but the red dress she had settled on – it had clung to her, complemented her figure – she looked gorgeous.

His mother had stayed with him for a couple of days after they had found Amanda's body and she had offered to tidy the clothes away but he had insisted she leave them where they were. It was not as if he would sleep in the bed anyway, not without his girlfriend by his side.

He thought about his mother for a while.

He knew that Amanda's death had hurt her deeply, although she hadn't said much. He suspected that was because a part of her blamed him for it, and why shouldn't she? He blamed himself, too. Elsa never said anything, of course, and had tried to be there for him, but he couldn't stand her fussing, preferring to be on his own instead.

Opening a can, he went and sat on the edge of the bed, the tears rolling down his face as he picked up a photo frame and stared at Amanda's face smiling back at him. She was so beautiful, so happy and carefree, and he had been so lucky to have her but he had ruined everything with his jealousy.

Instantly, his mind was back to that night, her last few moments.

She must have been so scared.

He would never be able to forgive himself for that.

Over the next few hours, Tyrone opened can after can, trying to blot out the pain.

He wasn't sure how the thought had come about but, as he sat there, it was the only thing that made sense, the only thing that would end the pain he was feeling.

It was late by now and the flat was in complete darkness.

Tyrone took out his mobile and tried to send a message to his mother. As garbled as it was, he hoped she would understand. Then he put his phone down on the bed, next to the photo of Amanda, and walked unsteadily to the bedroom window and opened it as wide as he could. The cold air hit him hard, causing him to step back and sober up slightly. It didn't change things, though. It was the only thing now, in all of this, that made any sense.

He knew he couldn't go on, not without Amanda by his side.

By the time his mother had looked at the text and realised that something was wrong, Tyrone's broken, lifeless body, was already lying in a pool of blood, having fallen from the twelfth-floor window of the bedroom he had once shared with his beloved Amanda.

Chapter Twenty

Before they knew it, January had ended and they were rushing headlong into February.

Despite their best efforts, the police were still no further forward in their investigation.

Whoever had sent the letters to the radio station had since gone quiet which, in one sense, was a relief for everyone working on the case, because they had all had a very real concern that they would soon be dealing with a third murder. On the other hand, they still had no solid evidence that would lead them to whoever was responsible for the deaths of Kate Palmer and Amanda Edwards.

This lack of progress had left everyone feeling frustrated, knowing that there was still a killer on the loose yet unable to link anyone to the crimes. As frustrating as it was for the officers involved, though, for the family and friends of the two women, it was excruciating.

For a long time, Janice Palmer had felt as though she was in limbo. She was desperate to bury her daughter but, because of the way in which Kate had died, they had to wait for the Coroner to release the body. This only added to the pain Janice felt, but procedures had to be followed, however distressing they were.

After a second post mortem had been carried out by an independent pathologist though, the Coroner finally signed the papers releasing the body, leaving Janice to get on with organising the funeral.

She would have liked Brian to have been a part of it, choosing the order of service, the casket, the number of cars and so on, but he was too distressed. He had sunk into a deep depression since that witness had come forward, telling the police what their daughter had been doing the night she was murdered.

Janice hated that woman with a passion she never thought herself capable of. Their lives had almost been ripped apart when they found out that their daughter was dead, but knowing what she had been doing on the night she died had completely destroyed them.

Seeing it reported in the papers, knowing that their friends and family and even complete strangers would be talking about their daughter and what she was doing had thrust them into what Janice could only describe as a living hell.

She had also grown to hate the press and everything they did just to get their story – knocking on their door, stopping them in the street, phoning them at all hours in the days after her daughter had been murdered. They all started off by offering sympathy but it still came down to the same thing: wanting an exclusive.

As if that wasn't bad enough, once *that* woman had come forward, every time a newspaper mentioned her daughter's name, it was preceded by the shameful label of 'prostitute'. 'Prostitute Kate Palmer', as though this somehow made her a lesser person, made her death more acceptable, an occupational hazard, almost as if her daughter had been asking for it.

Janice shook her head bitterly at this.

Her daughter hadn't deserved to die in such a brutal way, no matter what she was, who she had become.

After the second woman was murdered, though, Janice found it even harder to look at a newspaper. Amanda Edwards had been enjoying a night out. She wasn't a prostitute – just a young girl enjoying the festivities, and, although her heart ached for the girl's family, Janice couldn't help feeling both angry and hurt that she had received more sympathy in the press reports.

They had both been murdered. Both had lost their lives in a terrible way, and yet her daughter and the second victim were treated completely differently by mainstream media.

That in itself, had been hard enough to deal with but then the outpouring of sympathy following the suicide of the second woman's boyfriend, had almost driven Janice to despair.

She felt so awful for the man, of course she did, but a part of her wanted to scream 'What about me? Where's my sympathy? My daughter was important too!'

She knew it was illogical but that woman coming forward, the police releasing the information to the press, had made coping with Kate's death even harder. It had also had an impact on her relationship with her husband and she had no idea if they would ever be able to mend it.

Still, at least she would soon be able to lay her daughter to rest.

Tuesday 3rd March.

The date was etched on her mind.

Would she always remember it as much as she remembered the day her daughter was born, or the day her daughter died? she wondered.

She just hoped that the arrangements would do her daughter proud.

Perhaps, afterwards, she would feel some sort of closure. Maybe they both would and then they could try to rebuild whatever was left of their lives.

He had woken up in a bad mood this morning and was still feeling agitated now. Emily had also been crotchety since she had woken up and although his wife had been trying to placate their daughter, it was starting to irritate him, especially when Alison had to rush off to the bathroom, retching as she went. Emily was so clingy with her mother that as soon as Alison left the room it would set her off all over again.

He had no sympathy for Alison though. It was her own fault that she constantly had her head over the toilet bowl and he wasn't about to make things any easier for her. In fact, he was determined to make life as difficult as possible if he had to.

Ever since his wife had dropped the bombshell on him that she was expecting again, he honestly felt as though his life was falling apart.

He didn't *want* another baby.

She *wouldn't* see reason, which just left him feeling bitter and resentful.

They had done nothing but argue since she had told him and although he had tried to force the issue, demanded that she have an abortion, she had refused. It wasn't like Alison to stand up to him the way she had done lately. His wife hardly ever stood up to him, scared of what he would do, but there was something different about this. She wouldn't go along with what he wanted, even when he had threatened to hit her if she didn't make the appointment with her GP.

The contempt he had felt for his wife had magnified beyond all reason at this point and yet her defiance had concerned him. Scared that she might pack her bags and leave if he pushed it too far, he began spending more time at home where he could keep an eye on her. As much as he hated her, he was not going to let her walk away, no matter how awful things were. She belonged to him and he would decide when it was over.

Apart from going to work, he spent most of his time in front of the telly lately, or on his laptop, but it couldn't continue. He felt as though he was losing control and he desperately needed that control back again. There was only one solution and he knew he would have to do something soon, before his frustration completely overwhelmed him.

Chapter Twenty-One

The day of Kate's funeral had arrived. The day Brian had increasingly been dreading as it edged closer and closer. It was all wrong; no parent should ever have to bury their child – it wasn't how things were meant to be. The circumstances surrounding his daughter's death only made it harder to accept, and just thinking about it filled Brian with a dark, overwhelming sense of grief. If she had been in a car accident then perhaps he could have eventually come to terms with it, but the way in which she had died – it was just too much to bear.

Then there was the baby.

Finding out that Kate was pregnant had pained him, made him question just how much he knew his daughter, unable to comprehend the life she had chosen. She had selfishly placed the baby – his grandchild – at risk and now he had lost that too, along with any other chance he might have had at becoming a grandfather.

Once again, he could feel the anger steadily building; he felt trapped. Wanting – no, *needing* to escape from it all, but the house was slowly filling with friends and family, all grieving, all offering support. None of it meant anything to him, though, not anymore. Brian wanted to shout at everyone to get out of his house, to take their sympathy elsewhere, but then it seemed as if Janice was feeding off the condolences of the array of visitors. Perhaps it gave her the strength she needed to get through the day. Just seeing how easily she walked among their guests, though, talking to each one briefly, seeking comfort here and there, left a bitter taste in his mouth and he could feel the rift between them grow even larger.

Brian placed his cup heavily on the table and headed towards the back door. He made his way into the garden, striding purposefully towards the empty swing. There were many happy memories to be found here: of Brian holding his daughter in his arms, rocking back and forth on the nights she wouldn't sleep. Brian and Kate when she was a little girl, putting her trust in him as he swung her higher and higher, just enough so that she wouldn't fall off. After she first started high school, when she would confide her troubles in him – minor issues as far as he was concerned but they were serious to Kate and so he had answered in kind, helping her figure it all out. They were happy back then, so where had that trust, that wonderful father–daughter relationship, disappeared to? Why did she have to do what she had, become what she did? Why couldn't she have called them? He would have welcomed her back with open arms, of course he would. Knowing that Kate could no longer put her trust in him, her father, gnawed away at him and added to his grief. There were so many things he would have liked to say to his daughter, but now it was too late and he hated that.

He also hated how much he blamed his wife, as if she should have somehow known what was happening in her daughter's life, should have put a stop to it, prevented what ultimately happened. He recognised how unfair he had been lately – but there was nothing fair about what had led them to today's events. It was easier to be angry than to deal with the overwhelming grief, even if that meant that Janice bore the brunt of it. Looking up briefly he could see her standing at the kitchen sink washing some dishes and his heart began to ache even more. He knew he was pushing her away, knew that what he was about to tell her could quite possibly bring about the end of their marriage, but he honestly felt as if he didn't have any choice.

Janice had waited so long for this day, for the Coroner to release her daughter's body so that she could finally be laid to rest. She knew it wasn't going to be easy – she would never get over the death of her daughter, or the way in which she had died – and yet, she had woken up this morning with what could only be described as an overwhelming sense of relief. Arranging the funeral had given her a sense of purpose and, although she had no idea how she would cope beyond today, a dignified send-off was the one last thing Janice could do for Kate and she was determined that everything would run smoothly.

Brian, on the other hand, clearly had different ideas, and she was annoyed when she spotted him walking out into the garden rather than engage with their visitors. Things had not been great between them lately. Ever since the police had informed them about their daughter's secret life, about the baby she was carrying, Brian had seemed to be looking to blame someone and, unfortunately, Janice was closest to him.

Of course, the longer it went on, the angrier he had become until finally, last night, it had come to a head. He had said some awful things about Kate and she couldn't take any more. Their exchange of words had been so bitter, so hate-filled, that she wasn't sure they would ever recover from it, no matter how much she still loved her husband.

Watching Brian now, though, from the kitchen window, she only felt compassion at the sight of him. He looked like a broken man sitting on the swing, and although he had been so wrapped up in his own grief that he couldn't see what he was doing to their marriage, she desperately wanted to reach out to him.

Janice rinsed the last of the dishes, dried her hands on her apron, and made her way out into the garden. The hearse would be arriving shortly and she needed her husband to gather control of himself so that they could say one last goodbye. Standing beside him, Janice gently placed her hand on her husband's shoulder.

'It's twenty past nine' she said gently. 'The hearse will be here soon.'

The words hung in the air between them.

At first, she wasn't sure if her husband had heard her or even knew she was there, so she reiterated more firmly that it would soon be time to go. There was no mistaking the tensing of Brian's shoulders this time. He had clearly heard her, so she removed her hand and looked directly at him, waiting for a response.

Brian could see the look of pain in his wife's eyes. Knew that she would be deeply hurt, but he had made up his mind. There was never going to be an easy way of saying it so he figured he may as well just come out with it.

'I'm not going,' he said bluntly, and then, softer this time, 'I'm not going.'

Brian could feel the tension between them as he waited for it to sink in, unsure how his wife would react to what he had just said. He could see her hands clenching as she stood there and even wondered if she was about to hit him. He wouldn't blame her if she did. He knew how difficult he was making things for her but he couldn't help it. When she did finally say something, there was no mistaking the pain in her voice.

Choking back tears, Janice asked, 'What do you mean, you're not going? It's our daughter's funeral. *Your* daughter's funeral. You can't do this!'

Brian did not speak – couldn't even look his wife in the eyes. He knew he was hurting her. But the pain and the grief and the anger he felt was just too much for him to deal with, and he didn't know how he could cope with the funeral as well. Everyone would be looking at him, would know what his daughter was, who she had become and, as much as it pained him, he couldn't face it.

'Brian, please. Don't do this. Not today,' Janice cried desperately. 'The hearse will be here any minute. We have to go.'

'Why?' he spat. 'So people can stare at us, point fingers, criticise us for raising a common whore ...'

He knew he shouldn't have said it, but he couldn't help himself.

His wife's reaction though; stepping away from him, raising her hand to her mouth, perhaps to stop herself from screaming at him, even the look in her eyes, it was as if he was a stranger to her and not the man she had been married to for the last twenty-five years.

'She is still your daughter, Brian. Don't turn your back on her now,' she pleaded.

'She stopped being my daughter when she started selling her …'

'How dare you,' shouted Janice, cutting him off mid-sentence. 'Don't you *ever* talk about our daughter like that. *Ever!* Do you hear me?' Tears spilled down Janice's face. She wiped them away quickly. 'I am not going to let you spoil today. If you don't want to go, fine. But don't you dare insult our daughter's memory with your hatred.'

He had wanted to reach out then but Janice wasn't done.

'This is the one last thing I will ever be able to do for Kate and her baby. I don't care what anyone else thinks about what she chose to do with her life, she will *always* be my daughter and I'm going to make sure she has the best send-off that anyone could ever have.'

'I …'

'No!' She held up her hand to stop him. 'I don't want to hear it. We have nothing else left to say to each other. You carry on sitting here, wallowing in your won self-pity. I am going to get ready to say goodbye to my daughter.'

With that, Janice turned and made her way back to the house, leaving Brian alone on the swing. The tears started flowing then; everything that had led to that day had been bottling up, eating away at him, causing him to lash out, hurt the woman he had loved all these years and why? Why had their daughter chosen to sell her body to anyone who offered? She came from a good family. They *were* a good family and yet, she had chosen to do what she did. He wasn't sure he could ever forgive her for that.

Once the hearse had arrived, it was Brian's sister who came to find him and persuaded him to go to the funeral. She told him how much he would regret not going, how much he was hurting himself as well as his wife, how much the guilt would eat away at him in the years to come, and he knew deep down that she was right, that his wife was right, that he needed to go. Kate was still his daughter after all.

Walking outside as the funeral cortege prepared to leave, seeing his daughter's coffin in the hearse, with a single yellow rose placed on top, Brian could feel his grief threaten to overflow and, more than anything, he wanted to reach out to his wife, but perhaps it was too late for that now. Holding on to his sister, they walked towards the car directly behind the hearse. His wife was already in there, seated behind the driver. She didn't even look at him as he got in beside her, focusing instead on the few people who had gathered across the road to watch.

They were once so close and now, here they were, each wrapped up in their own grief that Brian couldn't help but feel an overwhelming sense of sadness and regret, as they set off towards the church.

Chapter Twenty-Two

'Ellie-Mae,' her father called from the bottom of the stairs.

It was the third time he had called her, but this time she knew she needed to get a move on because he had used her full name. Usually it was just Ellie or Els, and he only ever added 'Mae' when he meant business.

Ellie smiled to herself.

She loved her dad more than anything in the world and they had a close bond, which she couldn't ever imagine changing, even when he was calling up the stairs for her to hurry up.

Life had not been easy for Ellie.

At fifteen, her mother had finally succumbed to the illness that had plagued her for as long as Ellie could remember. It had been tough, seeing how ill she was just before she died, and, as much as it was a relief when her suffering came to an end, Ellie was still heartbroken.

'Cancer is a horrible disease,' she thought bitterly.

'Come on, Els, you're going to be late.'

Ellie looked up to see her father standing at her bedroom door. She hadn't heard him coming up the stairs, too absorbed in her own thoughts.

'Sorry, Dad. I was just thinking about Mum,' she replied sheepishly.

She was only nine when her mum first became ill and she didn't understand the implications of breast cancer at that age. She would walk in on her dad and her two older sisters talking in hushed tones with her mum but they would always stop whenever they realised that she was there and then her mum's eyes would fill with tears.

She was in and out of hospital for a while and then they were talking about secondary cancer. Ellie was in high school by that point and so she had gone along to the school library to look up what it meant on the computer. That's how she found out that her mum was dying.

She knew they had been trying to shield her from the worst of her mum's illness but at the same time, finding out the way that she did had hurt Ellie and she had reacted angrily, which she still felt guilty about.

'I miss her so much,' Ellie continued.

'She would have been so proud of you,' her father replied, sitting down on the bed next to her and giving her a gentle hug.

Ellie didn't doubt that. She knew how proud her dad was so it stood to reason that her mum would have been too. Despite everything that was going on with her mum, she had achieved excellent exam results at school and was now excelling at college. She was hoping to secure a place at Stafford University to study law and everyone was sure she would breeze through her A Levels.

She hoped so.

She would miss her dad, but Stafford wasn't that far away. Even so, she gave him a big hug as they sat there, telling him how much she would miss him when she went off to uni.

'I'm going to miss you too,' he replied, his voice faltering slightly as he kissed the top of her head. 'Now, come on. You really do need to get a move on otherwise you're going to be late.'

'I don't have to be in until eleven today, Dad. Plenty of time yet.'

'Not the way you move,' he chided gently. 'A sloth moves quicker in the morning.'

They both laughed at this, which lightened the mood somewhat.

Ellie playfully punched her father on the arm, grabbed her bag and made towards the door.

'Bet I can move faster than you, old man.' She laughed as she ran down the stairs, closely followed by Mark who was pretending to chase her.

Once she reached the kitchen, Ellie picked up the cup of tea waiting for her on the table and managed to drink half of it before her father walked in.

'See!' she teased.

Her father laughed and then offered to make her some breakfast.

'Don't worry, I'll grab something at college.'

With that, Ellie picked up her bag again and headed towards the front door.

'What time do you finish today?' her father called after her.

'Not until six.'

'Well, text me when you're coming back,' he reminded her.

'Will do,' she replied, shutting the door behind her.

Mark sat back down at the kitchen table with his own cup of tea. He would finish his drink, spend an hour or so job searching, then get on with the housework and preparing tonight's tea. Even though there were just the two of them at home now, there was always so much to do around the house. Still, it wouldn't take long and then he could take a walk down to his eldest daughter's house to spend time with his grandchildren.

They had all come a long way since Lisa died and, although the last few years hadn't been easy, Mark knew that she would be looking down on all of them, pleased with how things had turned out.

Chapter Twenty-Three

Just outside the grounds of St Laurence's, two areas had been cordoned off on either side of the wrought-iron gates in preparation for Kate Palmer's funeral. The first area was reserved for members of the press and their camera crew who had gathered to film the arrival of the funeral cortege, ready to broadcast across the nation on their respective news channels.

There had been a bit of jostling, pushing and shoving earlier as freelance photographers vied for the best position so that their photo would be the one that made the newspapers, but things had settled down for now, while they waited for the hearse to arrive.

The second area had been set aside for members of the public. Many didn't know Kate or her family, but they had been touched by her death in some way and had come to pay their respects. Others simply lived in the village and, although they were not close to the Palmers, had wanted to show their support by attending. Others still had a morbid curiosity and had chosen to come along for no other reason than that Kate's funeral was current news.

As the cortege pulled up, members of the public were visibly moved at the sight of the white coffin with the single yellow rose lying on top being driven slowly past them. Cameras flashed as photographers got their first pictures, and then again as the cars following the hearse passed by. Despite the family liaison officer warning them that Kate's funeral would generate publicity, Janice had not been prepared for this.

Today was one of the hardest days of her life, burying her only daughter, and yet at that moment, seeing the flashing lights of the cameras, she suddenly felt as though she would not be able to grieve properly without that grief being splashed across the newspapers or on the TV. After everything that had been printed about their daughter, these people didn't even have the decency to let them mourn in peace. Well, she wouldn't give them what they wanted. She was determined not to break down, at least not in public.

Brian hated the press intrusion. The stories they had printed about his daughter, about her lifestyle, had left him feeling ashamed, as if people would blame him for Kate's choices. He would never understand why, maybe would never be able to forgive her, but Janice was right. She was still his daughter and he was glad that he had come to say goodbye. As they stood waiting for the undertaker to instruct the pall-bearers, Brian sought out Janice's hand. And then he couldn't help the tears, knowing that both his daughter and his grandchild were lying in the coffin. Friends quickly gathered round to support him, but it was Janice's support he needed. He just hoped she could forgive him for everything he had put her through since Kate's death.

Janice squeezed her husband's hand, feeling such pain for him that her heart felt as though it was breaking all over again. She didn't have any words; she just knew she had to be strong, for both of them.

Signalling that they were ready to proceed, the pall-bearers lifted Kate's coffin out of the hearse. They slowly made their way into the church, with Janice and Brian, close family and friends walking behind.

As the coffin was brought to the front, members of the congregation sang the first hymn, 'In Heavenly Love Abiding'. Tears flowed freely, as they did throughout the rest of the service. It was a beautiful send-off, and Janice and Brian not only mourned Kate's death, but also celebrated her life; both would eventually find comfort in that.

Chapter Twenty-Four

They were sitting at the table eating their tea when the six o'clock news came on.

As the newscaster spoke, he could feel his heart rate begin to speed up and tiny goosebumps spread up his arms. Trying to keep the smile off his face, he watched as they showed the funeral cortege arriving at the church, people getting out of the cars behind and the coffin being carried inside. The voice of the reporter was solemn, as they once again talked about her death, where they had found her, how the person responsible was still at large.

He had wanted to laugh out loud as he listened, managing to stifle it with a cough instead. Quickly glancing across at Alison, he was worried that she might have noticed, but was relieved to see that she was too distracted with feeding Emily and so his gaze returned to the screen.

They had no idea at all. None of them. Even his wife sat there oblivious to the fact that this was his handiwork, that he was responsible for the deaths of the two girls. Clearly he was smarter than the police, smarter than his wife – they just didn't have a clue. This last thought pleased him more than he could have imagined and he suddenly had the urge to go back out there. Find someone else.

Pushing his plate away, his meal only half eaten; he felt restless causing his wife to look up at him.

'Is everything OK?' she asked, tentatively.

He looked across at her, briefly making eye contact before she lowered her head; her cheeks burning bright red as he stared at her. They had been arguing a lot lately and he could hear the concern in her voice; no doubt she was worried that they were about to have another row and he could have, easily. His wife's snivelling was getting on his nerves. She had blamed it on pregnancy hormones but every little thing would set her off and he couldn't be doing with it tonight.

'Everything's fine,' he reassured her after a short while. 'I'm just not hungry.'

Apparently satisfied with this, Alison returned to feeding Emily, a look of relief now fixed on her face. Even the tone of her voice had changed; it was much lighter as she encouraged their daughter to eat her dinner.

At that moment, he was surprised by just how much her indifference had irritated him. Glancing at his watch, he drank the remnants of tea from his cup then stood up and announced that he would be going down to the pub for a game of darts.

He had expected Alison to say something – ask why he had not mentioned it before now but she simply nodded, focusing all her attention on their daughter. She didn't even bother saying goodbye as he left the kitchen. His wife's lack of interest *really was* starting to grate on him. She didn't seem to care that he was going out and he could have sworn that she had the beginning of a smile on her face when he told her, even if she did try and hide it.

Well, he would show her.

He would show all of them what he was capable of.

'Hi, Dad. Just finished college. Off to the library with Lucy if that's OK.'

Mark read the text and sighed.

He would have preferred his daughter to come straight home but he was trying to give Els her independence – she would soon be eighteen after all. At least she had texted him to let him know.

'What about your tea?' he quickly texted back.

'Will probably go to Maccies and grab something.'

This was typical Ellie. It never occurred to her that her father would have prepared something for when she got home and this did annoy him somewhat; still, it wasn't worth an argument.

'OK. Text me when you're done and I will meet you at the bus stop. Stay safe.'

'I'll be fine, Dad. Love you xx'

'Love you too x'

As much as she irritated him at times, she was a good kid and sensible too. He did worry about her, more so after what had happened to those two women just before Christmas, but there was no way Ellie would ever get into a car with someone she didn't know. He would still rather go and meet her though.

He took the cottage pie out of the oven and dished up his own plate. Afterwards, he loaded the dishwasher and settled down to watch his soaps. His children used to tease him about this but Mark didn't care; he loved all of them – the dramas, the plots, the twists and turns of life in the fictional streets and villages, thankful that his own life was nothing like what was portrayed on the screen, despite everything they had been through.

At half past seven he hadn't heard any more from Ellie so he sent her a quick text. She replied that they were just making their way towards McDonalds. Just after eight o'clock, Ellie texted her dad to say she was waiting at her friend's bus stop and would be catching her own bus once Lucy's had arrived.

At eight thirty he sent her a message, asking if she had caught the bus yet.

Nothing.

Ten minutes later, he messaged again.

Still nothing.

Not wanting to panic, yet sensing something wasn't right, Mark called his daughter expecting her to pick up once it started ringing. Instead, it went straight to voicemail. This was unusual for Ellie as she permanently had her phone in her hand, but he dismissed it, thinking she was on the phone to one of her friends, so he left her a message.

'Ellie, where are you?' he asked. 'Call me as soon as you get my message.'

By nine o'clock, Ellie still hadn't texted or called and now Mark was pacing the floor, going to the front door to see if he could see her. This wasn't like Ellie; she always let him know where she was, given how much he worried about her.

He called his eldest daughter, Becky, to see if she had heard from Ellie. It was a longshot and, anyway, if he was honest, he just needed to talk to someone, to hear that he was worrying over nothing.

By the time nine thirty came and went though, Mark knew something must have happened, especially when he dialled his daughter's phone and it went straight to voicemail again. Frantic now, he called Becky a second time, unsure of what he should do. What if Ellie had been in an accident, or worse?

Mark tried to push those thoughts from his head. As Becky pointed out, it hadn't been that long since he had last heard from her and she was probably chatting away to some friends, oblivious as to what time it was. Still, she agreed to come over, leaving her own children with their dad so she could go and look for her younger sister, more for her father's benefit than anything.

Within five minutes, Becky had pulled up outside her father's house.

'Any news?' she asked as soon as he opened the door.

Mark shook his head.

'Honestly, Dad, she can be so inconsiderate at times.'

'Don't start!'

Mark knew how Becky felt about her sister; every opportunity she got, she would point out her flaws, criticising her, complaining about how spoilt she was and maybe that bit was true but right now, he was worried about Ellie and the last thing he needed was another argument with Becky over her sister.

She had apologised then, perhaps because she knew she had stepped out of line. It was enough for Mark. He couldn't stay mad at any of his children for long, so he had hugged her, letting her know that she was forgiven before filling her in on what had happened.

'Look, why don't we walk down to the bus stop,' she suggested, once he had finished. 'We will more than likely bump into her on the way and then I can get back home to John and the kids.'

Mark had been feeling useless, waiting round the house for Ellie to get back, so this seemed like a good idea. He didn't know what he expected but if his daughter *was* just down the road, chatting away to friends, he would have a few choice words with her about it later. Mark grabbed his coat, locked the front door, then they made their way towards the bus stop.

It only took a few minutes for them to reach it.

There was no sign of Ellie but, lying in the middle of the pavement next to a spilled cup of what looked like a chocolate milkshake from McDonalds, there was a blue satchel.

Mark recognised it instantly.

It was Ellie-Mae's.

Chapter Twenty-Five

'999. Which service, please?'

'Oh, God! Oh, God! Police. I need the police!' Becky was panicked, desperate.

'Connecting you now, caller.'

'Police emergency, how can I help?'

'It's my sister, she's missing,' Becky cried. 'She was on the bus and her bag ... oh, God! We don't know where she is ...'

'Ellie!' Mark shouted.

'We'll find her, Dad.'

'OK, what's your name?' asked the operator, his own voice remaining calm, trying to gather as much evidence as he could

'It's Becky ... Rebecca Walker,' she sobbed. 'My sister hasn't come home and we don't know where she is.'

'What's your sister's name?' the man asked.

'Ellie. Ellie-Mae. She hasn't come home and her bag ...'

'Ellie!' Mark said again, more desperate this time.

'OK, and how old is Ellie?'

'She's seventeen. Oh, God! We need the police here,' Becky screamed down the phone.

'Have you tried her friends?' asked the operator. 'Could she have ...'

'No. Her bag, it was on the floor. There's a drink spilled everywhere. What if something has happened?' She was crying now and the fear in her voice must have been unmistakable.

'OK, Becky, try and calm down for me. Where are you right now?'

'Lichfield Road, Aston. At the bus stop by Church Lane. Please hurry,' she pleaded.

'Becky, where are they?'

'It's OK, Dad, I'm calling them.'

'I'm dispatching a car to you now, Becky,' the operator continued, his voice still calm, reassuring. 'Who's there with you right now?'

'My dad. Please hurry. She hasn't come home and her phone is switched off. Oh, God! Please let Ellie be OK,' she sobbed down the phone.

'OK, Becky, someone is on their way. Try and stay calm for me, OK?'

'Where are they?' Mark cried out, clearly desperate for the police arrive and find his daughter.

'Dad, they're coming,' Becky cried. 'I can hear a siren.'

'OK, Becky, they should be with you any minute. Thank you for your call.'

The operator terminated the call just as the flashing blue lights came into focus.

Becky was filled with an enormous amount of relief at the distant sound of sirens and hoped they would now find her sister safe and well. It had seemed like an eternity since she first dialled 999 but now the sirens were growing louder and she could see the blue flashing lights rapidly approaching.

'They have to find her now,' she thought.

Guilt had been eating away at Becky ever since they had found Ellie-Mae's bag lying on the pavement. When her dad had phoned earlier that evening, she was convinced that her sister had probably stopped off with a friend – she was selfish like that, not that her dad would hear a bad word said about his youngest child. She was definitely the spoilt one in the family.

Seeing her dad now though, kneeling down on the cold pavement and clutching Ellie's bag to his chest, the guilt had magnified to the point where Becky felt it was stuck like a ball in the back of her throat.

At least the police were here now.

Becky tried to explain what had happened to the two officers who got out of the car, but she found it difficult to get her words out. Her father couldn't help; over and over, he kept screaming for them to find his daughter. The older of the two officers tried to calm Becky down and asked her to repeat, from the beginning, what had happened.

As Becky filled them in, the officers exchanged concerned glances; the younger officer went back to his patrol car to call in. They would require further assistance on this one; the circumstances surrounding the girl's disappearance was troubling, even to them.

They had no way of knowing what had happened to the missing girl but, given that her bag was found lying on the floor next to a spilled drink, it raised enough of a concern for them to act swiftly, especially as they were aware of the letters that had been sent to the radio station. The officers were also mindful of the fact that this girl had seemingly disappeared along the same stretch of road that Kate Palmer had been picked up on, albeit several yards further up, leaving them with an uneasy feeling that their suspect might have struck again.

They couldn't focus on that right now though.

While they waited for further assistance, the officers needed to gather as much information as they could about the missing girl, as well as securing the bag, which was now evidence. Turning his attention to the man kneeling on the floor, the officer crouched down to his level and explained why they would need to take the bag from him.

The man, however, was not ready to let it go, repeating over and over that if her bag was safe then Ellie was safe. The officer knew that it was illogical and while he could understand the reluctance, it was important that he handed it over.

'Mr Walker, can I, please?' the officer asked again, holding his hand out towards the bag.

With tears in his eyes, Mark finally released his grip on it and the officer quickly took it off him.

'Find my baby,' he pleaded with the officer. 'Please find her.'

Placing his free hand on the man's shoulder, as though that would comfort him in some way, the officer did his best to reassure him. He knew that he couldn't offer any guarantees but he had promised that they would do their best.

For now though, the officer suggested that Mark should go and sit in the back of the police car with his daughter. He gently led the distraught man to the car, where the other officer was still talking to Becky. Instinctively they reached out to each other, holding each other close, and the officer could only imagine the nightmare they had suddenly found themselves in. He was all too aware of the enormity of the situation and having down all they could by this point, he was now anxious for guidance on how they should proceed.

Thankfully, following the call for assistance, it didn't take long for other officers to arrive, including a police dog handler, and they quickly began a search of the immediate area. The arrival of extra emergency vehicles, their lights flashing, had people coming out of their houses to see what was going on. Word soon got round that a young girl had gone missing resulting in local residents also helping with the search.

Watching everything that was going on around him, Mark had never felt so helpless. As soon as he had seen the bag lying there, he had known it was Ellie's, and a feeling of dread had washed over him. Something awful must have happened to his daughter and he should have been out there as well, searching for her, but instead he was sitting in the back of a police car.

Consumed by guilt at his inactivity, he was just about to get out when the same officer he had handed his daughter's bag to, came back to the car and suggested that they return to the house in case Ellie turned up. They would be able to call off the search then, no harm done, and if she wasn't there they would need a photo of her anyway, so it made sense to head back.

Despite his initial reluctance, Becky finally managed to persuade her dad to do as the officer suggested. He knew, though, as soon as they pulled into Sycamore Road, that Ellie had not returned. He could see that their house was still in darkness; he began to cry, an agonising, gut-wrenching cry that completely overwhelmed him and he had to be helped from the police car.

Mark couldn't recall walking from the car to the house. It was all a bit of a blur but he must have done because he was now sitting in the kitchen, a box of photos on the table in front of him. The police officer had wanted a picture of Ellie; he could remember that bit and yet, he was now desperately trying to recall which one he had handed over. What if it wasn't a recent one? How would that help find her?

Mark couldn't think straight and it didn't help that the house was slowly starting to fill up; family, friends and neighbours all rushing round as soon as they had heard. He assumed that it was Becky who had made the calls, letting everyone know that Ellie was missing and he wondered how she could be so practical when his whole world was crashing down in front of him. He knew that wasn't fair but then she could have asked him before she had started phoning everyone. He would have preferred to be on his own as he waited for news but that wasn't likely now and whilst everyone only had the best of intentions, wanting to reassure him, convince him that his daughter would soon be home, he couldn't shake the feeling that something awful had happened and he had been plunged into a nightmare over which he didn't have any control.

As he headed back towards the city centre, he could see several flashing blue lights up ahead of him on the other side of the carriageway, right by where he had pulled the girl into his car.

Seeing them there caused a sudden rush of fear to rise up from the pit of his stomach and he could feel his hands becoming clammy as he gripped the steering wheel. Letting out a deep sigh, he tried to focus on the road. The last thing he needed was to draw attention to himself but, as he got closer to the flashing lights, he felt as though his heart would burst out of his chest at any minute.

He hadn't expected to see the police there and it had unnerved him.

Were they there because of the girl or had something else happened?

Had anyone spotted him?

Spotted his car?

He knew when he first saw her getting off the bus that it would be risky trying to get her into the car, especially as they were on a main road and there were houses nearby, but he couldn't help it and had acted on impulse. As soon as he had made a grab for her though, she had put up a struggle, dropping the drink and bag that she had been holding. In hindsight, he should have picked the bag up but he was worried that the girl's screams might have alerted someone and he just wanted to get away from there as quickly as he could once she was subdued in the car.

Driving past the scene now, he tried to see what was going on. There were four police vehicles, all with their emergency lights on, parked at the bus stop and several people milling round, some in uniform.

There were so many thoughts running through his head as he tried to weigh up any perceived risk he might face that his breathing was becoming laboured, and a trickle of perspiration began to run down his back, sitting uncomfortably at the base of his spine.

What if the police were to stop him now?

What would he say to them?

He had already dumped the body but he still had some of her belongings on him.

What if they wanted to search the car?

'Get a grip,' he muttered to himself.

Trying to reason with the thoughts in his head, he figured that the likelihood of them stopping him right now was slim. Even so, he needed to get as far away from the area as he could. Keeping an eye on his rear-view mirror, he steadily made his way towards the town centre. It didn't take long for the flashing lights to disappear from view, but he didn't start to relax properly until he was making his way over the Lancaster Circus flyover. Only then did he allow himself to think about what he had done that evening, the power he had experienced as she took her last breath, and that cold, calculating smile began to spread across his face once again.

Jim replaced the receiver and stood there for a few minutes, trying to process the news he had just heard.

'Everything OK?' asked Angie, coming out into the hallway.

Jim shook his head. This was not the end to the evening he had envisioned.

'Another woman has gone missing,' he said. 'Well, a girl, she's only seventeen.'

'Where?'

'Lichfield Road. Apparently, the father found her college bag when he went looking for her.'

'Oh gosh! That must have been awful,' Angie replied. 'Do you think it's related to the other two?'

'Similar description of the missing girl: long blonde hair, slim, petite. No sign of her yet though.'

Jim couldn't help but feel unsettled by this latest development. If the girl's disappearance was connected, he knew it wasn't looking good. Lifting his hands to his head, Jim ran his fingers through his hair and sighed so deeply that Angie strode across to him and took him in her arms.

'Are we going in?' she asked.

'There's nothing we can do unless they find her,' Jim replied, feeling helpless.

'Come on,' Angie replied. 'Let's go and get dressed and go in anyway. We can help with the search or the house to house. Anything is better than sitting here wondering what's going on.'

That was one of the reasons Jim adored Angie. She always knew just what to say in any situation.

Nodding, he followed her upstairs.

He hoped that this girl's disappearance was not connected to the deaths of the other two girls but he couldn't shake the awful feeling that the man responsible had struck again.

Chapter Twenty-Six

By the time they arrived at the possible abduction site – separately, of course, to avoid any unnecessary speculation that they were seeing each other – the immediate area was alive with activity as several police cars, all with their emergency lights flashing, lined the bus lane.

The report of the missing girl was being taken extremely seriously, especially given the circumstances in which she had disappeared, and there were now several police officers as well as many local residents all gathered round and awaiting instruction for a second, more detailed, search of the area.

Parking his car, Jim noted that the area around the bus stop had been cordoned off and, to the side of the shelter, he saw an empty McDonald's cup, its contents spread across the pavement.

Had that belonged to the girl, he wondered.

There was no sign of her bag, leaving Jim to surmise that it had already been secured by the first responding officer. Hopefully it would be able to provide some evidence to help them figure out what had occurred here tonight.

Once again, he found himself wondering if this girl's disappearance was connected to his investigation and as much as he didn't want this to be the case, gut instinct was telling him otherwise. For starters, the description of the missing girl was similar to the other victims and the significance of today's events had not escaped him, either.

The funeral of Kate Palmer had taken place earlier that morning and both her death and that of the second victim, Amanda Edwards, had once again dominated local news.

Had that prompted him to strike again?

He had been quiet for a while now, ever since that last letter back in January, so why tonight? If indeed, it was the same man.

Making his way over to the centre of the operation, Jim was impressed by the well-coordinated search, with everyone split into teams. He could also hear the force's helicopter overhead, seeking any heat source that might lead them to the girl.

Jim announced their arrival to the officer who appeared to be overseeing the search, and asked how they could be of help. At this stage, they were not officially part of the investigation as there was no direct evidence linking the missing girl to the other two women. Despite this he scanned the area, looking for anything unusual, or anyone who looked out of place, just in case.

The officer in charge, however, was clearly glad of the extra hands and directed the two detectives towards the search party on the opposite side of the dual carriageway, working their way towards the Birmingham and Fazeley Canal. This area was largely industrial, apart from a couple of derelict pubs.

Calling Ellie-Mae's name as they went, volunteers were checking buildings to see if they were locked, looking in wheelie bins, searching under shrubs and in bushes for anything that might hint at where she had gone. It was a large-scale search, perhaps one of the largest Jim had ever seen, let alone been a part of, and yet, despite the bitterly cold chill in the air, more and more people were willing to join in, all hopeful at that point of finding Ellie-Mae Walker alive.

It wasn't until he got back home that he thought about how risky his actions had been that evening.

He could so easily have been caught.

Of course, there was still a chance someone had seen him, seen his car, and this set his heart racing. If he was honest though, the added risk fuelled his adrenalin, making tonight's events even more satisfying, but now he felt on edge, worried that someone would be able to put him at the scene – and how would he explain that?

The trouble was, he couldn't help himself.

He had been making his way back towards the city centre when he first spotted the girl on the opposite side of the dual carriageway. As soon as he saw her get off the bus, he had felt an overwhelming urge in the pit of his stomach, so he quickly headed round the island, pulled up at the same bus stop and grabbed her from behind. The girl had been wearing headphones and had been distracted by her phone so she didn't hear him approaching until it was too late.

He pulled into the garage, locked everything up and went over to the workbench which ran along the back wall. He reached up for a blue plastic storage box that was sitting on the top shelf, placed it on the workbench, then removed a large black holdall that had been hidden inside. This he gently placed in front of him.

It was his pride and joy.

Running his hand across the top of the holdall, he couldn't help but smile, knowing what was in there. For a few minutes he thought about how he had come into possession of each of the bag's contents, reliving every moment, and then opened it up and added to his collection: gloves, phone – which he double-checked to make sure it was definitely switched off – bus pass, keys, college identification, purse and his most prized possession, her panties.

He wasn't sure how just yet, but he knew that many of these items would be useful to him over the coming weeks.

He zipped the holdall up again and returned it to the top shelf before going into the kitchen, locking the internal door behind him.

The house was in complete darkness so he assumed that both Alison and Emily were in bed.

Glancing at the clock on the microwave, he was suddenly irritated.

It was just gone ten thirty.

'Surely she could have waited up,' he thought bitterly.

Every night, lately, Alison would take herself off to bed as soon as their daughter had settled down, leaving him downstairs on his own, with only the TV for company.

Was it any wonder he did what he did, when she ignored him like that?

Perhaps that was a good thing tonight, though, as now he wouldn't have to engage in any sort of conversation with her, or listen to any more tales of every little thing Emily got up to. How she didn't find it boring was beyond him. He didn't care about what words his daughter mumbled, how many teeth were coming through, how far she had crawled across the floor, how she was trying to stand up. None of it interested him.

He set about making himself a cup of tea before settling down at the kitchen table, his mind still focused on the events of that evening. It was like nothing he had ever experienced before. The adrenalin rush had been so intense and afterwards, looking down at the dead girl, knowing what he had done, the power he felt in his hands as he had tightened the rope round her neck, watching the life drain from her eyes – it had almost been worth the risk of getting caught. Even so, he knew he would need to be more careful next time.

'*Next time!*'

Yes, he liked that thought.

He placed his empty cup in the sink then made his way up the stairs.

Stifling a yawn, he was suddenly feeling very tired and his bed seemed very enticing, despite the early hour.

He would sleep soundly tonight.

Within hours of Ellie-Mae Walker's disappearance, word got out on Facebook and more people arrived to help search for the missing girl; however, by 2 a.m., with still no sign of her, the decision was made to call off the search for the rest of the night. They would start afresh in the morning, widening the search area.

Despite the freezing temperatures and the rain that had settled across the city, there were still people willing to carry on and the way the community had pulled together would have a lasting impact on those who were there that night, with the police and members of the public working together to try and bring the girl home.

This was an unusual occurrence in Aston as there was a long history of an 'us against them' attitude, with many residents having no faith or trust in the police force. In the search for Ellie-Mae, though, there was a common ground that united everyone involved.

For Mark Walker, hearing that the search was being called off for the night was particularly difficult to deal with. He had wanted to be out there himself, searching for his daughter, but his family, friends, the police, had all suggested he stay at home in case she returned. The last few hours, though, had been a nightmare and Mark felt as though his heart had been ripped out of his chest as he waited for news. With the hours ticking by and no sign of his daughter, Mark started to prepare himself for the worst, waiting for someone to come in and say they had found a body. Of course, it would have destroyed him, but the not knowing was even harder to deal with and he had never felt as alone as he did right now, despite the house being full of people.

Under different circumstances, Mark was sure that he would have appreciated the support of his family, his friends, neighbours, even the police officer who had stayed in the house since bringing them back earlier, keeping him up to date with what was going on as they searched for his daughter. Instead he had been desperate for everyone to leave him alone. He just wanted his beloved Els, wanted her to walk through the door, laughing and joking around like she always did. He wouldn't even be annoyed with his daughter, just so long as he could hug her and hold her in his arms again.

As if on cue, the police officer announced that he would be leaving now that the search had ended for the night. Friends and neighbours also began to reach for their coats, offering words of comfort as they did so, along with the suggestion that Mark should try and get some sleep, as if that was going to make everything all right. He knew they meant well, knew it was difficult for them to find the right thing to say, but did anyone really expect him to sleep while his daughter was still out there somewhere?

Mark reached for his laptop and signed in to his Facebook account. He had been deeply touched when he heard about the support Ellie's disappearance was generating and wanted to make his own plea for help in finding her, even if that meant confirmation that she was dead. Setting his status to public, it only took a few seconds for Mark to think about what he wanted to say.

Please, if anyone has heard from Ellie, please let me know where she is. She didn't come home this evening and we are all desperately worried for her safety. If anyone knows where she is, tell someone, tell the police who are looking for her. I just want her back, where she belongs. Please help me find her.

Suddenly tears filled his eyes once again as he imagined his daughter's body lying in the undergrowth somewhere. Everyone had said he should have hope that night, that she would be found alive, but even if it was already too late, he still needed his daughter home, would need to lay her to rest, next to her mum.

Almost as soon as that thought entered his head, it was replaced with the image of a coffin – Ellie's coffin – and it was such a painful thought to even begin to contemplate that Mark broke down and sobbed uncontrollably. Rushing into the room, his other two daughters, Sonia and Becky, found him hunched over in his chair and they threw their arms around him holding him tight, as they all shed their tears together.

Chapter Twenty-Seven

By eight o'clock the next morning a mobile incident unit had been set up on the verge between Lichfield Road and Church Lane, providing a central area from which to conduct operational activities. The search area was being widened and more officers had been drafted in to help with this. There were also house-to-house enquiries which would need to be carried out in case someone had noticed anything unusual, or had seen Ellie once she got off the bus and had not yet come forward.

It was a hive of activity, even more so as several news crews had now arrived in the area, all vying for an interview with a senior officer, or stopping local residents and parents walking their children to the local primary school, desperate to talk to someone who knew the family and could give them an insight into how they were coping with the girl's disappearance.

It was intrusive at times, but this was also a double-edged sword because the press were able to get Ellie's photo out in the public domain, increasing the chances that someone may have seen her.

For the Walker family, though, their presence just added to the stress they were already under. The reporters were now camped outside their home and a couple of them had actually knocked on the door, hoping to speak with Mark. It had got so bad that the family liaison officer assigned to the Walkers had to request that a constable be positioned at the front door to prevent any further intrusion.

Just after 9 a.m., Detective Chief Inspector Alan Jones arrived at the scene, ready to give a press conference. Faced with a barrage of snapping shutters and camera flashes, he read out a hastily prepared statement, detailing what they knew so far and asking for any information that would aid in their search for the girl. Then, carefully folding up the sheet of paper to signal that he was done, he waited for the plethora of questions that would surely follow.

Almost immediately, the one question everyone wanted to know was whether Ellie's disappearance was connected to the murders of the other two women in Aston. Had he struck again?

It wasn't a question Alan Jones could answer. The truth was, at this point they had nothing to suggest that the cases were linked. All he could reiterate was that they were very concerned for Ellie-Mae Walker and would be doing all that they could to find her.

The implications of the missing girl being connected to the current murder enquiry had not gone unnoticed though. A third murder would mean they were now looking for a serial killer and if that was the case there was nothing to stop him from striking again, unless the officers working on the case apprehended him first.

Unfortunately, however determined his officers were, they were still no nearer to solving this case than they had been on the night the first victim had been discovered and the reporters gathered that morning were now demanding to know why.

Sitting at the kitchen table, Alison was on tenterhooks, a feeling she had experienced so often lately. This was hardly surprising, given her husband's erratic and increasingly volatile behaviour over the last few months. It had been a rollercoaster, not knowing from one minute to the next what sort of mood he was in, whether she could relax a little or remain on edge, fearful of the next attack, whether verbal or physical.

Both hurt.

Both were becoming more and more frequent.

She knew a lot of it was because of the baby. He had made it perfectly clear that he didn't want it, but it was her baby too and she could never have forgiven herself if she had opted for the abortion her husband had demanded. Truth be told though – his behaviour had been erratic even before she found out she was pregnant again and she was beginning to think that nothing she did would ever be right as far as her husband was concerned.

The whole situation had made Alison desperately unhappy and she often found herself crying at the slightest thing, but deep down she was still hopeful that her husband would eventually come round to the idea of another child, especially at times like this morning, for example. He had been so nice to her over breakfast, smiling, engaging in conversation, laughing a little at Emily as she tried to stand up.

There had been so little laughter in the house lately that Alison treasured those moments when his good mood lifted the tension. Of course, it didn't last. As soon as she had mentioned her plans for this morning – the clinic appointment – she could see the change in his eyes and felt the atmosphere that had settled itself in the room.

It wasn't the first time she had asked her husband if he wanted to go to the clinic with her. She had asked him when the appointment originally came through, but his mind had already been made up and she didn't want to push it. This morning though, sensing the good mood he was in, she decided to ask him again, hoping more than anything that he was starting to accept the baby now.

The look he gave her told her everything she needed to know and, from that point, she was fearful he would cause an argument giving her no choice but to cancel again. Thankfully he just went upstairs without saying a word, leaving her and Emily to finish their breakfast.

Alison sighed, glanced up at the clock, drank the last of her tea and took the cup over to the sink to place in the bowl with the other dishes. It wouldn't please her husband but she would have to leave the dirty dishes until later; she didn't want to be late.

She should have gone for her first antenatal check three weeks ago but had delayed it in case they wanted to examine her and saw all the bruises on her body. She knew she wouldn't be able to explain them and the last thing she needed was any investigation into how they had happened. Then her GP had contacted her, stressing how important the check-up was, and how they would need to book her in for a scan to give them a better idea of her due date, and she couldn't back out.

Alison figured she was around twelve weeks pregnant by now and knew she needed the scan, so had tried her hardest not to upset her husband over the last few days. She didn't want anyone to suspect that her marriage was in trouble, that she was suffering from domestic violence. It was just too embarrassing to contemplate.

Sighing again, more deeply this time, Alison quickly wiped away a single tear that had started running down her cheek. She didn't have time to get upset right now. Lifting Emily out of her high chair, Alison then reached for her all-in-one. It was still quite chilly outside, and she made sure to wrap the child up warm before securing her in her pushchair in the hallway. Alison reached for her own coat then went to the foot of the stairs to call up to her husband and let him know that she was about to leave.

He didn't reply so she made her way out of the front door, shutting it quietly behind her.

Watching her from the upstairs window, he could almost feel the bile in the back of his throat as he thought about their current situation. He despised his wife. She had promised him that she would lose the baby weight after Emily was born and she did, a bit, but her body never looked the same after that and then she was constantly eating, so whatever she had lost went straight back on. Now she was pregnant again and all he could envisage was her getting even bigger.

It repulsed him.

Made him feel physically sick.

The thought of running his hands over her body as they made love was enough to turn him off her. He hated the fact that her once taut stomach now wobbled beneath him.

Was it any wonder he looked elsewhere?

Desired younger, prettier, slimmer women than his wife?

Alison must have sensed he was watching her – she suddenly turned to look up at the window, causing him to step sideways before she spotted him. He wanted nothing to do with this baby and thought he had made that perfectly clear. It didn't stop her from asking if he wanted to go to the clinic with her though and he was beginning to think perhaps he hadn't made it clear enough. That was easily resolved though.

Thankfully, by the time he looked back out of the window his wife had gone. He finally felt able to relax for the first time that day, allowing himself to relive the events of last night all over again.

Chapter Twenty-Eight

There were some days when Jim hated his job.

Well no, actually, that wasn't quite true.

There were only parts of his job that he didn't like. Unfortunately, today was one of those days where he would have to endure something he hated doing: talking to grieving relatives.

Ellie Walker had been missing for over thirty-six hours now and they still had no idea what had become of her. There was no evidence that her disappearance was related to their current murder investigation but Inspector Goulding had suggested that Jim and Angie go and interview the father to get a feel for the family dynamics and find out if there were any other underlying reasons why the girl might have disappeared.

Gut instinct was telling Jim that this was nothing to do with the father. However, he was also aware that they wouldn't be doing their job properly if they didn't explore all avenues, consider all possibilities, no matter how difficult it might be. Even so, if the reports from the family liaison officer were anything to go by, the father was distraught, which would make their visit even more difficult.

Jim threw his pen on his desk, ran his fingers through his hair, held them briefly at the back of his head before scratching his scalp and letting out a long sigh as he did so. It was something he often did subconsciously, whenever he was feeling under pressure.

* * *

It was an action that Angie had grown used to by now and could recognise as a de-stressor.

'You OK?' she asked, a hint of concern in her voice.

'I am,' he replied with a slight smile. 'Just thinking about the missing girl's father. We need to go and speak to him this afternoon.'

Angie knew how difficult Jim would find this, trying to gather information while dealing with the raw emotions that the family would no doubt be experiencing. Truth be told, though, this only endeared him to her even more and, if it wasn't for the fact that they were at work, she would have gone over to him and given him the biggest hug ever. Instead, he would have to make do with a discreet smile for now.

Suddenly aware that several of her colleagues were watching the exchange between herself and Jim, Angie had the grace to blush slightly before clearing her throat and asking what time he was planning on visiting the Walkers' house.

She still wasn't ready for anyone to know about their relationship and would need to be more careful in future. Looking across at Jim, she was pleased to see that he no longer looked as tense as he had a few minutes ago. Satisfied that he was OK, her attention returned to the pile of paperwork on her desk.

Jim appreciated Angie's concern. That little exchange was just what he'd needed, even if it had risked exposing their blossoming romance. Not that he minded, of course, but Angie was calling all the shots as far as any announcement went and he respected that. Still, he couldn't wait for everything to be out in the open. Although all the cloak and dagger secrecy of their relationship had been fun, he often felt like a little kid with a big secret that he wanted to shout out across the rooftops before he burst.

Perhaps once this investigation was over, they would tell everyone.

Running through his notes again until he found what he was looking for, Jim then reached for the phone and dialled Mark Walker's number.

'Aston Strangler strikes again?'

As soon as he entered the kitchen, his eyes were drawn to the headline and he smiled inwardly. Memories of the events leading up to the girl's death suddenly filled his mind again and the familiar adrenalin rush he had experienced so often lately began to course through his body.

He picked up yesterday's newspaper from the table and started to read the article again. It still excited him, reading about the missing girl, and he had spent hours last night scrolling through social media. He had even found the father's Facebook page, where he was pleading for the girl to return home safely.

'Well, that's not going to happen,' he had thought gleefully.

As he carried on reading, though, his excitement began to dissipate, only to be replaced with a feeling of annoyance. It was the last paragraph that had had such a negative effect on him. The fact that the police were not linking the girl's disappearance with the other women he had killed. No evidence to suggest they were connected, apparently.

'Perhaps I should give them that evidence?'

He quite liked that idea but, as he started to think through the possibilities, he heard the front door open and close. Quickly placing the newspaper back where he had found it, he went over to the kettle to make a cup of tea just as Alison walked into the kitchen.

'I'm sorry I'm late,' she stuttered. 'There was a queue in the pharmacy but I needed to pick up my prescription for some iron tablets and didn't want to leave them.'

She was clearly flustered as she offered her explanation but he said nothing. He hadn't even noticed how long she had been out of the house as he had quickly fallen asleep after she left this morning, but he could sense the fear in her voice as she spoke, and this pleased him.

If only she knew!

He hated that woman so much, standing there all timid and mouse-like that it repulsed him and he knew it wouldn't take much for him to be free from her. Then again, that article in the paper had excited him, maybe more than he had realised, so she still had some uses and he couldn't help but smile.

His smile did not go unnoticed but there was something about it that didn't seem at all pleasant and Alison suddenly felt on edge, wondering if this was the start of yet another row. Thankfully, Emily was fast asleep so if he did start, she would hopefully smooth things over before her daughter woke up.

Hearing the kettle boil, Alison suggested making them both a cup of tea; if she behaved normally then perhaps this would blow over. It was ridiculous for her husband to be in a mod because she was delayed in picking up her prescription but his behaviour was becoming more and more unpredictable.

He didn't even acknowledge her offer; instead he slowly, deliberately, reached for a single cup and began making his own tea while she stood there.

It wasn't until he had finished taking his first sip that he finally bothered to speak to her.

'Where's Emily?' he asked, gruffly.

'She's asleep in the pushchair.'

'Good. Go upstairs.'

Alison's heart sank and tears sprang to her eyes, knowing what her husband wanted. Biting on her lip to stop herself speaking out, Alison inadvertently let out a deep sigh. She could do without his demands right now. The morning sickness she had been suffering from with this pregnancy, had left her feeling drained but at the same time, she didn't want to have another row with him.

'Why are you still standing there?' he seethed, clearly angered by the response to his order.

Alison knew this was only going to go one of two ways – do as he wanted or face the consequences, either way, he always got what he wanted, with or without her consent. With her stomach in knots, Alison placed the bag she had been holding, on the table before walking out of the door and making her way up the stairs.

After knocking at the door, they didn't have long to wait before it was opened by a young woman. She bore a resemblance to the missing girl and Jim wondered if it was her sister. By the look of her, it was clear that she had been crying; her eyes were puffy and red, which instantly made Jim feel uncomfortable.

This was not going to be an easy interview.

Clearing his throat, Jim took out his warrant card and showed it to the woman before asking to speak to Mr Walker.

'He is expecting us,' he continued, wanting, more than anything, to get this over and done with.

Standing aside, the woman invited the two officers into the house.

'He's in the kitchen,' she mumbled, then, more clearly, 'Have you found her?'

'Sorry – you are …?' asked Jim, wanting confirmation before he could give her any information.

'I'm Ellie's sister, Sonia. Sorry, I should have said.'

'Don't worry,' Jim replied. 'I just needed to check. It's just a routine visit, there's no news yet, I'm afraid.'

Despite the fresh tears that began flowing down the young woman's face, she led the two police officers into the kitchen where her father sat at the table. He didn't look up as they walked in, completely lost in thought, with photos of Ellie-Mae spread out in front of him. He had been holding one of the photos in his hands, staring intently at it.

'The police are here to see you, Dad.'

No response.

'Mr Walker?' Jim spoke this time, his voice louder and clearer.

Mark looked up, suddenly seeming aware that someone else was in the room. He apparently hadn't heard them come in. Dropping the photo he had been holding, he stood up, muttering an apology. 'Sorry … I …'

'Don't worry, Mr Walker. I understand. I'm Detective Sergeant Wardell and this is Detective Constable Watkins. I phoned earlier.'

'Yes, yes of course,' Mark replied. 'Is there any news? Have you found my Ellie?'

Jim could hear the desperation in his voice, and he wished that he could offer something positive, but at this stage they didn't know what had happened to the young girl.

'As I said on the phone, it's just a routine call, I'm afraid.'

Sighing heavily and with an anguished expression etched on his face, Mark sat back down in his chair.

'I need her home,' he said simply, almost as a whisper.

'I know, and we're doing everything we can to find her,' Jim replied. 'That's why I'm here. We need to ask you about Ellie's friends, anyone she may have had a falling out with, a boyfriend, perhaps, or any problems she was having at home?'

As soon as he said it, Jim regretted his words.

'*You think this is my fault?*' Mark shouted, standing up so violently that the chair he was sitting on fell backwards, crashing to the floor. 'My daughter is missing and you think it's my fault.'

'Dad!' Sonia exclaimed, rushing to pick the chair up again.

'Not at all, Mr Walker. That's not what my colleague meant,' Angie quickly soothed, trying to placate him.

'I'm sorry,' was all Jim could offer. He had not meant to offend the man and was thankful that Angie was talking to him and calming the situation down. Jim was feeling the pressure of this case but alienating the missing girl's family wasn't going to help matters. By the time they left the Walker house, though, Angie had managed to smooth things over and they now had a clearer picture of Ellie-Mae, who her friends were and what her home life was like.

'Thanks for that,' Jim said once they were sitting in the car. 'I should have phrased things better.'

'No harm done,' Angie replied. Placing her hand on Jim's arm in support, she gently squeezed it before suggesting they head back to the office.

Jim had been under so much pressure lately and having to interview the missing girl's father, knowing that there was a very real possibility that she had been abducted by the same man that had killed two other women, had been tough.

As he started the engine though, Jim was extremely grateful that Angie had been with him and not one of his other colleague. She always knew just what to say and made situations easier to deal with. She was one remarkable woman.

Alison sat on the bedroom floor looking at the chaos surrounding her and, once again, felt fresh tears, wet and warm, running down her cheeks. She didn't know how much more she could take and was seriously beginning to question how much longer she could stay with her husband, especially after today's outburst.

He had wanted to have sex with her when she got back from the shops. She couldn't call it lovemaking any more as there was very little love involved. As she had begun to undress he had walked in the room. She no longer felt comfortable with him seeing her naked. Since giving birth to Emily any confidence she had in her body had long gone and so she had tried to cover herself up but he was having none of it. Her husband could be so cruel at times, making disparaging comments about her body. Then, as soon as he had finished, she tried to cover herself up with her house-gown but that only resulted in her husband losing his temper. Ranting and raging about how much she had let herself go, how fat she was, how frumpy she looked, how she never made any effort for him anymore, how grateful she should be that he even wanted to have sex with her.

The venom in his voice had hurt Alison, reducing her to tears, which, of course, only served to infuriate him even more, resulting in him emptying all of her clothes out of the drawers and the wardrobe before dumping them on the floor and threatening to set light to them.

He had been in such a rage by then that Alison had suddenly felt very afraid of her husband – more than she ever had before. Thankfully, the phone had started ringing, disturbing Emily, which seemed to distract him. He stormed out of the bedroom, not before telling her just how much he despised her, how much he couldn't even stand being in the same room as her anymore.

A few minutes later she heard the front door slam shut, so she had gone to her daughter and brought her back to the bedroom, hoping to distract her with cartoons on the TV, so she could pick up her clothes again.

She wondered where her husband might have gone and how long until he would be back. She knew she was torturing herself now, but perhaps he had gone to meet the other woman she suspected he was seeing behind her back.

Did he really think he could keep his affair secret?

Some nights he didn't even bother to hide the smell of perfume that had transferred onto his clothes, which made her feel cheap, disrespected and worthless, especially when images of her husband frolicking with some blonde woman filled her mind for the umpteenth time. She knew the woman was blonde – she had found a few stray hairs attached to his clothes.

Was it someone he worked with? Did she even know he was married?

As much as it hurt her to think about it, Alison knew that their marriage was in deep trouble – had been for a while now, if she was honest. There was a part of her that desperately wanted her husband to ask for a divorce so that he could go and live with this other woman but then, on the other hand, he was still her husband and she had made vows when they married that she took seriously, even if he didn't.

It was pretty obvious that he didn't love her anymore, even though he would still insist on them having a physical relationship. If she was honest, she didn't love him either, not in the way she once had, and any physical contact just left her feeling used. She often wondered why he bothered when he could just go off to this other woman, but then she knew it was another way for him to control her, to show her who was in charge.

Over the last few months, she had noticed how controlling her husband was becoming – and not just when it came to sex.

He was also financially controlling, so even if Alison did leave, where would she go, how would she manage to take care of her daughter and the new baby? Every penny he gave her had to be accounted for so it wasn't as if she could squirrel a bit away, just in case.

Something had to change though. She sighed bitterly.

How many times had she said that over the last few months – and yet, nothing had. She was still scared of her husband, still treading on eggshells, still felt as though she were something he had scraped off the bottom of his shoe.

Well, maybe it was down to her to make things change.

The midwife had discussed a healthy eating plan with her yesterday and she knew it would be good for the baby if she could keep her weight in check, but perhaps it would also be good for her marriage if her husband started to find her attractive again.

Drying the tears off her face, Alison got on with picking up the clothes and returning them to their proper place. Maybe she did need to get some new outfits, make more of an effort with her husband. She was just so exhausted lately, what with Emily, the morning sickness, trying to keep on top of things. Still, she had to try and make their marriage work, for the children's sake if nothing else.

Deep down it wasn't what Alison wanted, but what choice did she have? She couldn't turn to her parents and there was nowhere else for her to go so she would just have to try harder to make her marriage work.

Chapter Twenty-Nine

Following Ellie-Mae's disappearance, the police were under growing scrutiny as mainstream media debated whether a serial killer was prowling the streets of Aston. Even across social media sites, people were asking just how safe it was and what the police were doing about it. There was a certain amount of anger directed at the police for failing to apprehend whoever had been responsible for the deaths of Kate Palmer and Amanda Edwards, and now, with the disappearance of another girl, the pressure was on.

The officers working on the case felt the frustration of local residents. Ellie-Mae Walker had now been missing for more than three days and they had no idea where she was or what had happened to her. Despite all the news coverage surrounding her disappearance, despite several reported sightings of Ellie, all of which proved fruitless, no one had come forward with any viable information. She had, to all intents and purposes, simply vanished into thin air.

For Jim, this case was turning into a nightmare.

Ever since Kate Palmer's body had been found over in Aston Park, they had followed lead after lead after lead, all of which led to nothing, and now the possibility that another young woman had fallen victim to this man had placed a heavy burden on his shoulders.

Surely he couldn't be this lucky – to avoid detection.

It was incredible to him that this man had managed to abduct and kill at least two women, and had likely abducted three now, without anyone seeing anything. Ellie-Mae's disappearance had not officially been linked to their murder inquiry yet; however,

Jim was in little doubt that they were connected. The girl's physical appearance was so close to that of the other victims, and the location she had disappeared from pointed to this being the case.

CCTV secured from West Midlands Travel confirmed that she had been travelling on the 67 bus out of the city centre and had alighted at the bus stop where her bag and the spilled drink had been found. They could now assume that this drink was Ellie's as the images taken from the bus camera showed her holding a McDonald's cup as she got off.

After that, though, nothing.

No one had got off at the same stop as Ellie, ruling out the possibility that she had been attacked by another traveller.

Had someone been waiting for her to get off the bus?

Attacked her from behind, perhaps, causing her to drop her drink?

Her father was meant to meet her but she hadn't texted him to let him know. Was that because she had planned to meet someone else?

Local officers had searched the immediate area, along with volunteers who lived nearby. Derelict buildings, grassy banks along the railway line as well as any other open areas that might have held a clue as to what had happened that night were searched. They had also searched Aston Park on several occasions in case he had taken her there, but nothing.

Sighing heavily, Jim threw his pen on the desk and got up to pour himself another coffee.

Looking round, he was surprised to see that the office was empty. A quick glance at his watch showed that he, too, should have gone home ages ago, but this case was pulling him in deeper and deeper, and, even though it was now late Saturday afternoon, he wasn't ready to call it a day just yet.

There were only remnants left in the pot and the liquid had long since cooled down, enabling him to drink it back in one go.

Jim grimaced as the bitterness of the coffee hit the back of his throat, then placed the empty cup on the side and returned to his desk where he began, once again, to sift through the mountain of information they had gathered so far throughout the investigation. He had already gone through everything several times by now but he couldn't shake off the feeling that maybe they were missing something. It was a laborious task but if it helped to solve their case he would happily go through it all again, even if it took most of the night.

Especially if it would help them find out what had happened to Ellie-Mae Walker.

Jim was painfully aware that wherever the girl was, the likelihood was that she had already been murdered, probably on the same night she was abducted. It was a sentiment shared by his colleagues but, for now, the official line was that they were hoping to find her alive, at least as far as any press reports were concerned.

He thought for a minute about the press conference that was due to take place tomorrow morning. Her father had finally been persuaded to take part, appeal for his daughter's safe return. It was a long shot, but maybe it would trigger a memory, or guilt someone into coming forward with what they knew – a wife, mother, girlfriend.

Someone, somewhere had to know something.

The question was, why had no one come forward yet?

Chapter Thirty

The press conference was one of the hardest things Mark Walker had ever had to do.

Faced with a barrage of flashing cameras, it was all he could do not to break down there and then as flash after flash picked up every facial expression, every detail of the grief now etched on his face.

When the family liaison officer had suggested he do the press conference, Mark had been reluctant at first. They had wanted him to plead for his daughter's safe return and yet, in his heart, he already felt she would not be coming home to him. Of course, there was always hope and, despite the fact he was not a religious man, he had prayed so much over these last few days. Deep down though, he had a feeling that, whatever had happened that night, it had resulted in his daughter's death.

It was a painful thought and one that tormented him greatly, but Ellie had never gone missing before and would not stay away from home out of choice. Something had obviously happened to her and the horrors that had filled his head since finding her bag abandoned on the pavement had aged him beyond belief. Still, they had finally persuaded him and now, here he was, sitting in front of a room full of strangers all waiting to hear him speak.

The man next to him, Detective Chief Inspector Alan Jones, had just run through what they knew about Ellie's disappearance, the bus she had caught from town, where she had got off. He had reiterated how concerned they were for her safety and asked for anyone with any information to come forward in order that she could be returned to her family.

With that, all eyes were now focused on Mark.

Clearing his throat, Mark tried to speak, tried to get the words out, but nothing happened.

Squeezing his arm in support, the inspector whispered in his ear, reminding him that this was for his daughter.

Mark took a sip of water, cleared his throat once again, looked straight ahead at the cameras and, voice cracking under the strain, he read out the prepared statement he had been given by the family liaison officer that morning, pleading for his daughter to return, begging whoever had taken her to let her go, unharmed, so that she could return to her family where she belonged.

It was an emotional appeal, especially when Mark began to describe Ellie, what she was like, how much she was loved. It was at this point that he broke down, unable to continue with the appeal. He had tried so hard to hold it all together but it was more painful than he could have imagined. Dropping his head in his hands, he began to sob and everyone in the room could feel his pain.

Stepping forward, the family liaison officer called a halt to the press conference.

Mark was helped to his feet and led from the room. All the while, the cameras continued to flash, his every movement recorded for the upcoming news bulletins.

Now, all they could do was wait, and hope, and pray, that the appeal would jog someone's memory and they would come forward with enough information to help find Ellie-Mae, to find out exactly what had happened when she got off that bus but, most of all, to put an end to the uncertainty that her family were now facing.

Chapter Thirty-One

The level of media coverage over the last few days had excited him more than he could possibly have imagined. Everywhere he looked there was mention of the missing girl, especially across social media, and someone had even set up a 'Find Ellie-Mae' page on Facebook.

He couldn't begin to describe the satisfaction he had felt as he read through the different posts, all hoping for her safe return. The press conference released yesterday had also been particularly satisfying, especially when the girl's father had pleaded for his daughter to come home.

They had been eating their Sunday dinner when the news came on and, as they watched the appeal, Alison had kept going on about that poor man, how awful it was for him. Of course, he had muttered his agreement with her, but inside he was almost fit for bursting. How he had managed to control himself he had no idea but he knew that he could not raise the slightest suspicion, so he put what he considered was a concerned look on his face while they discussed the situation. It was only later, once Alison had gone to bed, that he could watch it properly.

He had taken a great deal of pleasure from the father's pain as he sat watching the press conference last night. Perhaps even more than when the boyfriend of the last one sat in the same chair, but then, they had already found *her*. This one was still his little secret for now, which made it even more exciting.

Of course, the press conference wasn't the only thing he had delighted in recently.

The Birmingham Advertiser had dubbed him the 'Aston Strangler', which he thought had a rather pleasing ring to it, rolling off the tongue with ease.

'*Aston* Strangler,' he had whispered to himself.

'Aston *Strangler.*'

Yes, he had liked that, a lot.

It had also given him an idea.

He had felt extremely frustrated when there had been no mention of the first two letters he had sent to the radio station. Perhaps they had not taken them seriously. Perhaps they did not understand the significance of the set of keys. Or perhaps they were deliberately trying to anger him so he would make a mistake, give them the opportunity to arrest him.

He wouldn't put it past them to try and trick him like that but, whatever the reason, he had come up with a plan to make sure they didn't ignore him any longer, and he couldn't help but feel pleased with himself.

He was going to enjoy this.

He quickly typed a short note on his laptop and printed out two copies. Once that was done, he deleted the document, gathered the two sheets of paper and headed to the kitchen to find the pack of envelopes he had last seen in one of the kitchen drawers. Having located them, he headed out to the garage, went directly over to the work station and reached up for the storage box that held his black holdall.

Running his hand across the zip, it was all he could do to contain his excitement as he opened it up. He could remember every single incident that had added to the collection inside, and he was lost in thought for a while, staring at the contents. He knew he needed to focus though, in case Alison came looking for him. Not that she ever came into the garage, knowing it was out of bounds, but still, it wouldn't be the first time she had disobeyed him lately.

He removed two matching items and placed one in each of the envelopes, along with a typed note, before sealing them up and writing different addresses on each one. That done, he quickly placed them out of sight in the boot of his car. He would have to wait until tomorrow to post them – he would need to pick up a few stamps – but they would soon reach their destination and he couldn't help but smile at this.

He replaced the holdall in the storage container and made his way back into the kitchen, locking the internal door behind him before making sure all traces of what he had been doing had been cleared away. Satisfied that there was nothing out of place, he made himself a cup of tea before heading towards the sitting room where he settled down in front of the TV, switching between news channels, looking for the slightest mention of the missing girl.

It didn't take long for him to start drifting off.

As he began to fall into a deep sleep, images swirled round his head: of the girl, of the letters, of the game he was about to embark on. A deadly game that he was in control of and they didn't have a clue.

They would be sorry they had ignored him. He would make sure of that.

Chapter Thirty-Two

Mark Walker sat on his daughter's bed, cuddling her favourite childhood teddy, almost as if his life depended on it.

It had been a week since his daughter had gone missing. A whole week without hearing her bubbly, vivacious laugh, without clearing up her mess after her, or nagging her to finish off her homework instead of spending all her time on Facebook, posting selfies and being silly with her friends.

How he longed to have all that back again.

Every night since his daughter had disappeared he sat in her room, holding on to her teddy, praying that the police would find her. He had never experienced a pain like the one he felt now, had felt since the night he found her satchel. He had never imagined it would get any worse, and yet facing those cameras on Sunday morning had sent a whole new level of pain soaring throughout his whole body.

He hadn't realised just how difficult the press conference would be, how much hope he had placed on it leading to the police finding her, bringing her home, or, at the very least, bringing her body back home to her family so that they could give her a proper burial.

It had now been more than forty-eight hours since he had appealed for information from the public, pleaded for Ellie's return, but he had heard nothing from the police or the family liaison officer, nothing on the news. Still no sign of his beloved Els.

A gentle knock at the door interrupted his thoughts.

'Dad?' the voice called softly. 'I've made you a cup of tea.'

Drying his eyes, Mark informed Becky that he would be down shortly.

She had been so good since last week, staying over at the house after putting her own children to bed, taking it in turns with her partner to get them to school, cooking meals for all of them in the evening, just so that he was not in the house on his own – not that he had felt like eating much.

His other daughter, Sonia, had also done her bit and he was grateful to both of them – the way they had rallied round, tried to keep his hopes up that today would be the day that Ellie would walk through the door wondering what all the fuss was about.

They all knew that was never going to happen, but, for a while, each of them would get lost in the desire for everything to return to normal, to the way it had been a week ago, before she had disappeared.

Mark put Ellie's teddy back on her pillow, dried his eyes on the corners of his shirt and made his way down to the kitchen where his daughters were waiting for him.

Their immediate neighbours and other local residents had planned a candle-lit vigil for tonight at the bus stop where Ellie had vanished and had asked him to go along. It wasn't something he particularly wanted to do but his daughters had talked him into it. They had made t-shirts of Ellie which everyone was going to wear. The media would be there, as well as the police, the vicar from the local church, Ellie's friends.

'If it triggers someone's memory, surely that's a good thing,' Sonia had reasoned with him when she first mentioned it, and so he had agreed. The fact that he was now having second thoughts, didn't want to share his grief with anyone, well, he would just have to put that aside, for tonight at least.

Smiling at his daughters, he picked up his cup and took a welcoming mouthful of sweet, hot tea. He felt lost as he stood there, not knowing what he should do or say to lift the tension between the three of them.

'Thanks, pet,' he said finally, breaking the silence in the room.

'It's nearly time to go,' Becky reminded him.

'I know.' He sighed. 'Are you sure it's a good idea though?'

'We're doing this for Ellie, Dad,' Sonia said.

'I know, pet. I know.'

Mark placed his empty cup back on the table, then picked up a t-shirt that had been draped across the back of the chair and put it on. A picture of his youngest daughter adorned the front of it, along with the word 'Missing'. Mark felt the pain sting but he couldn't let his daughters down.

'Come on,' he said. 'Let's go and do this – for Ellie.'

The vigil for Ellie-Mae was very well received, despite the rain. Many people had gathered at the bus stop where she had disappeared the previous Tuesday. No one really knew what they hoped to achieve by being there but they had all come together to support one another, to support her family, and, in particular, her father.

They had also come to pray for her safe return and it didn't matter that night what religion anyone had, even if they had none at all, but, in a show of unity, they all linked hands and stood silently as the vicar of Aston parish church offered a few words of comfort.

It was a touching moment – one that would be broadcast across the nation, as news crews filmed the event, focusing on Mark and his daughters, intruding on the grief that was evident in their faces.

It would have been so easy to tell them to go away, but Mark and his family knew how much they needed the press in order to keep Ellie's disappearance on the front pages of the papers and at the top of any news bulletin. So they put up with the intrusion and focused all their energy on keeping the vigil going.

By the time it was over quite a few tears had been shed, as time and again friends, neighbours, even complete strangers, had come up to Mark to say a few words, all hoping that his daughter would soon return home and, in a way, he had taken some comfort from their support.

He still couldn't shake the thought that something terrible had happened to Ellie-Mae, but at that moment he was calm, and was glad his daughters had talked him in to doing this.

Once again though, it would be a waiting game before they knew if the publicity surrounding his daughter's disappearance had had the desired effect.

The following morning, as Jim walked into the office, he could feel the negative energy amongst his colleagues as they waited for the daily briefing to begin. The investigation into Ellie-Mae's disappearance had now entered its second week and there was still no news on her whereabouts, despite her having been missing for eight days. Although she was still officially considered 'missing', the investigation into her disappearance had unofficially switched from hoping to find her alive to searching for her body.

By now, morale was running at an all-time low.

Jim wasn't surprised.

The onslaught of criticism his team had faced was hard to ignore at times, especially when everyone seemed to have a negative opinion about their handling of the investigation. Even that day's headlines had screamed out how clueless the police were, how they had failed in their search for the missing girl.

It was frustrating for everyone involved and Jim felt every last bit of that frustration, but they still had a job to do. He began their regular morning briefing, updating everyone on any new information that had come in since yesterday, running through what they would need to do today, allocating the various leads his colleagues would need to chase up, reiterating how that one small piece of evidence could be the key to this whole investigation, trying to boost morale.

With the briefing almost at an end, however, Inspector Goulding made an appearance, and what he had to say left no one in any doubt that they were now officially dealing with a serial killer, despite the fact they still hadn't found Ellie-Mae's body.

The decision to keep the letters sent to the radio station a secret had been an operational one. At the time, senior officers had felt that releasing the information to the public could end up jeopardising the investigation, especially as far as copy cats were concerned, and the staff at BTH FM were only too happy to cooperate.

Earlier this morning, not only was another letter delivered to the radio station but an almost identical one was delivered to George Atwood, the editor of the *Birmingham Advertiser*. Given the contents of the envelope, he had immediately reported it to the police, but by the time two officers had been dispatched to collect it photographs had already been taken. This was big news and there was no way the police would be able to keep it under wraps this time.

Sure enough, within a couple of hours, a copy of the letter had been posted on the *Advertiser*'s Facebook page, raising questions as to the existence of any other letters the police might have received.

'I told them they would pay for getting it wrong and now she's dead.

Tell her father it's all their fault.

I'm not done yet!'

It was signed 'The Aston Strangler'.

Alongside the letter, the *Advertiser* had posted a photograph of a single pink glove, which had a silver glitter 'Princess' emblem across the back of it. The lack of sensitivity in posting the contents to their Facebook page had astounded the officers working on the case, but there was little they could do about it.

Concerned that Ellie-Mae's immediate family might see what had been posted on social media before officers had had the chance to discuss the latest developments with them, once the evidence had been collected and secured, Jim and Angie headed straight to Mark Walker's house for confirmation that the glove belonged to his daughter.

As soon as Mark saw it, he confirmed that it was – that she had been wearing them on the day that she disappeared. Ellie had loved the colour pink and, of course, she was his 'Princess', so the gloves had been the perfect gift last Christmas.

It was the confirmation they needed: Ellie-Mae's disappearance had officially become a part of the same investigation. A serial killer was prowling the streets of Aston and Jim couldn't shake off the growing unease he felt, as they returned to the station, wondering when he would strike next.

Chapter Thirty-Three

The news channels soon picked up on the latest development in the case, forcing the police to issue an impromptu press statement confirming that they had received other letters, letters they had decided to keep secret, letters that contained threats to kill again, and they had said nothing about them, had not warned anyone that there was a potential serial killer on the loose.

This bit made him chuckle: to think that at two murders he was just a murderer, but three elevated him to serial killer. Three meant he was much more important, showed just how clueless the police were, how there was no confidence in their ability to catch him.

'Serves them right for ignoring me,' he thought. 'What did they expect would happen once it got out that there had been other letters?'

He turned off the TV and settled back into the armchair, a smug, satisfied expression on his face.

The latest news reports had been pleasing. He knew he was holding all the cards now and it was time to show everyone just how clever he was, how incompetent the police were. He was going to have some fun with this. He would make sure of it.

As the investigation into Ellie's disappearance entered its third week, he began embarking on a letter writing campaign that would ensure the investigation remained at the forefront of everyone's mind.

The first lot of letters, one containing the missing girl's bus pass, the other her college ID, were sent to both the radio station and the local newspaper. Both were typewritten, both mocked the police in their failure to find Ellie-Mae Walker, both were signed 'The Aston Strangler'.

It had amused him, thinking about the reaction his letters would receive, and he felt an element of satisfaction knowing that the police had no idea who was sending them. That initial amusement, however, was soon replaced with a feeling of frustration that they still hadn't found the girl's body.

'They really *are* that stupid,' he thought as he scoured social media late at night looking for any information on the disappearance, whilst Alison was fast asleep in bed.

It had been exciting at first, reading and watching updates on the search for the girl, but it had gone on long enough now and was starting to bore him. There was only one thing for it; he needed to up the ante and as soon as he got the chance, he knew exactly what he was going to do.

It wasn't long before that chance arose. Two days after the last lot of letters had been handed over to the police, he was once again typing out a note on his laptop. Satisfied with his latest message, he printed out enough copies and carefully wrote the recipient's address on each envelope before dropping them into his local post box. He couldn't help but smile as they hit the top of the pile, waiting to be delivered.

This time, there were three identical typewritten notes: one to the radio station, one to the local newspaper, and the third was addressed to Aston Lane Police Station, care of Aston Strangler investigators. That bit had amused him a great deal and he couldn't help but laugh at his handiwork.

He was so clever!

So much smarter than the police.

The letters made that clear.

Taunting them, highlighting their failure to catch him, their inability to find the girl, their utter incompetence as they bumbled their way through the investigation.

His final line was a clear reminder of just how dangerous he was.

'*I'm not done yet!*'

And he meant it.

Jim Wardell was under no illusions that he meant it, either.

He held up an evidence bag containing the second letter sent directly to the police station, looked at it in dismay, then pinned it to the incident board next to the photos of the three young women who had fallen victim to this man. The contents of this letter were much the same as the first one that had been sent to Aston Lane a few days earlier.

'Disappointed that you haven't found her.
You're not looking in the right place.
Will you find her before I strike again?
You know I'm not done yet.
The Aston Strangler.'

It was clear to everyone that the sender was goading them, playing games with them, trying to get under their skin. The frustrating thing was, he had managed to succeed.

Officers working on the case were already under an enormous amount of pressure and these letters had done little for their morale, especially now they seemed to be increasing in frequency, thanks, in part, to George Atwood's decision to post the contents of the first letter he had received to the *Advertiser*'s Facebook page.

The backlash from that had added to the pressure they were under, but it was too late now, the information was out there and they had to try and ignore the criticism, although it was easier said than done.

It didn't help that the man responsible appeared to be one step ahead of the police. They had no idea who they were looking for despite the DNA evidence that had been recovered from the victims. There were no credible witnesses, no CCTV, nothing to point them in the direction of an arrest, let alone enable them to recover Ellie-Mae Walker's body.

Despite this, they were desperate to bring about an end to the case, voluntarily working unpaid overtime as they searched for Ellie, all the while knowing it was imperative that they caught him before they had a fourth victim on their hands.

Chapter Thirty-Four

Twenty-six days after Ellie-Mae disappeared, everyone's worse fears became a reality when a dog walker came across her remains, hidden in undergrowth beneath Spaghetti Junction.

It had started out as a typical Sunday for Jed and his dog, Max, but what he saw that day would change his life forever. It was something he would never have imagined as they set off that morning.

As it was quite mild out, Jed had decided that they would take a stroll along the River Rea before joining the Birmingham and Fazeley canal. From there he had planned to walk around the reservoir in Salford Park then reverse their route, heading home to a well-deserved fried breakfast. It would take them at least an hour and a half but, after the long winter that had seemed to linger these last few weeks, he was looking forward to it.

It was a walk Max was familiar with too; they had taken the same route several times before, although it was the first time this year. As it was still quite early in the morning, Jed decided to allow Max the freedom to explore off lead. He was a friendly dog and if they did happen to come across anyone else out for a walk, he knew Max would behave himself.

Max preferred being able to roam without the constraints of the lead as he could bound off, stop, sniff, mark his territory, then listen for Jed's whistle signalling that he needed to return, before repeating the process all over again. It was much more fun than walking along the roads by his owner's side and he was confidently exploring the grass verges as they made their way towards Salford lake.

As Max neared the gap in the metal fence that would take them into the park, however, he stopped suddenly and began sniffing the air. Something had caught his attention.

A short distance behind him, Jed noticed Max's sudden change in behaviour. His ears had perked up and his tail dropped as he stood still, staring off into the distance. As he whistled for Max to return, the dog lay down on the ground, growling at something ahead of him.

It was unusual for Max to ignore Jed's whistle, so he tried calling for him to return.

'Max. Max!'

The dog remained where he was.

It wasn't until he got closer to the dog that Max shot up and veered off into the undergrowth, where Jed could hear him barking and whining at something a short distance ahead.

'What is it, boy?' Jed called, wondering just what it was that had caused Max to behave this way.

Making his way towards the overgrown vegetation, he wasn't sure what he expected to find, possibly a dead bird or other animal judging by the smell that suddenly hit him.

What he actually found though was something he would never, ever forget.

He took hold of Max and quickly pulled him away, hooked his lead back onto his harness and then reached for his mobile and dialled 999.

It didn't take long for news to break that a badly decomposed body had been found in undergrowth on the edge of Salford Park.

The discovery dominated news coverage. Reporters were promptly dispatched to the scene in order to broadcast the latest updates and obtain footage of the comings and goings of both the police and scenes of crimes investigators, as they made their way to and from the white forensic tent that had been erected along the fence that separated the canal towpath and the park.

They were desperate to get any titbit of information, confirmation of identity, but the police were not prepared to make an official statement that Ellie-Mae had finally been found; the body was too badly decomposed for a visual identification.

Given the circumstances surrounding her disappearance, though, no one was in any doubt as to who it was, with many taking to social media to express their shock, their despair, their sadness and their outrage, offering condolences and opinions on what they would like to do to the man responsible for ending the life of such a beautiful angel.

The mood across the city on that Sunday morning was a sombre one.

Mark Walker had been preparing himself for this day ever since Ellie-Mae had disappeared. There had always been that slight glimmer of hope, but deep down he had known that she wouldn't be coming home.

He had been standing at the kitchen sink drinking a cup of tea when he saw the police car pull up outside his house. He knew, then, why they were coming. Rooted to the spot, he heard the bell ring, heard Becky making her way down the stairs, heard the door open and the officers asking to come inside.

Still he couldn't move.

Even when they began explaining what they had found, how they couldn't be sure it was his daughter but that he needed to prepare for the likelihood that it was, he remained transfixed on the police car out front.

Becky's cries, her husband rushing down the stairs, the family liaison officer arriving, the two police officers who had broken the news leaving them alone with their grief, it had all become a blur. He had no tears, they had already been spent, but he had suddenly felt so helpless, at a loss what to say, what to do, still not having that final confirmation that his beloved Els was with her mother now, yet at the same time knowing that she had finally been found.

The doctor would later explain it as shock and offer a sedative to help Mark sleep but, at that moment, the minute he saw the police car, he had nothing left other than to shut down and distance himself from what was going on around him.

At one o'clock on that Sunday afternoon, Detective Chief Inspector Alan Jones arrived at the location where the body had been found. His remit was to brief the growing number of local and national reporters who had been gathering since the news first broke, awaiting any information on the discovery.

With cameras flashing and people jostling to get as close as they could to the DCI, he cleared his throat, removed a carefully prepared typewritten statement from the top left pocket of his jacket and waited a few seconds before speaking.

'It is with a heavy heart that I can confirm that a decomposing body, believed to be female, was discovered on the outskirts of Salford Park by a dog walker at approximately seven fifteen this morning.'

'Is it Ellie-Mae?' someone shouted out.

Looking up from the prepared statement, Alan Jones quickly processed how to answer before commenting.

'At this stage, we cannot confirm identity. As you can appreciate, given the length of time the body has been here, it will need to undergo forensic examination before any hopes of identification can be made.'

'Have you informed Ellie-Mae's family?' someone else asked.

'The Walker family are currently being supported by specialist officers and will be kept up to date with everything that is going on. I would ask that you respect their privacy at this sad time.'

'Does that mean you *do* suspect that it is Ellie?'

'Sorry. I can't answer that,' Alan Jones continued, his voice giving nothing away. 'If I can finish by saying that, as you can appreciate, recovery of the body will take some time. Scenes of crime officers are currently preserving the area around the body so that a detailed examination can be carried out and any evidence secured. Now, I don't expect that the body will be moved before the morning so I would ask that you keep your distance and allow officers the space they need to do their jobs. Thank you.'

Despite a few more questions being called out, DCI Jones had said enough. Placing the statement back in his pocket he silently made his way back towards the waiting car, aware of the cameras following his every move.

By the time the footage was shown on local news, it had been edited so that immediately following the briefing, several people were shown bringing flowers and teddies up to the police cordon, handing them over to the female officer standing guard, who then quickly placed them with all the others.

The cameras panned out to the rapidly increasing shrine for Ellie-Mae Walker, zooming in on school friends, college friends, crying and hugging each other as they left their condolences, even though there had not been any official confirmation at that point.

Shaking his head in despair, John Campbell let out a deep sigh and took a sip of his tea before commenting on what they had just watched. In all his sixty-eight years he thought he had seen it all, heard it all, and nothing surprised him. Yet, watching the news today, he couldn't help but be moved by what played out before him.

'They need to bring back hanging!' he stated. 'Let the bastard hang for what he's done!'

'Grandad!' Melissa Campbell exclaimed. 'Hanging won't stop this sort of thing – look at America. It's not a deterrent.'

'Your grandad's right though, pet,' Ada Campbell interjected. 'That sort of person has no place in society. Imagine how that girl's family are feeling right now.'

'I get that, Gran, but hanging doesn't work. It …'

'A rope around *his* neck would stop *him* from doing it to anyone else, though,' John continued. 'Why should the tax payer have to pay for him to spend the rest of his life in luxury, probably in some hospital or something instead of prison, because he claims he wasn't responsible for what he's done. Not fully compos mentis.'

Her grandfather's last sentence had been loaded with so much sarcasm and vitriol that Melissa knew there was no point in arguing with him. She understood how he felt but they were at separate ends of the spectrum as far as capital punishment was concerned.

Mel was a student nurse and hoped to specialise in the field of mental health, working with patients who had committed terrible crimes yet *were* judged to be non-compos mentis, or not criminally responsible. Her grandparents didn't understand this and saw it as some sort of an excuse to avoid being punished for what they had done, and the three of them had had some interesting conversations since she had started her studies, unable to agree.

Despite that, she knew how scary it was, living in Aston right now, knowing that there was someone out there targeting lone women, knowing that she wasn't safe walking along the streets after dark in the area she had grown up in. She also knew just how much her grandparents worried for her safety.

Melissa had not had an easy start in life. Her mother – John and Ada's daughter – had become pregnant at seventeen and didn't know who the father was, due in part to her addiction to drugs. She had tried to fight her addiction when she found out about the baby, had been offered help to get herself clean, but she couldn't resist the temptation, leaving social services no choice but to make Mel a ward of court after her birth.

Not wanting their grandchild to be placed in foster care, John and Ada had stepped in and it was agreed that Mel would live with them in the interim until a decision could be made on her future. They had ended up adopting Melissa after her mum died from a drugs overdose, doing everything they could to ensure their granddaughter reached her full potential. It had paid off as well; she was now an undergraduate at BCU's School of Nursing,

Midwifery and Social Care and would be graduating later this year.

'*Mel*!'

Suddenly aware that her grandfather had been speaking to her, Mel quickly apologised and asked him to repeat whatever it was he had said.

'Always in a daydream, girl,' he mocked lovingly. 'I said, I don't want you getting the bus back on your own on the evenings now. Not while that sadist is still out there.'

She smiled at him.

'I'll be fine, Grandad. Honestly. You worry too much.'

'I'm serious, Mel. It's dangerous out there at the minute. Either call me and I'll pick you up, no matter what the time, or get a taxi, but I don't want you out alone after dark.'

'OK,' Mel replied softly. She knew there was no point in arguing; her grandparents were worried about her safety, and she loved them all the more for it.

'*Promise me*,' John said, his voice firm.

'I promise,' she replied.

Walking past the sitting room, he paused briefly in the doorway. Alison was in there, watching the local news report and he could just about hear the newscaster reading out the latest details. Perhaps if Alison had not been snivelling again, he might have heard more but instead he had to make do with the images – teenagers huddled together, mourning the death of their friend.

He already knew they had found her. It had come across the radio while they were still in bed this morning and they had discussed it – or rather Alison did – going on and on about how awful it was, how desperately sad she felt for the family, and then the tears had started, rolling down her cheeks, mingling with the drips running from her nose.

It was not an attractive sight.

Knowing how much her snivelling annoyed him, Alison had tried to blame it on pregnancy hormones and if he had not been so excited at the fact that they had finally found her, he might have had a few choice words for his wife. Instead, he had nuzzled into her, taking advantage of their time alone, while Emily was still asleep.

Having gone back to sleep himself afterwards, he was now feeling in a particularly jovial mood and he found himself smiling as he walked into the sitting room. Almost immediately, Alison was reaching for the tissues, a look of panic etched on her face.

'What's up with you?'

Quickly wiping away the tears Alison looked up at her husband and shook her head.

'I'm sorry,' she said, her voice barely more than a whisper. 'It's just that it's been on the news about that poor girl and I couldn't stop crying. I don't even know how I would cope if that was Emily.'

His heart had skipped a beat at the mention of his daughter. It was not something he had ever considered before and it had annoyed him somewhat, that she would even think it. He wasn't going to let it spoil his day though.

Sitting next to his wife on the sofa, he placed his arm round her shoulder, giving it a gentle squeeze. 'It's OK,' he replied. 'It is sad, especially for the family.'

The look of panic had now been replaced with one of surprise. The tears began to flow even more then and she buried her head into his chest, comforted by the consoling noises he was now making as he stroked her hair.

It wasn't until much later, after Alison had gone to bed, that he could switch on the laptop and absorb everything that had been broadcast that day. He knew, despite the fact that the police could not identify the body, that they had indeed finally found Ellie-Mae Walker and he was surprised to find that it was actually a relief.

It had been fun for a while, taunting the police over their lack of ability in finding the girl, but he had started to grow tired of it. Truth be told, his mind was becoming occupied with the urge to go back out there, to find someone else, to watch as they took their last breath, and he couldn't shake it off.

Chapter Thirty-Five

Making her way home from her latest work placement, all Melissa Campbell could think about was having a nice hot bath, slipping into her pyjamas and curling up with a good book. She had had one of those days that she would be glad to see the back of.

She was working at a mental health hospital over in Edgbaston and desperately wanted to make a good impression as she was hopeful of securing a permanent full-time placement there once she graduated.

Right from when she had woken up this morning, the day had not gone well at all.

She had woken up late to begin with, had to wait ages for her bus, and then, to top it off, a fatal accident on her way into town meant that she was stuck in traffic for a while. Arriving at her placement over an hour late, she was more than a little frazzled.

After that, things went smoothly until lunchtime. While getting a bite to eat at a local cafe she had absent-mindedly left her bag on the seat next to her. By the time she had realised and went back for it, her purse had gone.

Thankfully she still had her bus pass in the staffroom locker. She knew how her grandad felt about her getting the bus, especially after what had happened recently, but she was sensible, kept her wits about her whenever she was out. Besides, she hated the thought of making her grandad leave the house to pick her up, especially this time of night.

By the time her shift had finished it was dark outside and, as Melissa waited for the bus back into town she felt slightly apprehensive, a feeling that increased as she waited for her second bus back out of the city centre.

As the number 7 came into view Melissa felt relieved. She would soon be home, curled up on the sofa in her PJs. The journey from town to her stop on Witton Lane didn't take long as there was hardly any traffic on the roads now. Melissa alighted near the Sacred Heart church where she had spent many a Sunday, since her grandparents had raised her in their Catholic faith. Not that she went much anymore. It was more of a hatch, match and dispatch relationship these days, much to the chagrin of her grandmother. As she passed the church and crossed Grange Road, she could hear music belting out from the working men's social club and wondered, briefly, if her grandad was in there. She could do with a drink after the day she had had, but then she had an early shift tomorrow so it probably wasn't wise.

Melissa quickly talked herself out of the temptation and continued up Prestbury Road, crossing over to her side of the street as she met the junction with Whitehead Road. It wasn't long before she spotted the light from the front room of their house, shining through the curtains. She smiled, knowing that either one or both of her grandparents had waited up for her.

'With any luck,' she thought, 'there'll be a mug of hot chocolate waiting as well.'

She just hoped they weren't looking out of the window waiting for a taxi to pull up. Melissa wondered what she could tell them if they asked. She didn't want to tell them she had caught the bus home as she knew her grandad wouldn't be happy, so she concocted a story about getting a lift off a colleague who had dropped her on the corner. She didn't like deceiving her grandparents, but she didn't want to worry them. She had worried herself, jumping at shadows as she had made her way back through town, so knew how they would feel if she told them the truth. Still, she was now just yards from her house so she was finally able to relax.

She didn't hear anyone running up behind her until the last moment but, as she went to turn, there was already something at her throat, constricting her breathing and preventing her from crying out. She tried to claw at it, tried to release whatever was tightening around her neck, but she wasn't strong enough and within seconds she had slumped to the ground. There was no let up on the pressure around her neck, though, and her last thoughts before losing consciousness were of her grandparents, how this couldn't be happening to her, to them, not when she was so close to home, when she could see the light shining through the curtains.

Pulling the woman into an enclosed alley between the two houses, he knew he would have to be quick. There were too many houses, too many lights on, and he was fully aware that at any minute someone might spot him.

His final act when he was done with her was to take the same length of rope he had used to render her unconscious and finish the job. Those same feelings of excitement, of euphoria, of power that he had experienced before began coursing throughout his body once again.

He would never tire of feeling this way and wanted to experience it more and more. For now, though, he needed to make his escape before anyone found him here. However, just as he was about to leave, he could hear loud, raucous voices coming up the street. They were male voices and it sounded as though the men had been drinking.

He couldn't risk going back out onto the street just yet in case they stopped to question what he was up to. Panicking, he dragged the now lifeless body further towards the back of the alley and hoped that this wasn't their route home.

His heart was pounding as he heard the voices getting closer and his fight or flight instinct suddenly kicked in. Beads of perspiration began to settle on his forehead, stinging his eyes as they dripped down his face, but then he heard the men pass by and their conversation begin to fade.

Breathing a sigh of relief, he was certain that they hadn't noticed him and he could make his escape. He needed to get out of there and back to the safety of his car.

He edged his way towards the gate and peeked out to see if the coast was clear. There was no one else outside but many of the houses still had lights blazing in the front windows. Once again, his fear of being caught began to overwhelm him and his breathing became shallow as his anxiety levels soared. There was nothing else for it, though; he would have to run and hope for the best. Ducking his head so that his face was hidden in the lapels of his jacket, he ran out of the alley as fast as he could, straight across the road without any thought for passing vehicles, and made a beeline for his own car parked a short distance away on Whitehead Road. By the time he reached it he was out of breath and he felt a burning in the back of his throat as he hungrily gasped in the fresh air.

He jumped in the car and reached under the seat for the keys. He was about to drive off when, once again, he heard voices. He lay down across the passenger seat and, as soon as whoever the voices belonged to had passed, he started up the car, desperate to get as far away from here as possible.

As he drove, he allowed his mind to wander.

What would he have done if those men had stopped and seen the girl lying there?

He knew he was risking everything and yet he couldn't help himself. There had been an overwhelming urge to recreate that first night in Aston Park and it was too powerful an urge to resist.

It wasn't just that now, though.

Knowing that the police were hunting him, that he was smart enough to evade them had given him such a buzz that he was starting to enjoy the game; it was a game that he was in control of and that had excited him, almost as much as taking those women's lives had.

'The hunter has become the hunted.' He laughed. Yes, they were desperately trying to hunt him down but he was just too clever.

As he joined the A34 heading towards the town centre the flashing blue lights and two-tone siren of an emergency vehicle, rapidly approaching, interrupted his thoughts; he was on edge again as he watched them getting closer in his rear-view mirror.

Slowing down, a sense of panic began to overtake him as he envisioned them pulling him over, questioning him about his movements tonight, searching him and finding the girl's panties in his jacket pocket, her phone in the glove compartment.

What could he say to them?

Had someone seen him leaving the alley?

Did they know what he had done?

Trickles of sweat began to run down the side of his forehead again and he held his breath as the police car caught up with him, before letting out a deep sigh as it passed by, speeding on to its intended location.

Tension released he began to laugh, deep, gut-level laughter, becoming louder and louder as he drove.

Chapter Thirty-Six

Ada Campbell had spent the evening engrossed in her cross stitch while her husband flicked through the TV channels, making pointless comments which would require her to join in a conversation with him. She didn't often mind but the pattern she was working on tonight required her concentration so she had found it a little bit irritating.

Having counted out a particularly challenging row, she was suddenly aware that John had switched the television off and was now looking across at her, in what she assumed was a way to get her attention. Sighing to herself, Ada placed her stitching to the side and glanced up at him. Almost as soon as she raised her head, he was asking her what time Mel was due home.

'I'm not sure,' Ada replied. 'I know she's on a late shift today, though.'

'Didn't that finish at ten?'

There was an edge of concern in his voice, which Ada instantly picked up on, making her feel guilty that she had been irritated by his interruptions earlier.

'They're probably short-staffed and asked her to stay on a bit longer,' she said, trying to reassure him. 'You know what these hospitals are like. She will ring us once she's done.'

'I don't like her being out on her own, not at this time of night anyway. Give her a call love, tell her I'll come and pick her up.'

'I'm sure she'll get a taxi back once she's ready. She's a sensible girl.'

John was insistent though, so Ada went in to the hallway to ring her granddaughter's mobile. She didn't like ringing mobiles, aware of how much it cost to call them from a landline, but they had always been reluctant to own one themselves.

Still, she knew it would ease her husband's worries if she spoke to her granddaughter. She carefully dialled the number written at the top of the notepad, and quickly hung up again when it went straight to the answering service. She didn't bother leaving a message as she didn't like the way her voice sounded on those machines.

Turning to make her was back into the front room, she was surprised to see her husband in the doorway. She hadn't heard him get up.

'Well?' he asked.

'It must be switched off,' she replied. 'It went to that message saying she was unavailable. She's probably still busy at work. You know they can't have their phones on the wards.'

John didn't appear convinced.

'It's almost eleven thirty. She should be home by now.'

'She'll be home soon, chick. Why don't I make us a cup of tea while we wait?'

By the time they finished their tea it had just turned midnight and, with no sign of Melissa, John Campbell was anxiously pacing up and down in their tiny kitchen.

Something was terribly wrong.

Ada had tried to reassure her husband but, by now, she was also feeling concerned. Their granddaughter *should* have been home by now.

'That's it. I'm calling the police,' John announced.

Tears immediately sprang to Ada's eyes. She took hold of the rosary beads that had been lying on the table and began twisting them between her fingers, praying that her granddaughter was safe as she did so.

John held the phone to his ear for a few seconds and then looked towards his wife.

'Who do I call?' he asked, his voice strained.

'I thought you were going to call the police,' Ada said.

'I meant, do I call 999 or 101? I don't know what to say, though.'

'Let me call them,' she replied, standing up to take the phone from her husband. She dialled the emergency number. She wasn't sure if this was the right thing to do but John was right, Mel should have been home by now.

Watching him while she waited to be connected, she could see the concern etched across her husband's face. He suddenly looked every bit of his sixty-eight years as he sat back down on the edge of the dining chair.

Once she was connected with the operator, Ada explained her concerns. She had half expected him to tell her she was overreacting but, as he reassured her that officers would be with her as soon as possible, she began to cry. This wasn't like Melissa at all. She was always a sensible girl. Surely she wouldn't have got into a stranger's car? What if that man had taken her?

The very thought of it filled her with dread and she quickly reached out to her husband, seeking his reassurance that everything would be okay. There was little else either of them could do for now though, other than to wait for either Mel or the police to turn up at their door.

It was a neighbour who found Mel's body early the next morning.

Derek Hayden worked in construction – a messy job at the best of times and one that often saw him caked in mud. Derek had been married long enough to know that walking his work boots through the house would guarantee a cold shoulder and so, after finishing his breakfast, he picked his boots up from where he had left them at the back door when he'd got home yesterday, put them on, then went out the back way as he always did if he had his work gear on.

As he unlocked the back gate, Derek texted his colleague to let him know he was on his way to the regular meeting point where he could catch a lift to the site. If he missed the pickup it meant going a day without work, so he needed to hurry. There was little natural light in the alley and, although Derek's mobile gave off a glow, the fact that he was distracted with texting meant that he didn't see her at first, not until he was almost on top of her.

'*Bejesus!*' he cried, automatically making the sign of the cross.

Leaning against the wall, he stared down at the figure lying deathly still on the ground. As he shone the light of his mobile towards her face, Derek instantly recognised the girl. He also saw very clearly that she was dead, and, given the state she had been left in, it was obvious what had happened to her.

'Oh, sweet Jesus,' he cried again, taking off his jacket and placing it over the dead girl to preserve her modesty.

What did he do now?

Go and tell John and Ada?

No!

He couldn't let John see his granddaughter, not like this. The shock would probably finish him off, especially as he wasn't in the best of health, and besides, how would he even begin to tell them?

Perhaps he should call his wife?

She had still been asleep when he got up and he didn't want to disturb her. Didn't want her seeing what he now saw as he looked down. She used to babysit for the Campbells when Melissa was small and this would break her heart.

No, he couldn't call her either.

There was only one option.

As the tears began rolling down his cheeks, he dialled 999. There was nothing else Derek could do for the poor girl but he would stay with her until the police arrived. At least she wouldn't be here on her own.

Chapter Thirty-Seven

The news soon broke that another body had been found in Aston and, as Jim and Angie arrived at the scene, the area was already bustling with activity. Inspector Goulding had not yet arrived but the forensics team were there and technicians were setting up lighting in the confined space of the alley.

Residents had gathered in their doorways, talking to neighbours about what had been discovered. They were unaware then that it was Melissa Campbell, a girl many had known since she was a baby.

As they walked from the car towards the alley, Jim was aware of a sick feeling growing in the pit of his stomach. It wasn't because of what they would find once they got there. Jim had seen plenty of dead bodies throughout his career. It was more than that.

They had been expecting the killer to strike again – he had threatened to do so in his last letter, but Jim had hoped that they would have caught him by now. Truth be told, he felt the failure of his team that morning and it wasn't a nice feeling. He knew it wasn't their fault. Everyone had been working flat out on this case but that didn't stop Jim from feeling responsible.

At some point, he would need to speak to the dead girl's next of kin. Tell them how sorry he was for their loss – and he would mean it. At least he didn't have to break the news this time and he was grateful for that. He was still troubled by his visit to Mark Walker yesterday, having to let him know that they had positively identified his daughter. He hated that part of the job but fortunately, or unfortunately this time, the man who had found this latest body had made a positive identification and, given all the activity taking place right outside their home, the decision had been made for a uniformed officer to inform the dead girl's relatives, sparing Jim the task.

To think she was only yards from her home when she was attacked,' he mumbled, shaking his head in despair. He was becoming more and more frustrated with the way this case was going.

'Someone must have seen or heard something,' Angie replied.

Jim nodded. He wasn't as optimistic as his colleague but he appreciated her attempt at lifting his morale.

'Come on, suit up,' he said. 'I've always thought how fetching you look in white.'

Angie smiled. The tension had broken.

Alison heard her husband's footsteps across the landing and instantly she was on edge. He had been in a foul mood when she went to bed last night, complaining that it wasn't even nine o'clock and he would have preferred her to stay up with him.

Alison had tried to stay awake, but she was just so tired that she could hardly keep her eyes open and he ended up telling her to get out of his sight. It hadn't taken long for her to fall asleep and she obviously needed it as she didn't wake up again until six this morning. She didn't even hear her husband come to bed but he obviously had, as he was snoring away next to her when she got up.

As he began walking down the stairs though, Alison felt apprehensive as she waited to see what sort of mood he was in.

She needn't have worried.

As he came down for breakfast there was a definite spring in his step. He had slept so well last night that he didn't even hear Alison get up with Emily.

It wasn't just that though.

Switching the radio on once he had woken up, he managed to catch the tail end of the news.

'So they found her, then,' he had mused while he lay in bed; instantly feeling an air of calmness wash over him as he imagined the reports this new discovery would generate.

He got up then, determined to make the most of the day ahead; the sun was out and he suddenly had this urge to spend it outside, even if that meant he would be out with Alison and Emily.

Walking into the kitchen now, he bent down and kissed the top of his wife's head, causing her hand to pause mid-air as she went to feed their daughter her breakfast.

'Do you want a tea?' he asked as he reached for the kettle.

The look of confusion on Alison's face was unmistakable, despite her trying her best to hide it. He knew his question had probably caught her off guard, she wasn't used to him offering to do anything for her, let alone make her a cup of tea so he wondered what could be going through her mind. For some reason this amused him.

'Yes? No?' he asked, then seeing the quizzical look on her face, he shook the kettle before asking again if she would like a cup of tea.

'I ... er ... I can make it,' she stuttered.

'No, no, you carry on feeding Emily. She looks as though she's enjoying that, aren't you, pumpkin?'

He reached across and ruffled his daughter's hair, making her laugh and spit a mouthful of breakfast everywhere.

'Now, tea?' he continued before turning back to the sink to fill the kettle. He had started whistling then. Today was going to be a good day, he could almost feel it.

With breakfast out of the way, Alison was also hoping that it was going to be a good day, especially when her husband had suggested they spend some time together as a family, making the most of the mild weather they were having.

She had almost choked on her tea when he mentioned it, causing him to ask if everything was ok. It had been so long since they had done anything together, that it had taken her completely by surprise.

He was in the shower now. She could hear him singing She had no idea what had happened to put her husband in such a good mood but she was going to make the most of it, for Emily's sake if nothing else.

Jim and Angie took in their surroundings as they stepped into the alley. It was a confined space and there wasn't much room to manoeuvre, so they had to make their way towards the body in single file, careful not to contaminate any evidence that might still be there. Thankfully, the whole area was now lit up so Jim could see exactly where he was stepping as he led the way towards the body, still lying in situ.

As soon as he saw her, Jim recognised the similarities between this young girl and the other three victims: petite, blonde, eighteen to twenty years old. Crouching down near the top of the body, he carefully moved the girl's hair to get a better look at the rope that now lay loosely around her neck. There were several scratch marks both above and below the rope, leading him to think that she fought to free the restriction on her throat.

Moving down to her hands, Jim lifted each one to take a closer look. There was what appeared to be dried blood under her nails. They would need to bag her hands to preserve any evidence. No immediate signs of any cuts or bruises though.

'We need officers to start going door to door,' he said, looking across at Angie. 'Find out what anyone heard or saw last night.'

Angie nodded, writing something down in her notebook, before making her way back onto the street.

Alone now, he looked at the dead girl and his heart ached. As detectives, their job was to investigate these types of crimes, dealing with the evidence and not the emotions, but it was hard not to get emotionally involved. Still, he knew he had a job to do and so he made his own notes, detailing everything he had seen both on and around the body.

Once Jim had finished his examination of the scene he rose to his feet and carefully made his way back onto the street to join Angie. The natural light was a welcome relief as he exited the alley and he waited a few seconds as his eyes adjusted.

Angie enquired if he was feeling OK. Her concern was touching. Just one of the many things that endeared him to her and he smiled briefly.

'I'm fine,' he replied. 'Come on, we need to go and speak to her parents.'

'It's her grandparents, I believe, Jim,' she stated, looking at her notes. 'A Mr and Mrs Campbell.'

'Right, her grandparents, of course. Come on then, let's get this over with.'

They walked to the house immediately to the right of the alley. Jim knocked on the door, which was quickly opened by a uniformed officer. The first thing he noticed as they entered was how deathly quiet it seemed. He didn't know what he was expecting – tears, screams, distress – anything but the silence he was met with, and it unnerved him slightly.

As he was about to ask the officer how the grandparents were holding up, a door at the bottom of the stairs opened and an older man, possibly in his early seventies, stepped into the hall. He had clearly been crying – his eyes were bloodshot.

'Mr Campbell?' Jim asked, stretching out his hand. 'I'm Detective Sergeant Jim Wardell and this is Detective Constable Watkins. I'm so sorry we have to meet under these circumstances.'

There was a moment of awkwardness as the older man failed to spot the handshake gesture, so Jim quickly put his hand back by his side.

'Sorry, son,' the man replied in a thick Irish accent. 'I'm a friend of the family. John and Ada are through here.'

Standing aside, the man beckoned the officers into the sitting room then pointed towards the kitchen where Jim could see two figures sitting at the kitchen table.

While Angie waited in the sitting room with the man they had just spoken to, Jim stepped into the small kitchen and introduced himself. The look of despair on the faces of the girl's grandparents was heartbreaking. Jim couldn't even begin to imagine their pain right now.

Once again he offered his hand and expressed his condolences. The man returned the handshake and invited Jim to sit down, moving himself across to the seat nearest the wall.

Jim was aware of how close they all were, seated round the small table, but he graciously accepted and now sat opposite Ada Campbell.

Wiping away silent tears, the woman looked straight at Jim and asked him why.

It was a simple question but one he couldn't answer.

'I don't know, Mrs Campbell,' he replied, honestly. 'I really don't. I can only tell you how sorry I am for your loss and that we will do everything we can to find the man responsible.'

What else could he offer by way of condolence? It wouldn't bring Melissa back, wouldn't ease their pain, but it was genuine and he hoped that they would take some comfort, no matter how small, knowing that he was going to do everything he could to apprehend the man responsible.

Chapter Thirty-Eight

Jade Ellis was a sullen, moody teenager. Everything in her life was 'unfair and she made sure she let the world and its dog know about it at any given opportunity.'
Nothing was ever her fault.

She was currently on the second day of a three-day exclusion from school for fighting. It wasn't her fault though; the other girl had started it. If that skank hadn't bumped into her, Jade wouldn't have lashed out the way she did. Of course, the principle took great pleasure in informing her that they had no choice but to issue her with an exclusion since she was already on a final warning.

At the time, Jade just shrugged her shoulders and waited while they phoned her mother. They all hated her at that school anyway so it wasn't a surprise that she would be excluded and the other girl given a warning. Three days away from the place was just what she needed, as far as Jade was concerned.

Her mother however, had been furious with her petulant daughter and for over an hour after she had picked her up from school she went on and on about how difficult Jade was, how irresponsible she was, how she couldn't take any more time off work to deal with her daughter, how she was causing problems within the family. Jade did her best to drown her out. She had heard it all before and knew from experience that if she tried to defend her actions her mother would carry on even more.

Carol Hanson was well aware how much of a handful her daughter was becoming and the exclusion was the latest in a string of incidents that had caused ructions in the household, especially between Carol and her husband, Jade's stepfather. She only had herself to blame, though. She had spoilt Jade something rotten after she was born. Being a single parent, she felt as though she had something to prove and, by the time her husband came on the scene, the die had already been cast. Jade had been nothing but trouble ever since, even more so after her younger siblings were born.

This morning was a classic example.

When Carol had opened the front room curtains she immediately saw several police cars and officers swarming all over the place. It looked as though the street had been cordoned off and her first thought was perhaps another stabbing. Thanks to a few phone calls from her neighbours, though, Carol soon found out that a body had been discovered in one of the alleys over the road.

The rumours were rife but, shocking as it was, she still had to get the boys off to their breakfast club at the school where she also worked as a teaching assistant. Carol didnt like the thought of having to leave Jade home alone, especially if the rumours were true that the Aston Strangler had claimed his fourth victim. Not that she believed everything old Martha told her but still, she was nervous enough to warn her daughter to keep the doors locked and not to open the front door under any circumstances.

Jade had clearly ignored her mother, though, as a couple of hours later the police had called in to the school to ask if Carol would accompany her daughter to the police station so that she could make a formal statement about something she had witnessed last night.

Carol was not at all happy about this. For one thing, her daughter had not mentioned anything about it to her and for another, it meant she now had to leave work to act as an appropriate adult and she knew the head was already unimpressed with all the time she had taken off to deal with her daughter's dramatics.

Despite her annoyance, though, if Jade had witnessed something, Carol knew they had to go along to the station so that the officers could talk through what her daughter had seen and get it down on paper. She just hoped that Jade wasn't wasting everyone's time; that would be the final straw as far as she was concerned.

Jade, on the other hand, couldn't remember the last time she had felt this excited. There was a fluttering in the pit of her stomach and her whole body tingled as they made their way to the police station. She had never been in the back of a police car before and her excitement had been building ever since that policewoman had told her that what she witnessed last night was of vital importance.

Jade Ellis was important.

It was just a shame they had insisted her mother attend the station as well; she would have preferred to enjoy this adventure alone, especially since she realised, the moment her mother returned home with the police in tow, that she was not at all happy about being pulled out of work.

It wasn't Jade's fault though. She never asked them to fetch her mother so she had no idea why she would be so angry with her. OK, so she had ignored her mum's instructions about not opening the door to anyone but it wasn't her fault that she had forgotten. Her mum had been going on and on about how annoyed she was that Jade had been excluded from school and would have to stay home alone as she couldn't take any more time off work.

Then, of course, they found out about the dead woman and that had set her mum off even more. It was all Jade could do to try and block her out so it didn't register about keeping the doors locked. It was only afterwards, once her mother walked back in the house with the police officers, that she remembered their earlier conversation.

Glancing fleetingly to her left as they drove along, Jade immediately saw that look, the one her mother adopted whenever she was angry, still firmly fixed on her face and decided it would be safer if she continued to look out of the car window.

Despite her mother's obvious annoyance at the situation, Jade was determined to make the most of all the attention she was now getting. It felt good, knowing that she could help the police with their investigation and the officers who had spoken to her were being so nice, friendly even, laughing and joking and asking her lots of questions about herself. It was exciting as well, to be honest. Right from when that policeman had knocked at their door earlier this morning. He had smiled at her when she opened the door, asking to speak to either of her parents as they were investigating a serious incident. He never said what it was but Jade couldn't help blurting out that she knew it was about a dead woman.

The police officer had just smiled at her and asked again if he could speak to either her mum or dad. Jade had been quick to correct him, informing the policeman that she lived with her mum and stepdad. There was no way she ever wanted anyone thinking that Bob was her father.

He had apologised to her, and Jade had blushed slightly, but again he asked if he could speak to either her mother or stepfather. She couldn't explain why but she suddenly felt insignificant and not for the first time in her young life. It wasn't a nice feeling and it only increased once she had told the officer that no one else was home. He had closed his notebook then, thanked her for her time and turned to walk away.

She should have just shut the door, waited until her mum returned home from work, but it was as if her mouth moved before her brain even thought about what she was saying.

'I saw something last night,' she had said, stopping the officer in his tracks.

'Did you, now?' he had queried, turning back to her.

'I saw who went into that alley,' she had replied, almost without thinking.

As soon as she said this the officer had instructed her to wait where she was while he moved a short distance from the house and spoke into his walkie-talkie thing or radio, whatever they called it.

That was when Jade had begun to feel important. The officer's whole attitude had somehow changed towards her and she could have sworn that his eyes lit up the instant she had uttered those few words.

Jade had tried to listen in on what he was saying but she couldn't quite make it out, which had annoyed her slightly. She soon put that out of her mind though when, a few minutes later, a female officer walked over to the man Jade had just spoken to. She knew they were talking about her as every so often the policewoman would look in her direction. She wished she could hear what they were saying but, whatever it was, it was beginning to dawn on Jade just how seriously her words were being taken.

There was a moment when she wondered if she should just go back in the house and lock the door but curiosity had got the better of her. Then, as both police officers began walking towards her, she knew there was no backing out and although she had become very nervous she was also very, very excited, wondering what would happen next.

Everything moved very quickly after that; talk about making an official statement, fetching her mum from work, getting in the back of the police car and making their way to the station which, thankfully, wasn't that far away, especially as her mother's annoyance had only seemed to increase during the short journey.

Well, Jade wasn't going to let her mother spoil her fun today. This was her moment and she was going to make the most of it, that was for sure.

Jim was back at the station following his visit with John and Ada Campbell, pondering on that morning's events, aware that a dark cloud that had settled over him.

He glanced up at the fresh photograph that had been added to the board; he couldn't help but be mesmerised by the sparkling eyes that stared back at him, the smile so carefree, just like the other girls, all with their whole lives ahead of them. They would have had no idea, as they smiled for whoever was taking their picture, just what their future held, the danger they faced, and now they were dead.

How many more girls would they see up here? he wondered bitterly.

He knew he was maudlin now. He turned away from the board, walked over to the percolator and, as made himself a fresh mug of coffee, one of his colleagues walked in and informed him that a credible witness had come forward.

Jim's heart skipped a beat. Would this lead to the breakthrough they needed? Whoever was responsible for killing these girls had managed to avoid detection for months now, abducting and murdering his victims without anyone being able to identify him. Hell, he had even managed to kill his latest victim almost on her own front doorstep but perhaps his luck was running out now and the information the witness held would finally lead to an arrest, bringing to an end one of the most frustrating cases he had ever worked on.

'Has someone taken a statement?' he asked, trying not to sound as excited as he felt.

'They're bringing her in now,' his colleague replied. 'Young girl, so they needed an appropriate adult. Think her mum's coming in with her.'

This was good news as far as Jim was concerned. If they were bringing the girl in then whatever information she held had to be crucial otherwise they would have taken a statement at her home.

Jim walked back towards his desk, his mood now much lighter than it had been when he first returned to the office.

'Not long now,' he couldn't help but think. 'Not long …'

As if on cue, the inspector's door opened and he stood in the doorway. 'Right, listen up,' he bellowed. Almost immediately, the whole room settled into a complete hush as all eyes turned towards him.

'As some of you will have heard, we have a credible witness who has come forward and given us the name of a potential suspect who she saw going into the alley where Melissa Campbell was discovered early this morning.'

'Finally!' someone called out, echoing the sentiment of everyone in the room. There was suddenly an excited buzz in the air as the officers on MIT hoped they were close to ending this case.

'Yes, well, settle down, eh. Let's get excited when we charge the bastard. Until then, there's still plenty of work to be getting on with.'

Jim knew Goulding was right and while he completely understood why the atmosphere in the incident room had lifted, he hadn't forgotten that they had been here once before, when they were about to arrest George Lawrence, and look at how that had turned out.

The man had not been entirely innocent, of course, having stolen Kate Palmer's bag and disposing of it but Jim had felt responsible – pushing for his arrest, convinced he had done it.

It was a painful memory, one he didn't want to dwell on and so his attention returned to his inspector, who was now talking about their witness.

'Right,' Goulding had continued, 'our witness is only thirteen, so kid gloves are needed when interviewing her. Jim, Angie, I want both of you to take her statement. Run through everything she saw last night and make sure she leaves nothing out. I want her to be very sure about what she witnessed. The last thing we need right now is to go arresting the wrong man again.'

Jim instantly felt the sting of his inspector's last comment but this wasn't time to dwell on it. Nodding his head in confirmation, he stole a brief look at Angie, offering what he hoped was a discreet smile before turning his head back towards the inspector.

'As soon as everything is down on paper,' Goulding continued, 'I will lead the arrest team and hopefully we will have him in custody before the day is out, with a signed confession to boot!'

Once again, a murmur went round the room as the inspector named the officers who would accompany him on the arrest. Jim was surprised to find that he would not be involved in that part of the investigation; he would have liked to have been part of the arrest team. Seeing the look on their suspect's face when he slapped the cuffs on him would have given Jim a great deal of satisfaction, especially after all this time. Still, at least he would be working with Angie and the information their witness held would hopefully help bring about an end to this case. He just hoped the witness wasn't a typical petulant teenager; he wasn't feeling particularly patient at this point.

A loud clap of hands brought Jim out of his reverie. Looking up, he briefly locked eyes with his inspector, who was clearly still after everyone's attention.

'One last thing,' Goulding said. 'I know this goes without saying but just a reminder that whatever information we have stays in this room. Reporters are milling around, given this morning's events, and I don't want loose lips jeopardising the arrest.'

Chapter Thirty-Nine

J ade Ellis was positively brimming with excitement now that she was at the police station. Everyone was being so nice to her. Well ... almost everyone.

Her mother still looked as though she was sucking on a lemon.

Jade giggled out loud at this thought, causing her mother to throw another one of her disapproving looks. Jade didn't care though. Her mother had been glaring at her almost from the get-go, right from the minute she walked back in the house, and although she had remained silent whilst they were in the police car she had plenty to say to Jade now that they were alone. Mainly about why Jade had not said anything to her this morning before she had left for work. Not that she could have got a word in edgeways, the way her mother had been going on at her.

'You had better not be wasting anyone's time, my girl, I'm warning you,' she had seethed after they were shown into the ... what had the policewoman called it? Oh yes, the interview suite.

Looking around her, Jade decided that she liked it in here. It was just like a sitting room really, with teddies and toys and books and squishy pillows.

Yes, she liked this room.

It was even better when the policewoman who had been with her earlier came back in the room with a can of coke, just for her.

Totally ignoring her mother now, Jade sat down with the policewoman and they chatted about school, about friends, her favourite pop group and what she liked doing, whilst she asked what it was like being a policewoman, announcing that this was what she had always wanted to do when she left school.

'Since when?' her mother had interjected. 'I thought you wanted to be a hairdresser?'

Why did her mother have to butt in?

Ignoring her, Jade continued with her conversation. Talking to the policewoman was nothing like the conversations she had with her school friends. It was so much more grown up and at least the policewoman was interested in her, in the things she liked, and didn't just treat her like a little kid.

Before long, however, two more officers came into the room, putting an end to their little chat. Not that Jade minded, especially since these two appeared to be much more important. They didn't even have to wear a uniform and when the man said that they were detectives, that they needed to talk to her about what she had seen last night, how important her information was, how important she was, Jade had felt like she would burst at any minute.

At that moment, it didn't matter what her mother thought, it mattered what Jade thought and it mattered what she had to tell them. Whatever that was, she just knew that they would be hanging off every word and that was the best feeling of all.

As he entered the room, Jim sensed tension and looked back at Angie, raising an eyebrow, wondering if she could feel it too. The shrug of her shoulders signalled that he hadn't been mistaken.

It wasn't the girl. She was happily sitting in the middle of the sofa holding a cushion across her stomach with one hand and a can of coke in the other, talking animatedly to the policewoman sitting next to her.

Turning his attention to the woman standing behind the sofa, Jim was surprised at just how unhappy she looked, seemingly more engrossed in reading the info posters on the wall than the chatter going on in the room. He found her standoffishness odd, given the circumstances, but then they had asked her to leave work so she could act as her daughter's appropriate adult.

Jim closed the door firmly and everyone turned their attention towards him. He smiled at the young girl, then asked her mum if she would like to join them; he sat down on one of the chairs. Angie followed suit and took the other empty chair, leaving a space on the sofa next to Jade for her mum. Carol, however, declined, apparently preferring to remain standing, which caused Jim to raise his eyebrow and look across at Angie again.

Ignoring the tension, Jim turned his attention to their witness. She was small for her age and, despite her attempts to look older by smearing thick black eyeliner under her eyes, she looked younger than her thirteen years, perhaps even more so, surrounded as she was by all the adults in the room.

'Thanks so much for coming in at such short notice,' Jim began with a smile, Inspector Goulding's suggestion of kid gloves still fresh in his mind. 'I'm Detective Sergeant Jim Warden and this is Detective Constable Watkins.'

Jade smiled back at Jim, clearly enamoured with him given the flush of red spreading across her cheeks.

'I'm going to be a policewoman one day,' she gushed. 'I told you that, didn't I?' she continued, turning back to the policewoman.

Jim watched as the girl's cheeks flushed bright red. He got the feeling that she was enjoying all this attention without realising, perhaps, the significance of her testimony. Still, he just needed to make sure they got it all down on paper and the best way to do that was to keep her on side.

'I'm sure you will make a great detective one day,' he replied, enthusiastically.

No sooner had he said it though, that he heard an unmistakeable tut coming from the direction of the girl's mother. Looking up at her, Jim could see how annoyed she was at being there and the tone of her voice only confirmed this.

'Can't you just get on with it?' she had asked. 'I'm supposed to be at work, not stuck here listening to small talk!'

'I apologise, Mrs Hanson,' Jim replied. 'I know you've had to leave work to come here and I do appreciate it.'

'Yes, well …'

'Right then,' he continued, ignoring the negativity in Carol Hanson's response. 'You know why you're here, don't you, Jade?'

She nodded.

'And you know how important it is that you tell us everything you can remember about last night?'

Again, she nodded.

'Good girl.' Jim smiled. 'Now, Detective Watkins is going to write down everything you tell us. If you're not sure about something, don't be scared to say you're not sure. We might ask some questions along the way to try and get a better understanding of things but there's nothing to be worried about, OK?'

'I'm not worried,' she replied simply. 'I know what I saw – who I saw!'

'And you had better be telling the truth, my girl,' Carol interjected, 'otherwise you'll be in a lot of trouble!'

Jade blushed, clearly embarrassed by what her mother had just said.

'I'm sure Jade understands about telling the truth and how important it is – isn't that right, Jade?' Jim said soothingly. The last thing they needed was for mother and daughter to be at loggerheads; that would make the interview process far more difficult than necessary and they didn't have time for that right now.

He could see that their young witness was almost shrinking into the sofa, her eyes fixed on a spot on the carpet in front of her. Addressing Jade again, in what he hoped was an encouraging voice, Jim asked if they could start at the beginning. It did the trick. Taking a quick swig of coke, Jade adjusted how she was sitting, making herself taller, raising her eyes to meet the detective's, then she began to relate exactly what she had witnessed the previous night.

'I was in my room listening to some music. *She* had sent me to bed early but I had my earphones in so she wouldn't hear me.'

'She?' Carol spat, but Jade ignored her, creating an uncomfortable silence before she continued.

'Anyway, I was bored so I looked out of the window to see if anything was going on.'

'Do you know what time it was?' Jim asked.

'I don't know but it was dark out.'

'Did you have your bedroom light on?'

'No. I didn't want to get into any more trouble. I'm always in trouble lately and I was supposed to go to bed ...' She trailed off and her mother spoke up again.

'And why are you always in trouble?' she spat. 'Go on, tell them why you had been sent to your room.'

Jade hugged the cushion she was holding and bent her head, avoiding eye contact with anyone.

Once again, Jim found himself trying to smooth things over. 'Let's not focus on that for now.'

There was obviously some tension between the girl and her mother but Carol Hanson wasn't helping the process. Whatever their issues were, the girl's statement had to take precedence and he was grateful that Angie had also picked up on this as she was now politely asking the woman if she could try and keep quiet so they could proceed with her daughter's witness statement.

'Fine, fine, just get on with it,' she replied, leaving Jim to once again focus on Jade.

'So, you're in your room and you're looking out of the window. Was anyone out there?'

'Not at first,' Jade replied. 'It was quiet out there. Sometimes a car went up Bevington Road, but there was nothing going on outside.'

'Then what happened?'

'I got my gown as I was cold and then, when I looked outside again there was a man and woman standing over the road by where, you know ...'

'Where?'

Jim needed the witness to be specific, without putting any words into her mouth.

'Where they found her body,' she replied.

'OK, and what were they doing when you saw them?' he continued, carefully watching her face as he waited for her response.

'They were kissing!' She giggled. 'Not a little kiss though. They were going at it.'

'What do you mean by that, Jade?' he asked her, wanting to be sure of everything she told them, especially if this confirmed that the victim knew her killer.

'Their hands were moving everywhere and their lips looked like they were glued together – like they were gonna have sex.'

She blushed as she said this.

'OK, and what happened after that?'

Again she giggled, but she quickly composed herself and answered Jim's question.

'Well, they were kissing for a bit and then he sort of pulled her into the alley but she wasn't fighting him or anything. I think she wanted to go in there, probably so they could do things …' She looked embarrassed as she said but it didn't stop her from embellishing 'You know, sexual things.'

For a few seconds, everyone was quiet. Jim broke the silence. 'So, did you see who it was who went into the alley?'

They were now at the most important part of their interview. They needed her to officially name the man she had mentioned to the uniformed officer earlier, so that his colleagues could go and arrest him.

'I didn't see the woman's face,' she replied, 'so I don't know who she was but the man …'

'Did you see who he was, Jade? Did you recognise him?' Angie asked, looking up from the statement she had been writing.

Jade knew she couldn't back out now. She had already told that policeman earlier who she had seen going into the alley, so it wasn't as if she could turn round now and admit that, actually, she hadn't seen anything after all. Besides, he deserved it, she reasoned with herself. Threatening to call the police on her after she had forgotten to pay for a chocolate bar last week. Grabbing hold of her as she went to leave the shop, leaving a slight bruise on her arm. Who did he think he was?

Looking up at the detective she announced, almost in a whisper, 'It was Mr Corcoran.'

'*What?* Charlie Corcoran from the corner shop?' her mother asked, obviously incredulous at her daughter's allegations. 'Really, Jade?'

'Yes, Mr Corcoran,' Jade cried indignantly, not appreciating the accusatory tone of her mother's voice. 'I *saw* him!'

'I swear you had better be telling the truth,' Carol warned.

'You never believe anything I have to say,' her daughter retaliated. 'Well, I did see him and he went into the alley with the woman and then he came out on his own and walked back onto Bevington Road, so there!'

She started crying now, her breath coming in short, sharp sobs, prompting the uniformed policewoman who had been sitting next to her throughout the interview to offer her a box of tissues. Quickly blowing her nose before there was an embarrassing drip, Jade looked directly at the detective again and, in a quiet voice, reiterated that it was Mr Corcoran who she had seen across the road last night.

'I need to know that you are absolutely sure about that, Jade,' he stated cautiously. 'You understand why, don't you?'

She nodded, her sobs easing off.

'And you understand why it's important to tell the truth. There's a dangerous man out there and we need to arrest the right person.'

'I know what I saw,' she responded, her voice barely audible. 'Mr Corcoran went into the alley with a woman. I don't know what they did in there but he came out on his own. I don't care if you don't believe me, but I saw him!'

The detective smiled at her and Jade knew he had bought it. She knew her mum would go mental if she discovered that Jade had lied but what else could she say. She had to stick to her story now, there was no way of backing out without being in serious trouble.

'*I did see him*!'

'That's OK, Jade. You've done really well, so far. I have a few more questions though if you don't mind?'

Jade liked the detective. He had been so kind to her, so she was more than happy to answer his questions.

'Tell me how you know Mr Corcoran.'

'He owns the corner shop up on Albert Road. I go in there for my mum when she wants milk and stuff, and,' she paused before continuing, 'he sells me cigarettes for her too, so I always go in there.'

It was Carol's turn to blush now and Jade couldn't help but think that it had served her right, after all the times her mum had embarrassed her since they had been at the police station.

'OK,' the detective continued, ignoring her mum's embarrassment. 'Now, did you see the woman come out after Mr Corcoran had left?'

'I was looking out the window for a while after he left and I didn't see her again.'

'And it was definitely Mr Corcoran?'

'Yes,' she replied, firmly. 'It was definitely Mr Corcoran.'

Chapter Forty

As soon as they entered the incident room Inspector Goulding made a beeline for Jim.

'Are we good to go?' he asked. 'Is she positive about who she saw going into the alley last night?'

'The girl is adamant about who she saw,' Jim replied, 'but the mother …'

'Did she witness anything?'

'No. She has doubts about her daughter's statement though, practically called her a liar in front of us.'

'What did you think? Did you two think she was lying?' Goulding asked now, turning his attention to Angie as well.

'Her statement never changed, no matter how often Jim questioned her about what she saw,' Angie responded.

'There's clear hostility between mother and daughter,' Jim added. 'She wasn't happy about being here, for starters.'

'Forget about her then. If the girl is definite as far as ID is concerned, then we pick him up.'

Jim knew the inspector was desperate for an arrest – they all were – and Jade Ellis was adamant about who she'd seen last night but, if he was honest, the mother's reaction had unsettled him. Perhaps it was just a typical mother–daughter family dynamic but, as he watched his colleagues getting ready to pick up Charlie Corcoran, he no longer felt as pissed off as he had earlier that he wasn't a part of the arrest team. As adamant as their witness was, there was a niggling doubt in the back of his mind that perhaps they weren't as close to solving this case as he had hoped.

Unfortunately, his inspector didn't want to listen to those doubts; he was more concerned with getting an arrest and bringing an end to a case that had haunted them for months.

Charlie Corcoran was busy serving one of his regular customers, when two men he had never seen before walked into the shop. Almost instantly he recognised they were police officers and his interest was piqued.

Were they there because of the poor Campbell girl, he wondered. Not that he could tell them anything, but he had already heard from old Martha before they walked in how the police were going door to door. He would have thought that uniformed officers undertook that job, though.

'Be with you in a minute,' he said with a smile, the tone of his voice calm, relaxed.

Charlie could have sworn that he saw a scowl flicker briefly across the one man's face as he exchanged a glance with the other. This puzzled him slightly but he carried on serving Martha, putting it down to the stress the officers must have been under, especially if Martha was right and this latest murder was connected to the others.

The man who had scowled stepped forward then. He obviously wasn't interested in waiting.

'Charles Corcoran?' he asked, an authoritative tone to his voice.

The atmosphere in the shop instantly changed. There was something off about the way the man had spoken to him and Charlie wasn't quite sure where this was leading. Still trying to remain jovial though, he winked at the woman before replying. 'That's me for all my sins, eh Martha.'

She was about to reply but the man interrupted her.

'Charles Corcoran, I'm Detective Inspector Goulding, Aston Lane CID,' he stated, moving towards the back of the counter, 'and I'm arresting you on suspicion of murder.'

'*Murder?* Now hang on just a minute,' Charlie spluttered, clearly shocked at the situation unfolding in front of him.

The man had lifted the hatch on the counter by now and was standing directly in front of Charlie with a pair of handcuffs in his hand.

Charlie's first instinct was to try and push him away. This had to be some sort of joke. Why would they be trying to arrest him for murder? His actions clearly didn't go down well though as the second man was also behind the counter then and there was a brief struggle as they attempted to secure the handcuffs.

They obviously meant business though as it wasn't long before Charlie felt the cold metal on his wrists, pinching his skin as they locked into place. He still tried to protest his innocence but it was falling on deaf ears.

It wasn't until the scowling man read out the list of charges though, that Charlie really felt as if the wind had been knocked out of him and he quickly sat down on the stool behind him before his legs gave way.

It didn't make sense. Anyone who knew him would have known they had made a mistake. He could never kill anyone let alone do what they had suggested. Sure, he was a bit of a flirt but he would never do that to a woman. The whole thing was ludicrous.

Looking across at Martha, he was desperate for some support; what she could do exactly, he didn't know, but as he looked at her with her mouth agog, his heart sank. He had known Martha a long time and there was no way she would be able to keep quiet about what she had just witnessed.

Sure enough, she was making her excuses to leave now and hurried towards the door, glancing back at him one last time before she stepped outside. It wouldn't be long before the whole neighbourhood heard about his arrest now and he suddenly felt nauseous.

No sooner had Martha left though, then two uniformed officers came in. This time, the door was locked behind them to prevent anyone else entering the shop. The scowling man had then asked them to start searching the shop. Charlie didn't know what for; they didn't say, preferring to tip his shop upside down instead.

He had asked who was going to clean up the mess they were making but the officers ignored him. All Charlie could do was look on in dismay as they went through everything in the shop.

After what had seemed like an eternity, the officers must have been satisfied that there was nothing of interest to be found as he could hear them talking about taking him back to the police station before searching his flat.

The police officer who had originally spoken to him, now came over to where he was sat and took him by the arm.

'We're going to take you to the station now,' he said, leading him towards the front door. 'Word of advice though, let's not make this any more difficult than it needs to be.'

Charlie had already realised there was no point in him protesting. The officers obviously thought that he was guilty so his only hope was that they would sort it all out at the station.

As soon as they left the shop, Charlie kept his head down until he was safely inside the police van that had been parked up outside. It didn't stop the group of teenagers who had gathered, no doubt curious to find out what all the commotion was about, from calling out to him.

'Oi oi, Charlie mate, what they got you for?' asked one of the lads as he zipped about on his bike.

'Who's been a naughty boy,' another piped up, causing a roar of laughter.

Charlie didn't answer them and he was glad when the van door slammed shut behind him. Sitting on the hard seat, the cold metal from the handcuffs digging into his wrists, he buried his head in his hands as he waited for the van to set off. It was all he could do to stop himself from crying, as the enormity of the situation hit him.

He couldn't believe this was happening.

Murder!

Murdering those girls!

John and Ada's granddaughter!
It just didn't make sense.

Thanks in part to Martha Fletcher, word quickly spread that the Aston Strangler had finally been arrested, even before it had made the news headlines. Unfortunately for Charlie Corcoran, many of those discussing his predicament belonged to the 'no smoke without fire' school of thought. It didn't matter that several of the older residents had known him for over twenty years, ever since he had taken over the shop from old Mr Johnson. The police had arrested him for murdering those poor girls and they wouldn't have done that without any evidence.

There were a few locals who didn't believe he was capable of such a thing and leapt to his defence, for all the good it did. There were also those who were cautious about believing tittle-tattle; after all, they hadn't forgotten local feelings when George Lawrence had been arrested. As it turned out, the police had got the wrong man but despite that, George still had to be moved by the council after his arrest; he had become a target for vandals and his flat had been attacked on more than one occasion.

Now, whether it was an act of mindful vandalism by bored teenagers or the result of months of fear and pent-up frustration, no one would know for sure, but within a couple of hours of the police finishing off their search of the shop, the outside was daubed with graffiti, making it clear to anyone passing by that Charlie Corcoran was 'Murdering Scum'.

As if that wasn't bad enough, the press was also running with 'Local Shopkeeper Arrested' headlines. They didn't name Charlie but pictures of his shopfront were plastered all over the news. A few of the residents were interviewed and asked to give their views on the man currently in police custody. The interviews which were given air time were not at all favourable and, by the end of the day, Charlie was facing a trial by media with no way of defending himself. They had decided on his guilt and that was all that mattered.

Chapter Forty-One

They had spent the day visiting both the Nature Centre and Cannon Hill Park and he had to admit that it had been enjoyable, making a change from all the hostility between them lately. He couldn't even remember the last time they had had such a good day and he was still feeling quite relaxed by the time they got back home.

He hadn't heard any news all day though and was eager now to get online and read up on the latest reports about the girl he'd killed last night. Leaving Alison to sort out their dinner he made his way into the sitting room, settled himself on the sofa and switched on the laptop. As soon as it had powered up he went straight to Facebook, typed a few letters into the search bar then waited a few seconds for the *Birmingham Advertiser's* home page to pop up.

It excited him, the way they talked about him, the fear they instilled in their readers as they detailed his crimes. His ability to pounce without being seen, almost as if he were a ghostly figure lurking in the shadows. Yes, that had pleased him, knowing that people were afraid of him and he couldn't help but smile as he recalled some of the reports he had read recently. Within seconds of the Facebook page loading, however, his smile had dropped and he stared at the screen.

He couldn't believe what he was reading, but every link he clicked on said the same.

They had done it again!

Feeling the rage start to build up inside him he slammed the laptop shut.

How dare they!

Well, he wasn't going to stand for it.

He needed to think this through. Were they doing this on purpose, trying to get him to make a mistake? He stared vacantly into space, trying to control his anger, pounding his fist into the palm of his hand.

Alison walked into the room. 'Cup of tea,' she asked lightly.

The look on his face as he turned towards her was enough for Alison to realise that the pleasant day they had enjoyed was now at an end.

Chapter Forty-Two

The incessantly high-pitched shrill that had suddenly interrupted her subconscious grew louder and more annoying by the second. Claire Maynard grudgingly reached out her hand to switch off the alarm, grimacing at the cold air as she did so.

The silence was welcome and Claire was tempted to roll over and go back to sleep. 'Just another ten minutes,' she promised herself as she tried to snuggle back under the warmth of the duvet.

One look at Jasper, however, and she knew he had other ideas.

As soon as he saw her hand reach out to switch off the alarm, he had immediately raised his head and was staring at her, no doubt waiting for a sign that the day was about to start.

Claire couldn't help but laugh and that was enough for him to pounce on her, nuzzling his nose under the duvet, desperately licking her face until she acknowledged him, all the while his tail wagging in excitement.

As much as she would have welcomed those extra few minutes of slumber, Claire gave in to his 'attack', and pushed the duvet away from her so that he could see her properly.

'OK, OK,' she cried, ruffling the top of his head. 'I'm awake now!'

Jasper rolled over onto his back, offering his belly for a good rub. He was all legs though and almost fell off the bed in his excitement.

'Oh, Jasper!' Claire laughed again as she stopped him from landing in a heap on the floor. 'You're such a silly dog!'

He was her silly dog though, and Claire loved him to bits.

She had picked him up from the dogs' home shortly after the council had awarded her this flat when she was just seventeen. After growing up in foster care and then a care home when her foster mother could no longer look after her, having a place she could call her own was important to Claire. Equally, having someone to share it with – someone she loved and trusted – made it even more special, which was where Jasper came in.

He was always there to greet her when she got back from work, knew when she was feeling down and needed her face washed or a loving paw on her lap, loved snuggling under the duvet with her as she watched a movie – he was the perfect housemate really. He also made her feel safe – not that he was much of a security guard. In Jasper's case, looks were definitely deceiving; he was as soft as anything, scared of his own shadow at times, despite the fact he was a great big hairy mutt of a hound.

Recent events had demonstrated to Claire just how vulnerable she felt living on her own and, although she didn't venture out after dark and no longer had to rely on public transport having recently passed her driving test, she still felt scared going out without Jasper by her side. Thankfully, the police had finally made an arrest after a witness had come forward and identified him following the death of another poor girl. Not that it made her feel any safer, but at least he was no longer out there roaming the streets, looking for his next victim.

Claire didn't want to think about that now though. Today was going to be a good day, despite having to get up at such a ridiculous hour. Swinging her legs out of bed, she let out an involuntary shiver as she quickly located her slippers. Her flat was always cold but she would soon warm up once she went in the kitchen and light the gas ring.

'Come on, you,' she called to Jasper, who was now sprawled across the bed she had just vacated. 'If I've got to get up, so do you. Let's have breakfast and then walkies.'

Waking with a start, he was suddenly aware of how cold it was. Hardly surprising since he had fallen asleep in his car. The events of last night came flooding back as he shifted in his seat. He had not experienced a rage as intense as he had in those moments before he stormed out of the house. Even now, several hours later, he still felt worked up over what had happened.

He had been annoyed after reading the news that the police had made an arrest, accusing someone else of being responsible for his actions. *As if* anyone else would be as clever as him, to commit such an act. It wasn't right, and the more he sat there thinking about it, the more annoyed he became; the evening ended in one almighty row.

'*Bitch*!'

He almost spat the word. The hatred dripped off his tongue.

He knew he had been unreasonable, taking his frustrations out on his wife – snapping at her, finding fault, picking an argument over the slightest thing. Sensing a change in her husband's demeanour, Alison had decided to take herself off to bed early, which infuriated him even more. Perhaps if she had been asleep when he made his way to bed the row wouldn't have happened, but she was still awake watching something on the TV as he entered the bedroom. Out of spite, as soon as he got into bed he reached for the remote and turned to the sports channel.

'I was watching that,' she had said to him, but it was the tone of her voice that he didn't appreciate, instantly setting him off.

'When you start paying the bills, perhaps then you can choose what to watch,' he had replied angrily, incredulous that she actually had the cheek to object to him watching the TV himself.

She had sighed at this point, but said nothing else. Instead she went to get out of bed, but this was like a red rag to a bull. He grabbed the back of her hair and pulled her back down on the bed.

'Where do you think you're going?' he had demanded.

'I'm going downstairs to watch the TV so that you can watch your programme up here,' she had replied, irritating him even more so that he held on tighter. 'Please. You're hurting me!' she had cried then.

For a few seconds he held her there, wondering which way to take the situation, before finally letting go. Alison sat back on the bed, waiting for whatever came next.

'Get out of my sight,' he had growled at her. 'You can stay down there as well. I don't want your fat ugly body anywhere near my bed. You sicken me!'

She had said nothing, simply picked up her dressing gown and left.

He must have fallen asleep not long after that because the next thing he knew, it had just gone 1a.m. There was no sign of Alison and at first he wondered where she was, but then he remembered their earlier encounter. He quickly pulled on his jeans and went to look for his wife.

She wasn't in Emily's room. His daughter was there, though, fast asleep in her cot, so Alison wouldn't be far away. Making his way downstairs, he could see the glow from the television coming out of the sitting room, where she had left the door slightly ajar. He pushed it open gently with his foot, and saw his wife fast asleep on the sofa. He didn't know why, but this made him angry.

He went to the kitchen and filled a glass with cold water, then made his way back to the sitting room. He walked over to where his wife was sleeping and threw the water at her face; she woke with a start.

'What are you doing?' she had screeched at him, sitting up quickly. 'What is wrong with you?'

He hadn't expected Alison to speak to him like that and he instantly felt the blood pumping at the side of his temples as he battled to keep his temper under control.

It was no good though.

He grabbed Alison round her throat with one hand and the other he bunched into a fist, hovering it in front of her face.

'Don't you ever speak to me like that again,' he snarled.

He could see the fear in her eyes as she tried to struggle to her feet whilst raising her hands to protect herself. She looked pathetic, the water still dripping off her face, her lip quivering as she looked from his face to his fist then back to his face. He had never hated anyone as much as he hated Alison at that moment and he had no idea how he managed to control himself. He pushed her back down onto the wet sofa and leant over her, his face so close to hers that he could feel her breath on his cheek.

'You disgust me,' he said simply, before standing back up, grabbing the remote and switching the TV off.

He wasn't done though.

'Now, get this straight once and for all,' he spat at her. 'I pay the bills. I tell you when you can watch my TV.'

It was petty.

He knew it was petty but he had felt the need to reassert his authority after the way she had spoken to him. But then she had said something he wasn't expecting. He wasn't entirely sure he had heard right at first because she had started snivelling again, but, when he had asked her to repeat what she had said, her voice was clearer.

'I want a *divorce!*'

There was no mistaking it that time.

Instantly, he saw red.

How *dare* she suggest a divorce. *He* would be the one to decide when it was over!

He struck her cheek with the remote that was still in his hand, then threw it across the room. He flipped the coffee table over, the glass shattering instantly and spreading across the sitting room floor. The force with which the glass had broken shocked him and, scared at what he might do if he stayed, he turned and walked into the hall, slamming the door behind him. He stormed out of the house with his car keys and soon found himself back in Aston. It was familiar territory – he knew the area like the back of his hand. Pulling into a side road, he had every intention of calming himself down and then heading back home, but instead had quickly fallen asleep.

A clinking of keys and the distant sound of a heavy door slamming shut woke Charlie abruptly from his sleep. Almost immediately he realised that this nightmare he had found himself in was still very, very real and his heart sank.

He had thought it was some sort of sick joke when he was first arrested, that this couldn't be happening to him. Even when they got to the custody suite and the officer read out the charges again he was almost expecting someone to say that they had arrested the wrong man – only it wasn't a joke. He was still here.

Adjusting his eyes to his surroundings he sat up on the edge of the hard bed and wrapped the coarse blanket they had given him tightly around his shoulders, almost like a cocoon.

'A safety blanket,' he thought bitterly, still unable to believe everything that had occurred over the last – how long? Automatically, he looked at his watch to see what time it was before recalling that they had taken it off him when he first got here.

How long had he been here now?

There were no windows in the cell, nothing that would signal if it was even morning. He had obviously fallen asleep, which surprised him given the situation, but had no idea how long for. Briefly, he contemplated calling someone to the cell door. He was desperate to hear that this ordeal was coming to an end as they realised it couldn't have been him, that he would never have done what they had accused him of doing to those poor girls, but what if they still thought he was guilty? Dropping his head into his hands, he let out a low moan as the enormity of his situation hit him all over again.

How could the police have made such a mistake?

Why would someone even name him as a suspect?

Who had he pissed off so much that they would try and pin these murders on him?

There were so many questions running around in his head, and no answers.

When the police officers had mentioned during the interview that there was a witness, he was convinced they were just trying it on, trying to trick him into confessing to something he hadn't done, but, having spoken at length to the solicitor they had provided him with, he now knew that someone out there *had* named him, had told the police they had seen him going into that alley with the dead girl on the night that she was murdered.

Racking his brain, he tried once again to think of anyone who hated him so much that they could have done this, but no one immediately sprung to mind. Charlie was pretty easy going, always tried to get on with everyone – even the detectives who quizzed him for what seemed like hours after he was booked into custody. Trying not to lose his temper as question after question was fired at him, questions he was revolted by.

Not that it made any difference. He was convinced that the police officers had already decided he had committed these awful crimes, despite his protestations. So much for 'innocent until proven guilty.' If only he had an alibi he could have cleared up this mess, but he had spent that night alone, going over the accounts for the shop. He hadn't made any phone calls and there was no one who could verify his whereabouts.

The sound of the metal cover over the door hatch interrupted his thoughts, sliding down far enough to enable a face to peer inside.

'Tea?' the voice asked pleasantly enough.

'Yes, please,' Charlie replied, then, almost as an afterthought, 'what time is it please?'

'Six o'clock,' came the reply, before the hatch was closed again, leaving him alone with his thoughts.

Chapter Forty-Three

After making herself a cup of tea, Claire was now hurriedly eating a bowl of cornflakes. Aware that the clock was ticking and wanting to take Jasper to the park for at least half an hour before she had to leave for work, she needed to get a move on.

Claire had an eight-hour shift ahead of her and would have to leave Jasper in the flat on his own while she was out, but she figured that he would be OK; he could have a longer walk as soon as she got back.

That was the only downside to owning a dog – Jasper needed his daily walk, especially since Claire lived above a garage and had no garden to let him go and do his business in. Since she was going to be out all day, she couldn't leave him until she got back. Thankfully, the park was just around the corner from her flat so they didn't have far to go.

Claire dumped her bowl in the sink, quickly got herself dressed, washed her face, brushed her teeth and sorted her hair, then grabbed a handful of doggy waste bags and stuffed them in the pocket of her coat. She picked up Jasper's lead and made her way down to the front door. Jasper's excitement was unmistakable as he bounded after her, almost causing a collision on the stairs.

'Oh, Jasper,' she said, laughing. 'You silly sausage. Come on, let's go walkies.'

Locking the door behind her as they left, Claire didn't think an early morning walk in the park would be dangerous. It wasn't as if it was dark out now and besides, they had arrested the man who had killed those women so she wasn't as cautious as she might have been.

He turned on the engine and adjusted the temperature, welcoming the instant blow of hot air that warmed up the car. Despite the sudden heat, he still felt chilled to his bones – a lesson not to ever fall asleep in his car again.

After a few minutes of holding his hands next to the heat vents and rubbing them together vigorously he started to warm up, and his focus switched to thinking about what was going on at home.

He knew that he would need to head back and try to sort things out, just in case Alison *was* thinking about leaving. He couldn't have that and figured he would have to apologise – not that he should; she was the one in the wrong.

He began making his way back towards town, his mind focused on what he would say when he got home. Rounding a bend however, he spotted someone ahead of him and his mind instantly switched to the woman he now saw walking down the road.

He turned into Burlington Street and checked in his rear-view mirror.

She had a dog with her.

Perhaps she was going to the park.

Could he do it?

There was the dog to consider.

What if it tried to attack him?

The park was also quite open, which increased his risk of getting caught. His heart was pumping by now though and he could feel the adrenalin coursing through his veins.

Could he really do it?

It would show the police how stupid they were.

Would show everyone he meant business.

Continuing along Burlington Street, he then turned left into High Street then left again into Phillips Street, where he pulled up near the park entrance. He had full view of the park from where he was now parked so he would soon see if that was where the woman was headed.

'Come on, *come on*,' he muttered to himself.

Letting out a long deep breath, his whole body suddenly felt on edge. His palms were becoming sweaty and his anxiety levels were about to go through the roof as he waited to see if the woman and her dog were heading towards the park. He knew he would be taking a huge risk, but he didn't care at this point and desperately hoped that she was heading in his direction.

He only had to wait a few minutes, although it seemed much longer. As soon as he spotted her walking along the grass verge towards the entrance he couldn't help but smile to himself.

He inched the car forward so that most of it would be obscured by bushes if she happened to look across, then reached under the passenger seat and felt around with his hand until he found what he was looking for. The length of rope he stuffed into his coat pocket. He opened the glove box and took out a small plastic container, along with a beanie hat and a pair of glasses. Using the rear-view mirror, he took the lenses from the plastic container and placed them carefully in his eyes, changing their colour from brown to blue.

After blinking his eyes several times he set about making sure that the beanie hat covered all his hair before adding the glasses to complete his disguise. Glancing at himself in the mirror he was pleased with how he now looked, and paused for a minute to consider just how clever he was, especially in changing his eye colour. That had certainly been a smart move – one that would hopefully work in his favour should anyone happen to spot him.

Heart racing, he took a final look around him to check that the coast was clear before cautiously getting out of the car, leaving the keys in the ignition. He moved round to the rear passenger tyre and crouched down as if he was inspecting it, waiting for the right moment to enter the park.

He tried not to look at her while he waited.

He didn't want to make her nervous.

Out of the corner of his eye, though, he watched as she made her way along the path towards him.

Chapter Forty-Four

By the time Emily had woken up, shortly after six o'clock, Alison had managed to clear up the broken glass that she could see and just needed to run the vacuum over the floor in case there were any tiny shards lurking anywhere. The last thing she wanted was for Emily to end up cutting her feet whilst she was roaming around the sitting room in her baby walker, or worse still, cutting herself as she shuffled across the floor.

For now, though, they were settled in the kitchen.

Emily was sitting in her highchair with a sippy cup of milk and a biscuit, while Alison set about making herself a pot of tea. Sighing to herself, she didn't know what to do anymore.

She felt worthless.

'You sicken me,' had been ringing in her ears, ever since he had said it.

It was the way he had said it that had hurt her the most, even more than the slap he had given her with the TV remote. There was such a hatred in his voice that the words had cut her to the core. Married life wasn't meant to be like this; they had been so happy once upon a time, so why did her husband despise her so much now?

She didn't have the answer to that, she just knew that things had started to change when she found out she was pregnant with Emily, and he had become increasingly more violent in the months following her birth. Emily would be one soon. She was picking up on things, especially the atmosphere in the house, which wasn't good for her, for any of them really, and with a new baby on the way she needed to make a decision: stay and work on her marriage, or leave and start a new life away from her husband.

Alison wiped away a stray tear and carried her tea over to the table; she sat next to her daughter. She didn't want Emily to see that she was upset and had done enough crying in the hours immediately after her husband had stormed out.

Emily soon interrupted her thoughts.

'Muma! Muma! Muma,' she chanted, banging her cup up and down on the tray of her high chair.

'Oh, sweetheart,' Alison sobbed, as her daughter gave her a beaming smile.

Lifting her daughter out of her seat, Alison gave her the biggest cuddle, squeezing her tight until Emily squirmed to break free of her hold.

At that moment her mind was made up. She would telephone her parents later and ask them to send her some money so she could catch the train down to Hayle. She could spend a few days with them while she worked out what to do next. That would mean admitting that her marriage had failed, but what other choice did she have?

She *was* scared though. Actually, she was *terrified* that her husband would follow her, cause a scene in front of her mum and dad, try and snatch Emily away from her, but she couldn't stay in the same house with him anymore, not knowing from one minute to the next if he was going to flare up at her. She was exhausted with it all and although she had so desperately wanted to make her marriage work, she now realised that it never would, not like this.

With a heavy heart, she placed her daughter back in her highchair and then got on with making their breakfast. She would make them both egg and toast – not that she was hungry, but they had a busy day ahead of them and the baby still needed nutrients even if she had to force it down.

As she entered the park, Claire had a quick look round and concluded that it was empty. With no other dogs in there, she took Jasper's lead off him and stood watching for a bit as he bounded off. He had such a funny run, with his legs going all over the place, that she couldn't help but laugh at him. She soon called him back to her though – not that he listened; he was far more interested in rolling around in something he had found in the grass.

'Jasper!' she called again, louder this time, firmer.

He still ignored her but at least he had the grace to look at her this time before rolling over again. Shaking her head, Claire made her way across to Jasper. Taking the outside path, she noticed a man out on the street. He appeared to be having car trouble and, although she wondered what was going on, he didn't even look her way, so she discounted any risk.

By the time she had caught up with him, Jasper had finished rolling in whatever it was that had caught his attention and once again he ran ahead, sniffing and spraying as he went. Before long, she recognised the tell-tale signs that he was about to defecate and, sure enough, she was right. They were right by the bins, which pleased her as she didn't fancy having to carry his poop around with her.

Claire opened one of the bags she'd brought, but it was fiddly, especially as the wind kept blowing at it so that she couldn't get it to do what she wanted. By the time she had opened it, Jasper had finished and had run ahead of her again, leaving Claire to pick up his squidgy deposit. With her attention focused on picking up Jasper's mess, Claire didn't hear the man approaching her from behind. As she bent down, though, something suddenly tightened around her neck, catching her by surprise.

By instinct she grabbed at the rope, trying to stop it from constricting her breathing. She was panicking, but within seconds everything she had learned at her self-defence class came flooding back to her. She bent her knee and stamped as hard as she could on his foot, resulting in him slackening the tension on the rope slightly, then she attacked him with her elbow, connecting with his side. This winded him, and his grip on the rope all but released.

As soon as it did so, Claire screamed for all she was worth, causing her attacker to turn and run.

Hearing a commotion, Mohammed Ibrahim, who had just entered the park saw that something ahead of him wasn't right – there seemed to be a struggle taking place between a man and a young woman. For a split second, he wasn't sure if he should get involved but then the woman slumped to the ground.

'Oi,' he shouted. 'What's going on?'

The man ignored him and ran out of the gate and onto Phillips Street.

Unsure of what had just happened, the newcomer rushed over to the girl, who had now been joined by a rather large dog. He had spotted the dog when he first entered the park, which had made him nervous, but it didn't seem vicious. Besides, the girl clearly needed some help.

'Are you OK, love?' he asked, concerned Mohammed didn't know what to do. He didn't want to get involved in a domestic but the girl was obviously distressed. He knelt down next to her.

The young woman was clutching her throat, unable to speak, as tears ran down her face.

Mohammed could see friction burns and abrasions beginning to form around her neck, and there was a length of rope on the floor. He still wasn't sure exactly what had occurred but did his best to reassure her.

'It's OK. It's OK. He's gone. You're safe now.'

Claire began to sob, her whole body shaking as she tried to process what had just happened. Tried to figure out who it was that had attacked her, to make sense of it all. Claire had never been so scared in her whole life. Then it hit her. What if that was him, the man who had killed those other girls? But the police had already arrested someone. Surely they couldn't have arrested the wrong man *again*?

Fear coursed through her body now and she began to dry retch. What would have happened to her if she hadn't been able to fight him off, if the man who was talking to her now had not come into the park when he did?

'Was that your boyfriend?' the newcomer was asking her as he draped his coat over her shoulders. 'Did you know him?'

Claire shook her head, unable to get any words out.

The man reached into his back pocket for his phone and dialled 999.

'Shit! Shit! Shit! Shit! Shit!'

What the hell was he thinking?

He could have been caught back there.

This realisation sent a chill through his whole body. His face turned deathly pale and his hands began to shake. He gripped tightly on the steering wheel as he navigated the backstreets, heading towards town. Although he tried to focus on the road ahead, his mind kept jumping to what had just happened.

She was only a petite little thing and he wasn't expecting her to fight back the way she had. She had caught him off guard, especially when she connected with his ribs, making him instantly flare up. In his rage, he could have easily overpowered her but, just as she started screaming, he saw someone else coming into the park and knew he had to run.

He was worried now though.

What if she had seen his face?

Would she be able to give the police a description?

What if they were able to put together a photofit of him?

What if Alison saw it?

What if she could identify him, could see past his disguise?

'Shit!' he exclaimed again. Why had he been so stupid?

Slamming his hand on the steering wheel in frustration, he was suddenly gripped by a sharp pain that caused him to draw in a deep, ragged breath. Clutching his ribs, he pulled over to the side of the road to investigate the reason for his discomfort.

He lifted his t-shirt and saw the beginnings of an angry-looking contusion at the point where the woman had hit out at him.

'Fucking bitch!' he muttered.

How was he going to explain this to Alison?

He leant back against the head rest and closed his eyes, trying to think of what excuse he could come up with. He was suddenly hit with a more terrifying thought, which caused him to sit bolt upright.

What if they had managed to get his car registration number as he drove off?

By now, he could feel his heart beating rapidly against his chest wall and a bitter bile had come up at the back of his throat, burning his tongue. He felt as though he was going to pass out. He opened the door and leant out to vomit onto the road by the side of the car.

Chapter Forty-Five

As soon as the call came in to the police control centre, an immediate response was put out to all available officers, requesting their attendance at the scene of an attack at Phillips Street Park, and the time in which the first car arrived was impressive.

It was clear to the first responding officers that the woman was in a state of distress, however, they needed to ascertain what had occurred and bit by bit they were able to piece together the events leading up to the 999 call.

The discarded rope was bagged and tagged for evidence.

A statement was taken from the man who had come to Claire's aid, and he was then allowed him to continue on his way. His details were noted down, as the police would need to talk to him in greater detail later, once they had established exactly what had happened that morning.

More officers arrived at the scene and an ambulance joined them. It was felt that, given her obvious distress, Claire should go along to the hospital to be checked out. This was more of a precaution than anything else. There were a few marks around her neck but other than that she didn't appear physically hurt. However, she had clearly gone through a traumatic experience.

* * *

All Claire wanted was to get back to the security of her flat. Besides, she had Jasper to consider. What would happen to him if she went to the hospital? Then there was her job. What would they say if she didn't turn up? Not that she could face work right now.

She couldn't stop crying, for starters, and there was no way her managers would want her serving customers in this state.

Despite her initial reluctance though, one of the officers managed to persuade her that it would be for the best. She would take Jasper home, make sure there was food and water down, if Claire let her. She would also contact her manager at work, let them know Claire wouldn't be in to do her shift.

By the time the paramedics had wheeled Claire to the ambulance, the area was a hive of activity, with blue flashing lights and uniformed officers everywhere. As the doors closed on the commotion though, Claire suddenly felt relieved that she was away from it all. She still couldn't stop shaking, despite the extra blankets the paramedic had given her. All she could think was that she had very nearly become the next victim of the 'Aston Strangler'.

* * *

Every single officer at the scene of the attack was thinking the same thing. That also meant that the person who had been locked up at the station since yesterday afternoon, the person they had suspected of committing these crimes, was quite possibly innocent.

There was no proof yet that this attack had been carried out by the same man and there was always the possibility of a copycat. If today's attack was connected, though, it was certainly a worrying development, as not only would they have an innocent man in custody, but the attacker had never struck in broad daylight before.

Either way, it was felt that the woman who had been attacked this morning had had a lucky escape.

* * *

After parking the car in the garage he carefully removed the blue lenses, placed them back in their plastic container and added some solution to prevent them from drying out. He took off his beanie hat, found the glasses, which he had flung in the back of the car when he made off from the park, then placed them carefully in his hat along with the contact lenses and solution. He left them on the passenger seat; he would return them to the safety of the holdall once he got out of the car but, for now, he sat there, quietly contemplating what he was going to do.

It was a tremendous relief when he had pulled into his road and there were no police cars surrounding his house. Throughout the drive home, he had been imagining all the worst possible scenarios of what could be waiting for him when he got back and had begun to dread the moment he would turn the corner.

Perhaps they hadn't registered his number plate after all?

Letting out a deep sigh, his mind switched from the fear of being arrested to the second biggest problem he had in his life – Alison.

It was her fault that he had nearly been caught this morning. If she had just kept her mouth shut instead of spouting that rubbish about wanting a divorce, he would never have left the house in a rage. Would never have spotted that girl. Would never have tried to grab her.

What if she was being serious about wanting a divorce, though?

This thought troubled him.

As much as he hated Alison right now, he was not going to let her walk out on him, and there was no way he was going to let her take his daughter.

Grudgingly, he knew he would have to put this right.

Before locking the car, he took off his jacket and placed it in the boot behind the tyre well, took the holdall from its hiding place and put the glasses, hat and contacts in there, then made his way into the kitchen through the internal door which separated it from the garage.

The kitchen was spotless and there was no sign of either Alison or Emily.

A quick glance in the sitting room – that was empty too. The broken glass had been cleared away and the table turned upright again. Everything was as it should be, everything in its place. It was just so quiet.

It hit him then.

Had she left him?

Pausing briefly, he strained to hear just the tiniest sound from his daughter but the house was in complete silence. Instantly on edge, he bounded up the stairs, two at a time and pushed open the bedroom door. Relief washed over him as he saw Emily sitting on their bed, playing with her favourite teddy.

He glanced across at Alison. She had been folding some clothes in a neat little pile on the edge of the bed, next to some toiletries and a few of Emily's toys, but now it was as if she was frozen to the spot as she stared at him, a look of panic in her eyes.

'What are you doing?' he asked, his voice quite calm, which surprised him, considering the rage that was once again beginning to bubble up inside.

'I … I can't do this anymore,' she replied, her own voice so quiet and strained that he was barely able to hear what she said. The fear in her voice was evident, though, and he knew then that he would need to be careful how he played this one out.

Sitting on the edge of the bed, he put his head in his hands and began to sob.

'Oh, Ally,' he cried. 'I am so, so sorry.'

Looking at her through blurred tears, he asked Alison to forgive him, promised her that he would change, blamed it on the pressure he was under at work.

'I'm so tired,' she told him. 'I haven't slept since you stormed out. I never know what sort of mood you're coming home in.'

The look on her face had softened now and he wondered if she had believed him; believed that he truly was sorry.

He hoped so.

Calling her *Ally* had been a smart move. He had not called her that in a long time but he had sensed a change in her when he did. The fear he had heard when she first spoke, had dissipated; it had been too easy.

'I …' she began, hesitating briefly before continuing. 'I can't carry on like this. Emily, the baby – it's not fair.'

'Don't leave … please,' he begged. 'I don't know what I would do without you.'

Taking hold of her hands, he looked up at her, his eyes pleading for forgiveness.

Alison began to cry, prompting him to rise from the bed and wrap his arms around her. He felt her flinch when he first touched her, but then her body softened into his and he started stroking her hair as she cried into his shoulder.

Despite the pain he was still experiencing in his ribs, despite the contempt he was harbouring for his wife, he stood there making soothing noises and promising that everything would be all right, until her tears were spent. Finally pulling away, he took hold of Alison's hands and sat her down on the bed, sat down next to her and called Emily over to them.

'We're a family, Ally. You, me, Emily, the baby.' As he said this, he placed his hand on Alison's stomach. It was the first time he had properly acknowledged their baby. 'Please don't leave,' he pleaded again, only softer, gentler this time. 'I promise I will change, take some time off work so that we can spend more time with each other.'

'I can't take any more,' she whispered.

'I know,' he replied, stroking her hair again. 'I don't blame you for hating me but I can change. I can, Ally. I can change and we can be a happy family, just like you always wanted. All of us, together. You just have to give me that chance to put things right.'

'That's all I've ever wanted, for us to be a proper family,' she cried.

Throwing her arms around his neck, she nuzzled in to him.

It that at that moment that he knew that he had convinced her to stay. She had believed his lies and he couldn't help but smirk as she hugged him. He had honestly expected more resistance, more of a fight, but now, she was like putty in his hands. She was pathetic.

* * *

At the hospital, Claire was unable to come to terms with the gravity of the situation she had found herself in. Knowing what could have happened, what *had* happened to those other poor women and the very real possibility that she could have been next had hit her hard and she was in a state of shock.

This must have been frustrating for the police officers who came to interview her; she was finding it difficult to give them a full account of what had occurred in the park that morning.

It wasn't her fault though.

Her mind was blanking out the finer details and she struggled to recall what her attacker looked like, even what he was wearing, so the doctor who was treating her suggested that the police leave it a day or so, to let her come to terms with what had happened.

* * *

It wasn't the outcome the police were hoping for, especially if her attacker was the same man responsible for the other rapes and murders. The sooner they had a description of him, the better, before he tried to attack someone else. Still, there was nothing more they could do at the hospital so they took the doctor's advice and left Claire to recover from her ordeal, if indeed, she ever would, focusing instead on their second witness, Mohammed Ibrahim, the man who had come to the woman's aid.

They already knew that he had been on his way to work that morning, cutting through the park after he got off the bus, to save a bit of time. Mr Ibrahim didn't usually catch the bus as a colleague often gave him a lift, but he had gone on holiday and so it was perhaps a stroke of luck that he had been walking through the park at the time he did.

The officers assigned to the case certainly thought so, not only because he had most likely prevented the woman from being abducted, but also because he could now give the officers a bit more detail about what he had witnessed that morning.

He told them it was the dog he had noticed first. It was quite a big dog and it was running loose, putting him on edge as he wasn't keen on them. Obviously this had distracted him somewhat so he didn't see the initial attack but, next thing he knew, he heard a woman scream, saw a man running away from her, before she then collapsed to the floor.

'I didn't know whether to chase after him or help her,' he said repeatedly throughout his interview.

'What can you tell us about the man?' the officer asked.

'He was a white man,' Mr Ibrahim replied, then paused a while as he thought about what he had witnessed that morning. 'He was taller than the woman, oh, and he wore glasses. I didn't get a good look at him as he was too far away and then, of course, he had run off by the time I reached the woman.'

'What about his build?'

'Build?'

'Yes,' said the officer, 'was he fat, thin, muscular?'

'He had a dark jacket on so I don't really know but he wasn't fat,' Mo replied, clearly aware that it wasn't much help to the officers.

'Did you see what else he was wearing? Anything that stood out?'

'He was wearing dark clothing, maybe all black. Oh, he had a black hat on too. Maybe he was wearing jeans but I couldn't see.'

'Don't worry. What happened when he ran? Where did he go?'

'He ran out on to Phillips Street, the exit by the back of the houses and I think, yes, I'm sure he had a car waiting. I didn't see him getting into a car but the back end of a car screeched away shortly after he disappeared.'

Now they were getting somewhere.

'What can you remember about the car?'

'I didn't see what make it was, not that I'm that good with cars but, it was a black car. I only saw it for a second but it was definitely black.'

Writing the colour in his notebook, the officer was satisfied that they had got all the information they were going to get, from this witness. Bidding him goodbye, they made their way back to the station so that his evidence could be updated on their records. With any luck, the information provided by Mr Ibrahim would soon lead to an arrest, especially now that they could narrow down the car the man had used to make his escape.

Chapter Forty-Six

He had been home for a couple of hours now.

Freshly showered and shaved, he had put his clothes straight into the washing machine, along with the rest of the darks, before adding detergent and setting it on a hot wash.

* * *

Alison was thrilled with the change in her husband. He had never volunteered to do 'woman's work', as he called it, before today. He really *did* want to change.

She knew it would take time for their marriage to recover but he was clearly trying and so she had to give him the benefit of the doubt.

She was also feeling slightly guilty.

He had slept in the car for a couple of hours, on their local pub car park, and had obviously slept awkwardly as he had strained his back. Every so often she could see him wincing, but he didn't complain. He didn't even want her massaging it, to try and relieve the tension in his muscles; he had said he felt like he deserved it for upsetting her so much.

Now they were sitting at the kitchen table with a pot of tea, discussing their future, the arrival of the new baby, how they would move forward. She could see that her husband was still on edge, no doubt worried that she was still going to leave, so she tried her best to reassure him, called her mother back while he was there to let her know that she wouldn't be going to stay with them after all. Letting her know that she had had a long talk with her husband and they were going to try and sort their differences out. Alison knew her mother was worried about her situation but she had to try and make her marriage work.

* * *

It had come as a bit of a shock to learn that Alison had been serious about leaving and taking their daughter with her. The anger he had felt as he listened to her talking to her mother was threatening to overwhelm him and he knew he was on edge, despite trying to remain calm. It wasn't just the realisation that she was *actually* going to leave, though, that had him feeling like this. He was still half expecting a knock at the door and dozens of police officers to come barging into the kitchen to arrest him at any moment.

How he had managed to remain so calm was beyond him, but at least he could explain it away by telling Alison he was still scared that she would leave, which she fully accepted. She had even started her snivelling again, taking hold of his hand and telling him how much she loved him, how much she wanted them all to be a happy family.

It was then that a local news report flashed on the TV. As soon as he heard 'attack in local park' his heart almost skipped a beat and he could feel the hairs on his arms rising.

Quickly glancing across at his wife, he wondered if she had she noticed, but she was too focused on the screen. Not that there was much detail on the news report, just that a woman had been attacked in a park in Aston, close to where four other women had been found murdered.

There was no description of the attacker.

Nothing linking *him* to the morning's events.

Unintentionally, he let out a relieved sigh.

Alison, apparently mistaking this for disgust at what had happened, asked him if he thought it was the same man that had murdered the other women. She was only making conversation but he had wanted to laugh at that.

The whole situation just seemed so surreal.

Offering a shrug of his shoulders, he attempted to change the subject. Alison clearly wasn't done with discussing it though, giving her opinion on the recent attacks, how awful it must have been for those poor women, for their loved ones, and how much she hoped the police would hurry up and catch the sick, twisted animal responsible.

The animal!

The sick, twisted animal!

That was what she had called him and she had said it with such disgust that he felt the rage start to build up inside him again. So much so, he quickly made an excuse and left the room. He knew he couldn't risk flaring up at her, especially when he had only just persuaded her to staying with him.

At that moment, though, he hated her more than anything.

She really, truly, disgusted him.

'Well, maybe one day,' he thought bitterly as he headed towards the bathroom, 'she will find out just what sort of a sick, twisted animal he really is and when she does, she will only have herself to blame!'

* * *

As soon as the news trickled through to the incident room at Aston Lane that there had been another attack, Inspector Goulding was furious. All too aware of the ramifications of having arrested the wrong man again, he immediately ordered Jim and Angie to go straight to their witness's house and speak with the girl who had come forward the day before.

The unease Jim had felt yesterday with the girl's statement; the way her mother had behaved towards their witness, had now manifested. The question was, had she just been mistaken, or had she deliberately lied. Perhaps the inspector shouldn't have rushed to arrest Charlie Corcoran but then, at the same time, he also knew how desperate everyone was to finally bring about an arrest. Even so, they wanted to arrest the right man and now he was wondering if it was because of yesterday's arrest that the real suspect had broken with his *modus operandi*, attacking the girl this morning.

Turning into Prestbury Road, Jim couldn't help but notice the sea of flowers outside both the Campbell's house and the alleyway where their granddaughter had been discovered. The sheer number of bouquets had grown immensely since news broke yesterday morning, with people wanting to offer condolences.

'I wonder if they will find any comfort in those?' he mused, nodding towards the display.

Angie had just shrugged and he felt a tinge of embarrassment then. He had often wondered how a bunch of flowers could possibly offer comfort to anyone in circumstances such as these, but it was one of those things that had become popular over recent years so who was he to question it?

Seemed as though Angie shared that view as well, saying as much when she did speak and Jim found himself wishing that he had never mentioned it.

After parking the car, Jim and Angie wasted no time in getting out and knocking at the door. There was no answer, so Jim knocked again, louder this time. A knock that clearly meant business. It did the trick; he could hear movement from the other side of the door and a key turning in the lock.

'Yes?' queried the man standing in front of him.

Showing his warrant card to the man, Jim quickly introduced himself then explained that they needed to question Jade again about what she'd seen the night Melissa Campbell was murdered. As he was explaining his reason for visiting, Carol Hanson came to the door, two boys in tow, ready to leave for school. This was too important, though, and Jim knew he would have to delay her.

'Mrs Hanson, we need to speak to your daughter, with you present, I'm afraid,' he said.

Sighing at this and clearly not amused at having to be delayed, Carol Hanson turned to the man who had opened the door, explaining that they were the officers who had interviewed Jade yesterday. Stepping aside and opening the door wider, the man – most likely Jade's stepfather, Jim assumed – motioned for the detectives to come inside, which they did, following Carol into the front room.

After declining a drink, Jim and Angie waited whilst the woman went back out into the hall and almost screamed her daughter's name. Three times she called before Jim heard footsteps above them, making their way down the stairs and towards the room where they now sat.

All eyes were on Jade as she stood in the doorway causing her cheeks flushing bright red. She looked like a deer caught in headlights; her hands were trembling and she shifted nervously on her feet.

Jim watched her for a few seconds, still trying to figure out if she had just made a mistake in identifying the man they currently had in custody or if she had simply made the whole thing up.

It didn't take long for the tears to start, giving Jim a clear indication that she had indeed, deliberately lied to them. Did she have any idea of what she had done? The ramifications were immense, not just for their investigation but for Charlie Corcoran as well. They had noticed the graffiti on the shop's shutters as they drove past. How would he move on from this? They would have to deal with that later.

After clearing his throat with a quick cough, Jim addressed the young girl, suggesting she take a seat, but Jade remained where she was, standing in the doorway.

They didn't have time for this and so he spoke again; this time his voice was stern with no hint of the friendliness he had shown before. 'Jade. We need to talk to you about what you saw the other night, and I want the truth this time.'

There was no time for niceties and although Jim knew he sounded harsh, he needed the truth. The tears had turned to loud sobs now but had no sympathy, at least not for the young girl standing in front of him. Charlie Corcoran, on the other hand …

'What the hell have you done?'

Jade's mother was glaring at her now, waiting for an explanation. The anger in her voice was unmistakable and it wasn't just reserved for her daughter.

'I told you she was lying!' she screeched at Jim. 'Would you listen though? It's your fault as much as hers. Stupid, stupid girl!'

Carol Hanson was angry and she had every reason to be, although Jim felt her anger was misplaced, given that it was her daughter who had lied, who had wasted police time and had caused an innocent man to spend the night in a police cell. He was angry as well, but Jim still had a job to do.

'Mrs Hanson, I appreciate how you feel but it's important that I talk to your daughter and clear this up.'

'There would have been nothing to clear up if you had just ...'

'*Carol!*'

It was the man who had opened the door, an air of authority in his voice cutting the woman off mid-sentence. 'Let them do their job!'

He wasn't done. 'And you,' he continued, turning towards Jade, 'sit down there, *now!*'

Keeping her eyes transfixed on the floor, Jade immediately obeyed the man, who Jim was now sure was her stepfather.

'Thank you Mr er ...'

'Hanson,' the man replied, confirming Jim's assumptions.

'Well, thank you, Mr Hanson. Now, Jade. I want the truth. What did you see the other night?'

The girl's response was barely audible through her tears but they all heard it.

'Nothing. I didn't see anything. I'm so sorry!'

Chapter Forty-Seven

It wasn't until the next day, once Claire was back home, Jasper closely by her side, that she could give a full account of what had happened to the police. Through tears she recounted how the park was empty when she first got there, and although she had noticed someone who she had assumed was a man bending over at the back of a vehicle, as if there was a problem with his tyre, he had not attempted to look in her direction and so she had felt relatively safe. Plus, she had reasoned, it wasn't dark out and she also had Jasper with her.

She never thought, for one moment, that she would be attacked.

When the officer asked her to describe the car, Claire was embarrassed to admit that she had gone out without her glasses that morning. All she knew was that it was a dark coloured car and even though they had pressed her for more details, there was nothing else she could tell them about it.

Moving on to the actual attack was difficult for Claire, having to relive what had happened made her even more emotional so she was grateful when the officers suggested she take her time.

Hugging Jasper closer to her, she went through how she had bent down to pick up his mess then the next thing she knew there was something tight around her neck, restricting her breathing. It had all happened so quickly that she had been caught by surprise, but she reacted instinctively and began fighting him off.

The police officer asked her to describe him then.

The man she had come face to face with; the man who had attacked her; the man whose image she had not been able to get out of her head since the attack had happened. She described it all to the police officer, not wanting to miss out any detail, hoping that they would finally be able to arrest him so that she could start to feel safe again.

They had asked her then if she could sit down with one of their sketch artists to help them produce an image of the man who had attacked her.

She nodded at this request; but they would have to come to her flat; she couldn't face venturing outside.

Not yet.

Not while he was still out there.

As soon as the officers left, Claire hurriedly locked the door behind them and made her way back up the stairs to her bedroom. She sat on the bed where Jasper quickly joined her. He could have no idea what was wrong but he seemed instinctively to know that his owner needed him right now; he had hardly left her side since she got back home yesterday afternoon.

Burying her head into the scruff of his neck, Claire once again found herself sobbing as images of the man danced around in her mind, taunting her, laughing at her, showing her what would have happened if she had not been able to fight him off, if that stranger had not disturbed him.

She had never felt so scared in all her life and probably wouldn't begin to feel safe again until the man who had attacked her was locked behind bars.

* * *

It was a feeling shared by many in Aston, that afternoon – along with fear, anger, disbelief and a lack of confidence in the police that they would ever apprehend the man that had terrorised their neighbourhood for months now.

* * *

'Haven't Got a Clue!'

'Keystone Cops!'
'No Trust in Local Police!'

The headlines screamed negativity, highlighting the failure of the police to arrest the Aston Strangler.

It didn't seem fair; every single officer involved in the investigation had worked tirelessly, following lead after lead, but it was a heavy burden on their shoulders: to arrest the right man before he struck again.

Morale was at an all-time low and this was not helped by sensational headlines, which only served to increase tension out on the streets. The escalating tension was understandable; the recent attack had raised many questions.

Had the man struck again? In broad daylight? In the local park where children played, where they cut through on their way to and from the local schools, where people walked their dogs, where they took a short cut to catch a bus into the city centre, or to get to the local shopping centre?

Within hours of the failed attack extra uniformed police officers were brought in to patrol the area, in a bid to reassure local residents. However, there was still a growing sense of unease and this had created an atmosphere of unrest in the neighbourhood especially after the announcement that the man arrested following Melissa Campbell's murder had been released without charge, resulting in appeals by both local councillors and the area's most senior police officer for everyone to remain calm.

* * *

Three days after the incident in the park, Claire Maynard sat down with a police sketch artist and described the man who had attacked her – tall, slim, white, thick glasses, unshaven and the coldest, most piercing blue eyes that she had ever seen. Unnaturally blue, with no light behind them.

It was a difficult process but, once they were finished, she stared at the completed drawing, tears streaming down her face as she looked at the eyes of the man who had attacked her. Those piercing blue eyes stared back at her and a shiver ran down her spine..

Claire felt sick.

Although it was only a sketch of the man, those eyes were so cold, so calculating, and still haunted her nightmares. She could only hope now that someone would come forward and identify him.

Within hours of the sketch being completed, the image was released to every news outlet reporting on the story. It flooded social media, trending on both Facebook and Twitter, and posters, along with a detailed description of the man, started appearing in shop windows across the city. Someone, somewhere, had to know who this man was and it was only a matter of time now before he was apprehended.

* * *

The moment he first set eyes on the sketch he felt as though he was going to have a heart attack, right there and then. His first fear, when Alison walked into the kitchen that afternoon, a copy of the *Birmingham Advertiser* in her hand, was that she would recognise his face staring back at her once she had chance to study it properly, without Emily distracting her.

As soon as he saw it he spotted the resemblance and his heart was in his mouth. Even if Alison didn't notice, what if someone else did? He was on tenterhooks as his wife read the report and was surprised that she didn't connect him with the image of the man on the front of the paper.

The coloured contact lenses had been a smart move. He had first come across the idea after watching a TV programme on American murder suspects and their crimes early last year, and had taken to wearing them, along with the glasses, whenever he went out at night. It had obviously worked, as the different eye colour had changed his appearance somewhat. The picture showed a scruffy, unshaven face, thinner than his, wearing the reading glasses he had bought from the pound shop.

There was still a slight concern in the back of his mind that someone he knew, maybe one of his colleagues, would recognise him, but, if Alison hadn't managed to identify him from the sketch, the chances anyone else would were looking slim.

The colour of the car was also a stroke of luck, as far as he was concerned. That they had got it so wrong proved that he was invincible, that the police had no hope of apprehending him. OK, so he had had a setback when the girl managed to fight him off, but that wasn't going to stop him. He would just make sure he was better prepared next time. For now, though, he would settle for sending another letter to both the newspaper and radio station.

Let them know how lucky that woman was.

How the next one wouldn't be so lucky.

He smiled to himself as he pictured the contents of the letter in his mind.

Events in the park had scared him but he knew he wasn't done yet, not by a long shot, and taunting the police, mocking their inability to catch him, well, that was almost as exciting as planning his next victim.

Chapter Forty-Eight

It had now been two weeks since he had persuaded his wife to give their marriage another chance and since then, everything had settled down at home. Alison was trying her best to make a go of things. She was watching what she ate, had been more attentive to his needs, especially in the bedroom, doing whatever he wanted to keep him happy, to make their marriage work.

He had gone along with it as well, playing the doting father, the loving husband, helping out more around the house, taking more care of Emily, even going to one of the ante-natal visits with his wife.

The atmosphere in the house was much calmer, *he* was much calmer, managing to keep his temper in check, but he knew it wouldn't last. She still irritated the hell out of him but he hadn't expected things to blow up the way they did. He had been so angry last night and he knew he had hurt her badly this time.

After reversing his car out of the garage, he stopped briefly to look up at their bedroom window and wondered if Alison was awake yet. He was beginning to regret not going into the bedroom to speak to her, to see if she was ok.

It had all started when he first heard the news that a homeless man had been set upon; kicked and beaten to death in Aston Park. He wasn't paying that much attention to begin with, but when the newscaster stated that the police believed this attack had occurred because of mistaken identity – the man's attackers thought it was him – he had immediately focused on the TV, rewinding to play it back from the beginning. As he'd listened to the report, the police officer describing it as a frenzied and sustained attack, he felt the blood drain from his face and was momentarily stunned at what he heard.

What if he had been in the area, looking for another victim?

What if they had rounded on him?

Attacked him?

He knew, then, that he would have to change location – it was now too risky over in Aston, which had annoyed him. He knew Aston. Knew the back roads like, well, the back of his hand.

It wasn't the only thing that had annoyed him though, as he listened to the news.

It was also reported that West Midlands Police had taken the decision to call in outside help, asking West Mercia Police force to liaise with them on the investigation. The extra manpower had unnerved him – and angered him – as it meant that it would be even harder to carry out his next attack, leaving him feeling frustrated about the whole situation.

He knew he shouldn't have taken it out on Alison though, and while she only had herself to blame, winding him up the way she had, he knew he would have some serious making up to do later.

Although Alison had been awake for a while now, she didn't dare move while she could still hear her husband in the house. At some point, he had come up the stairs and stood at their bedroom door – not saying anything, just standing there. It had unnerved her and although Alison had her face turned away from him, she could feel his eyes boring into her. Pretending to be asleep, Alison had silently willed him to go back downstairs.

It wasn't until she heard his car reversing out of the garage and driving off that Alison could force herself to get up. However, as soon as she tried to stand, a sharp pain tore across her lower abdomen where her husband had used her as a punching bag, causing her to fall back on the bed. Looking down at her stomach, she could see several angry-looking purple, red and blue contusions intermingled with the greens and yellows of previous bruising. Gingerly, she placed her hands over the slight bump which was beginning to take shape and began to sob – deep, gut-wrenching sobs.

For the life of her, she couldn't understand what had gone wrong. Everything had been so peaceful lately and they were becoming a proper family again. Then, yesterday afternoon, for some unknown reason, her husband's mood had switched. Once again, she had found herself tiptoeing around him, hoping that he would calm down again and they could go back to playing happy families again.

Despite his mood, the rest of the day had passed without incident and Alison had felt relieved that he had not started an argument when she settled Emily down and was ready for bed herself. Her last thought, as she began drifting off to sleep, was that her husband was changing at last.

She should have known better.

With her pregnancy draining her of energy, Alison quickly fell asleep, almost as soon as her head had hit the pillow. She had no recollection of her husband getting into bed but he was lying next to her when she woke up after hearing her daughter through the baby monitor.

More often than not, lately, Emily slept through the night, but for some reason last night she had been fretful and wasn't settling back down again. After a couple of minutes of crying, Alison went to get up to see to her daughter but her husband immediately flew into a rage, angry that she would wake up as soon as she heard Emily but had ignored him when he came to bed. He was so angry that he had refused to let Alison leave the room, despite the fact that their daughter was crying.

She had tried reasoning with him but to no avail. He threw the baby monitor against the wall, smashing it, ranting about how he had had enough of the child's wretched snivelling before turning on her, criticising her; her weight, her appearance, how much she disgusted him. It was as if the last two weeks had meant nothing as the bile spewed bitterly from his mouth, and all the while she could hear Emily crying.

Desperate to go to her daughter, Alison stood up to her husband, but his rage then turned to violence. After a few minutes Emily had cried herself back to sleep but, for the next hour, Alison suffered both physical and emotional abuse at the hands of her husband. Eventually, he had stormed off downstairs, leaving Alison in a heap on the bedroom floor.

She didn't see him again for the rest of the night and, apart from the brief period where he stood in the doorway earlier, he had left her alone. She had been absolutely terrified of him last night. The look in his eyes as he laid in to her had scared her beyond belief, and she was relieved that he had left the house without any further confrontation.

With fresh tears beginning to spill down her face, Alison carefully lifted herself up off the bed again, put on her gown and slowly made her way to her daughter's room. As soon as she saw Emily, happily playing in her cot with her favourite bear, more tears began to fall. Alison had felt so guilty that her daughter had cried herself to sleep last night, that she had not been able to comfort her, and yet she didn't seem to be affected by it in any way.

Even so, Alison had made up her mind: there was no way she could stay any longer; he wasn't going to change, no matter how much he promised her that he would. Her parents had told her to keep hold of the money they had forwarded to her account when she was going to leave last time, just in case she ever needed it, so she knew she had more than enough to catch the train down to Hayle.

It would be a fresh start: Alison, Emily and the new baby, away from her husband's violent episodes. She just needed to pull everything together before he returned.

Rush hour traffic was frustrating!

He had hit the Bristol Road now and traffic into the city was crawling along at snail's pace, making him regret offering to cover for a colleague at work. With little else to do other than sit and wait it out, his mind kept going back over last night's events. For days he had tried so hard not to lose his temper, but, finding out about that man who had been killed and then his wife pretty much ignoring him for the rest of the day, well, it had set him off.

God! He hated that woman so much.

It was all her fault.

If she had just spent the evening with him instead of going to bed early, he wouldn't have got so angry with her. It didn't matter that she had been making more of an effort lately, she had ignored him last night. Didn't even acknowledge him when he got into bed and yet, as soon as Emily needed her she was awake, getting up to take care of the snivelling brat. It wasn't right and he'd flipped, unable to control the rage that had been bubbling up inside him. It was only the look of sheer terror in her eyes as he laid in to her that had stopped him from carrying on, and he had stormed down the stairs, falling asleep on the sofa until his alarm went off, waking him with a start.

Almost immediately, the reason *why* he had slept on the sofa had come flooding back and he'd rushed up the stairs to check on his wife. The relief he felt when he saw her asleep in their bed was immeasurable; she hadn't left him, hadn't called the police to report what he had done and, although he knew that it would take more than just a few tears to get her to forgive him this time, he was convinced he could smooth things over.

The sudden beep of a horn interrupted his thoughts and he realised that traffic was beginning to move freely again. He lifted his hand to the rear window by way of apology, turned up the radio and made his way in to work.

Chapter Forty-Nine

Having been caught up in traffic thanks to an accident in the Queensway tunnel, Jim arrived at Aston Lane station slightly later than he had planned. Despite this, he couldn't help but whistle to himself as he walked into the office and there was a definite spring in his step, prompting colleagues to ask what it was that he was so happy about.

Ignoring the ribbing that followed, Jim busied himself with organising the day's tasks.

His ritual remained the same – coffee, whiteboard, desk.

Every now and then, he would glance up at the door, waiting for someone to make an appearance. He didn't have to wait long before Angie walked through the office door. As she did, her eyes met with his for a brief moment, before she also made her way to the percolator.

Angie stifled a yawn with her hand and a smile played at the corner of her mouth as she thought about their evening. She blushed. She had stayed over at Jim's house again last night, and neither of them had got much sleep.

Quickly looking round at her colleagues, Angie was relieved to see that they were all too busy with the investigation to spot her blushes. She still wasn't ready to let everyone know about their relationship, preferring to keep everything on a professional level at work. Thankfully, no one had noticed that she was still wearing the same clothes that she'd worn yesterday, and the furtive glances she and Jim were stealing had gone undetected.

With Emily sitting contently on her bed, distracted by her favourite TV show, Alison began taking clothes from their drawers. She knew she wouldn't be able to take everything with her, but she could figure all that out later. Even so, it was surprising just how much she would need to pack for her daughter and the bag she had originally planned to take with them wasn't going to be large enough after all. It didn't matter, though; they had a black holdall somewhere and she would just use that.

Thinking that it was on top of the wardrobe, Alison reached up to check, but as she did so a sharp pain ripped through her stomach, resulting in a sudden urge to vomit. She rushed to the bathroom, bent over the toilet bowl and retched until there was nothing more to bring up. She knew breakfast had been a mistake and, although she had only eaten a bit of toast, more for the baby's sake than anything, she regretted it. The morning sickness was a lot worse with this pregnancy but, at that moment, she wasn't sure if it was morning sickness or fear that had brought on this bout of vomiting.

Whatever it was, she didn't have time to start feeling sorry for herself. She needed to find the holdall so she could pack their stuff and get out of there before her husband returned home from work. It was only after she had turned the bedroom upside down that Alison remembered where it was. Her husband had used it to take some items to the charity shop a while ago now and had never brought it back into the house afterwards, preferring to leave it in the garage instead. She had no idea why and had no reason to question it; it wasn't as if she'd needed the holdall – well, until today.

Alison carefully picked Emily up off the bed, aware of the pain still grumbling across her abdomen, carried her down the stairs and sat her in the baby walker before picking up the internal door key for the garage.

'You wait there,' she cooed, 'while Mummy goes to get something. We're going on an adventure. Just me and you.'

Emily smiled at this.

Alison had no idea if she understood what was going on but Emily was happy and that was all that mattered.

Unlocking the door, Alison felt apprehensive. She knew it was illogical but her husband had always insisted that she never come into the garage. He had created some drama about this being the only place in the whole house that was totally his and she had kept away, not having any reason to go in there anyway.

As she turned on the light, it struck Alison just how daft it was that her husband wanted the garage all for himself when there was nothing special about it anyway. She looked around for the holdall and was dismayed when she couldn't find it. She was about to go back in the house when she saw something poking out of the top of one of the plastic storage boxes on the shelf above the work station. She carefully took the box down and retrieved the bag, happy that she could now get out of there.

Alison didn't open the holdall in the garage. Instead she headed back into the kitchen and placed it on the table. She was on a mission now. Handing Emily her sippy cup, Alison went back upstairs to collect the clothes she had left on the bed, a few toys, some toiletries and a few other bits and pieces. It took a couple of trips but she soon had everything they would need piled on the kitchen table.

It was a relief, knowing that she would soon be on her way to her parents', away from this house, away from her husband and everything he had put her through. All she had to do was pack their things then phone for the taxi.

Once she did open the holdall, though, Alison was surprised to find it wasn't empty. Not only that, but the contents surprised her. She had suspected that her husband had been cheating on her for a while now, but what was women's underwear doing in the bag? All sorts of things started going through her mind. Did he have a fetish? Was he wearing them?

It didn't matter now.

She tipped the bag upside down, deciding she would leave the items on the table. As they came out, though, something else also fell onto the table. Several newspaper cuttings held together with a rubber band now lay on top of the pile of underwear. Alison raised her hand to her mouth.

She immediately recognised the photo on the top cutting. A young girl in a yellow bridesmaid's dress.

What were these in the bag for?

Why had he saved them?

With trembling hands, she removed the elastic band and looked at each cutting. All four girls were there, as well as press reports of the girl who was attacked, and then there was the police sketch.

It didn't make sense.

Searching the rest of the bag Alison found several other items, but it was a small, round, plastic case that caught her eye. She opened it and looked in disbelief at the contents: piercing blue contact lenses. The colour drained from her face and Alison thought she was going to be sick again. She needed to sit down. She couldn't believe what she had found.

Alison stared at the sketch properly for the first time.

It couldn't be, could it?

Her husband didn't wear glasses but, take them away, change the eye colour and then, well

'*Oh my God!*'

She suddenly felt light-headed and found herself gripping the corner of the table, trying to keep her composure. The tears were flowing now, though. She couldn't believe what was lying on the table in front of her. Couldn't stop the thoughts swirling round in her head that she had been living with the man who had killed those girls.

'*Oh my God!*' she muttered, again, the bile rising at the back of her throat. There was something else.

Something she hadn't realised before.

Looking at the pictures of the four women, it suddenly struck Alison just how alike they were, how much they resembled her, with their long blonde hair and petite frames, albeit when she had first met her husband, before the weight gain, the tiredness, before becoming a mother!

With the tears still rolling down her face, there was only one thing to do.

Alison quickly put the contents of the bag back in the holdall, securing the newspaper clippings with the same elastic band she had just removed. Even touching them made her feel sick to her stomach but she couldn't leave them on the table now. She phoned for a taxi, put Emily's coat on, grabbed a jacket for herself then left the house. Emily was getting heavy and she was still hurting from last night but she didn't have time to struggle with a pushchair.

Chapter Fifty

Following the homeless man's death, the amount of pressure that the Murder Investigation Team was under had increased significantly. They were facing criticism from all sides – the press, the public, community leaders, their own superiors and, although it was understandable, the pressure was unfairly ascribed as far as Jim was concerned, especially since stranger abduction and murder was one of the hardest crimes to solve, and in this case there was nothing to link the victims to the perpetrator other than time and place.

Jim knew how much effort his colleagues had put into the investigation – the hours spent following each lead, watching every bit of CCTV footage, following up on door-to-door enquiries, taking statements, and yet it was all to no avail; the investigation had stalled.

Desperate to bring about an end to this investigation before they had another victim on their hands, the powers that be had bowed to that pressure and reached out to neighbouring West Mercia police force, hoping that fresh eyes would succeed where Aston MIT had so far failed. The decision was not a popular one and, as Jim walked into the briefing room with Inspector Goulding on that Monday morning, the atmosphere was somewhat tense.

It didn't get any easier once the briefing began.

Taking his place at the front of the room, Inspector Goulding announced that officers from both forces would be split into five sub-teams, so that they could begin sifting through the mountain of evidence relating to each of the murder victims and the attempted abduction. Possible witnesses would need to be re-interviewed. CCTV would need to be viewed all over again, only this time with an officer from West Mercia, just in case something had been missed the first time.

Morale had never been so low. However, Inspector Goulding pressed on, choosing to ignore the collective groans that had rippled around the room as he allocated the day's tasks. Jim and Angie were both assigned to the attempted abduction in Philips Street park.

Snatching a discreet look at his colleague, Jim gave her a brief smile, which Angie quickly returned. She was pleased that they would be working together; they had discussed trying out a new restaurant at lunchtime and this would make it easier to get away for a while, to enjoy each other's company, away from the pressures of work.

She stood opposite the police station.

Trying to balance Emily in one arm and the holdall in the other, Alison was aware that the pain across her abdomen was steadily increasing. She knew she had to go inside, tell them what she had found, but she still couldn't quite believe it. All this time she had thought her husband was cheating on her, had blamed herself for not being able to lose her pregnancy weight, for being so tired in the year since Emily had been born, for not wanting to have sex with her husband like they used to. She had been feeling guilty all this time, and yet he must have been going out and killing these women then coming home to her. Why else would he have the underwear? The newspaper cuttings?

How could she walk into the police station and tell them that her husband was a murderer?

She couldn't even believe it herself.

He wasn't that man.

When they had first met, everything had been so wonderful and she was blissfully happy. Her husband was charming, funny, handsome and she was slim, had a perfectly toned body and naturally blonde hair, which her husband loved. She always used to tie it up but her husband would insist she leave it down, would run his fingers through it, telling her how beautiful she looked.

After Emily was born she didn't even have time to wash it some days, so it was easier to tie it up again. Her once slim body had long gone and now she had a stomach lined with stretch marks, no longer as taught as it had once been, but she had Emily now and Emily was far more important to worry about than her figure, even though she knew it repulsed her husband.

Aware that Emily was starting to become restless and fidgety, Alison knew they would have to make their way across the road and go into the police station. Trying to readjust her daughter in her arm, a searing pain spread across her stomach, causing Alison to drop the bag. She was sweating now, with beads of perspiration across her forehead and she felt as though she was going to be sick.

'Are you OK, Miss?' asked a young policewoman.

Alison hadn't noticed the woman walking over to her, but she was thankful that she had. She didn't feel well at all; the morning sickness, the pain in her stomach, it had been getting steadily worse. She had also started to feel light-headed.

'Let me hold the little one, get you some help,' the officer suggested.

She could hear voices but they were swimming round in her head; distant and muffled. Opening her eyes, everything around her was a blur. It felt safer when she was wrapped in a cloak of darkness and she desperately wanted to close them again. She knew she wasn't alone though; knew someone was speaking to her, even if it did sound like a jumble of words. Her head was beginning to hurt now as well and instinctively, she raised her hand to touch the source of the pain.

Ouch!

Suddenly everything was becoming clearer.

She must have fainted.

Hit her head.

She had been holding Emily.

Where was she?

That was when the panic set in and Alison desperately tried to get up. Someone kneeling beside her – a policeman, judging by the uniform – thought better of it, though.

'Lie still,' he had suggested. 'You've taken quite a knock to the head.'

She couldn't lie still though. Struggling to get to her feet, she called Emily's name. She could feel the tears brimming now, threatening to roll down her cheeks.

'Emily,' she cried again.

'Is that your daughter? It's OK, she's safe. We've taken her inside,' he said soothingly.

Relief washed over her and for a brief second, Alison felt herself relax but then the pain was building in her abdomen again and she suddenly felt the urge to vomit. Turning her head to the side she managed to throw up on the pavement, retching until there was nothing more to bring up.

'We've called an ambulance,' the officer continued. 'See if we can get you sorted out. Is there anyone we can ring to come and take care of your daughter?'

'No!' she almost screamed, as she started to cry.

The pain in her abdomen was becoming more intense and she instinctively placed her arm across her stomach.

'The baby, I … I'm pregnant.'

'That explains it.' He smiled sympathetically. 'My wife was the same when she was carrying our son. Let's get you and the baby checked out. Make sure everything's OK.'

Alison couldn't think about that now though. Struggling to her feet, despite the officer suggesting she lie still until the ambulance arrived, Alison insisted that she needed to get Emily, needed to talk to someone. Pointing to the bag, she mumbled incoherently as she tried to explain what she had found.

Suddenly, pain ripped through her abdomen, a level of pain Alison had never experienced before. Her last thoughts before losing consciousness were of her baby and the very real fear that she was about to miscarry.

The incident room was buzzing with activity.

Officers on Jim's sub-team were reading through the witness statements taken from Claire Maynard and Mohammed Ibrahim. A question was raised over the colour of the car seen leaving the scene immediately after the woman was attacked.

Although Mr Ibrahim had stated that the car was black, this couldn't be substantiated by the victim who could only remember a dark coloured car. What if Mr Ibrahim had been mistaken?

Now that a seed of doubt had been planted, Jim knew it was a possibility.

Had they wasted precious man hours trying to locate the wrong car?

It was agreed that both witnesses would be re-interviewed as soon as possible, with Jim and Angie going to see Mohammed Ibrahim to determine just how sure he was about what he had seen that day.

Jim called the number they had for their witness, hoping he would be available that morning. As luck would have it, he was off work and was happy for the officers to call round.

Replacing the receiver, Jim was suddenly feeling more optimistic. Although it hadn't been a popular decision, perhaps everything would start to come together now that West Mercia were on board.

However, within seconds of his call to Mr Ibrahim the phone rang and, as Jim listened to the voice on the other end of the line, his heart sank. The radio station had received another letter, the contents of which were similar to those they had already received: mocking the police, blaming them for his actions, telling them he wasn't done yet. The implications of the letter were clear – they would soon have another victim unless they could positively identify their man.

After taking the call, it was agreed that Jim and Angie would also go and collect the letter, once they had concluded their visit with Mr Ibrahim. If the murderer had followed the same pattern of behaviour, the chances were that the *Birmingham Advertiser* would also be calling in to inform them that they had received one as well. Jim was certainly expecting the call.

The phone rang a second time as Jim and Angie were getting ready to leave the office. Instead of the *Advertiser*, however, it was from another police officer, based over in Rubery. Jim started to feel excited as the officer related some events from that morning and information regarding a holdall.

Was this it?

Their big break in the case?

He would need to inform his inspector, however, looking over towards his office, Jim saw that it was empty. Asking his colleagues if they knew where he was drew a blank so at that point, Jim suggested to Angie that she should go and interview Mr Ibrahim and pick up the letter herself, while he headed over to Rubery to find out the significance of the holdall that had been found.

Once he arrived at the station, Jim was shown though to an office where the bag had been placed. As he searched through the contents, Jim noted several newspaper clippings reporting each murder, the foiled attack, and the sketch of the man they were hunting, all neatly folded and secured with a rubber band.

Nine pairs of knickers were also contained within the bag.

They knew that all four women were found without them. The three women who had been raped had also reported that their knickers had been taken but that only accounted for seven pairs; they had nine. Were there more victims out there who had not been discovered? Women who had been raped – or worse? They had no way of knowing, but the feeling that they would soon find another body was not a pleasant one, and filled Jim with dread.

He knew he couldn't think about that right now, though, so Jim put it out of his mind and continued with his search of the bag. On opening the small white plastic case he was surprised to discover that it contained a pair of blue contact lenses.

Had the man changed his eye colour?

Suddenly, he recalled something the last victim had said as she made her statement.

'Unnaturally blue, with no light behind them.'

It made sense now and Jim knew that they were finally on to something.

What he didn't know was whether the woman had found the bag or if she knew who it belonged to, but it was imperative that they spoke to her to find out what she knew. Unfortunately, the woman had been taken to the Queen Elizabeth Hospital, having collapsed with what they suspected was a miscarriage.

Not wanting to waste any more time, Jim headed for the QE's Accident & Emergency Department where he found the woman sitting up in a cubicle. She was attached to a drip and did not look at all well, but she said she felt OK to talk.

'Have you arrested him yet?' she asked after Jim had sat down.

'Arrested him? Who?' Jim looked puzzled.

'My husband,' she said simply, before starting to sob.

The policewoman on the other side of the bed offered her some tissues and Jim waited a few moments before continuing.

'Why don't we start with your name?' he asked, gently.

'It's Alison,' she replied. 'Alison Carter.'

'And your husband?' he asked urgently, as everything began falling into place.

'Eddie. Eddie Carter. He's a radio talk show host over at …'

'Was that your husband's bag?'

'I found it … in the garage.'

The colour drained from Jim's face as he remembered that Angie was going to call in at the radio station after she had finished talking to Mr Ibrahim, to pick up the letter.

Chapter Fifty-One

Eddie Carter had just finished a two-hour show and it had gone well. It was nothing like he was used to, it was a more relaxed broadcast, but he had enjoyed it. The day was turning out better than he had expected. Getting to the station around seven thirty this morning, he had just time to go through his mail before going on air. Finding yet another letter he had insisted that his assistant report it to the police while he went and did the show.

Smiling to himself, he thought about how stupid they all were, not realising that he had been posting them, making sure he opened the envelopes in front of others, acting all shocked and concerned. They had no idea how much that had made him laugh.

He tried to call Alison on his mobile to tell her he would be home around twelve thirty.

No answer.

That was strange. Why wasn't she answering?

After trying a couple more times he could feel himself getting angry again; he wondered where she was. It wasn't like Alison not to answer her phone. She knew better than that.

Slamming the door of his office shut, he went and sat at his desk, closed his eyes and began massaging his temples with his fingertips, trying to calm himself down before any of his colleagues noticed something was wrong. It wasn't easy – his mind kept drifting back to his wife and where she might be.

The shrill of the phone soon interrupted his thoughts. He picked it up on the fourth ring, and listened as the woman on the reception desk informed him that a police officer was there to see him.

Immediately he wondered if Alison had phoned them and that was why she hadn't answered him. Panic started to take over, and then the receptionist informed him the officer was there to pick up a letter. Calming down again, he asked the receptionist to send the officer up and he would meet him at the lift. Her reply pleased him. It was a female officer, Detective Constable Angela Watkins. He liked Angela Watkins, she reminded him of his wife when they were first married.

As he replaced the receiver, a plan had started to formulate. *He couldn't, could he?*

Eddie's heart rate started to increase the more he thought about it and a slow smile spread across his face. He knew it was reckless but he couldn't help himself.

As Angie came out of the lift, Eddie Carter was there to greet her as promised. She smiled at him, shaking his outstretched hand.

'Good to see you again,' he said politely.

Angie liked Eddie. He was such a charismatic man and certainly knew how to make people feel at ease. He also had a certain boyish charm about him and his wife was one lucky woman. Not that she was looking, of course. Her relationship with Jim was progressing nicely and he had met her parents last Sunday for the first time, which had been a huge success.

Aware that she still had hold of his hand, Angie blushed slightly and removed it.

'Good to see you, too,' she replied. 'I've come to pick up the letter you received this morning.'

'Yes, of course,' he said. 'It's perfect timing actually. I was just about to make my way to the police station with it so we need to go down into the car park. I've left it in my car.'

'Oh OK. I'll follow you then.'

Stepping back into the lift, Angie had planned on giving Jim a quick call to let him know she was nearly finished at the radio station but then she found herself asking about the late night show Eddie hosted and the call was all but forgotten for a while.

Jim couldn't help but worry that Angie might be in danger.

Realising how irrational his thoughts were, he tried dismissing them. There were enough people at the radio station that she wouldn't be at risk. Besides, Eddie had no idea that his wife had come forward so would most likely carry on with the pretence that he had received this latest letter. All the same, Jim needed to let her know. He quickly dialled her number but it went straight to voicemail.

After trying another couple of times, he started to panic, and phoned his inspector to tell him what he knew and his concerns for Angie. They needed to go and pick Eddie Carter up now. He was too far away himself but it wouldn't take a patrol car long – they were pretty much just round the corner from the radio station.

At least they now knew who was responsible – but how had he not realised? He could kick himself. He had worked on cases before where the guilty party had somehow got themselves involved in the investigation, whether that was by giving interviews to the press or hanging around at a crime scene. Jim couldn't believe he had missed it, but there had seemed nothing odd about the bloke. He appeared quite genuine and yet had managed to deceive them all.

Heading for his car, he just hoped that Angie was OK.

'Sir,' a voice called behind him. It was the young policewoman who had been sitting in the cubicle with Alison Carter. 'I'm sorry, I overheard your phone call and radioed my sergeant. He suggested that I drive you in the squad car.'

Jim was relieved at this. It would take at least twenty minutes to get from the hospital to the radio station if he was driving; he would have to stick within the speed limit whereas this officer could navigate the traffic quicker with blue lights flashing.

However reckless it was, the temptation was overwhelming and Eddie couldn't stop thinking about all the ways he could pull it off.

It seemed far too easy.

Could he actually go through with it though?

They had engaged in small-talk in the lift. Eddie wasn't paying much attention though. All he could think about was how much the detective reminded him of Alison.

'With her hair down, it was probably a similar length as well; would probably look better too. He could never understand why they would let it grow and then wear it tied up. He had been tempted to reach over and pull the bobble out but then that might have spooked her a bit and so he had resisted.'

Once they reached the car park, the detective told him that she was going to make a quick phone call while he retrieved the letter. It would be a waste of time – he knew that. The car park was situated under the building so trying to get a signal was nigh on impossible. Still, it would give him a bit of time to sort out what he needed.

'Not wanting to alert the woman to anything untoward, he explained that she might have a problem with it and hoped she wouldn't insist on going back upstairs.'

'You're right,' she had confirmed after trying a couple of times. Her focus was back on the letter again then and they started making their way towards Eddie's car, which was situated on the far side of the car park.

It only took a couple of minutes before they had reached the car but in that short time, Eddie only had one thing on his mind and the more he thought about it, the stronger the urge was becoming.

Glancing around him, he wanted to make sure there was no one else down there. No one who would see what he was about to do.

Wanting to put the detective at ease, he smiled at her as he opened the car door and began looking through the glove box.

'I'm sure I put it in here earlier,' he told her. 'No, hold on, I think I put it in the boot.'

She was preoccupied with her phone again as he walked round to the boot of his car, no doubt trying to get a signal. She had even turned her back on him while she waited.

This was too easy.

Keeping an eye on the detective, Eddie carefully took out a length of rope from the back of his car and within a second he had tightened it around the unsuspecting woman's throat. Angie dropped her phone as she tried to get the man off her.

Dropping her phone, the detective tried pulling at the rope which was now constricting her breathing; tried to get herself free from the restraint around her neck but it was no good, Eddie had no plans on letting go, not now. She would be able to identify him and he couldn't have that.

As she stopped struggling, Eddie gripped the rope one last time, wanting to make sure she was dead, and then placed her in the boot of his car. He threw a blanket over her to hide her from view. He would hide her properly later. Somewhere they wouldn't be able to find her, not for a while at least. He was already starting to think about the letters he would send to himself, taunting the police, knowing they would be desperate to find their colleague. Oh, yes, this would be fun.

Eddie wiped the sweat off his forehead, picked up the woman's phone and threw it in his car, which he locked before heading back upstairs. He wasn't expecting the police officers to be there as he stepped out of the lift. Wasn't expecting them to arrest him and couldn't understand how they had found out, but one officer definitely said he was being arrested for murder. Before he knew it he was in handcuffs, and people he knew, work colleagues, had all stopped what they were doing, watching what was unfolding before them.

He knew it was over. Knew they would find that policewoman in the boot of his car. As they headed back to the lift he relaxed and started to laugh. The game had switched now but he was still going to play it his way.

Chapter Fifty-Two

As they arrived at BTH Radio, Jim saw the ambulance ahead of him, blue lights flashing, and knew that something was wrong. Throughout the journey he had been trying to contact Angie but her mobile continued to go straight to voicemail. He could see Angie's car just a short distance ahead of the ambulance, so he knew she was still there.

After entering the building he was directed to the underground car park reserved for staff members. The mood was solemn as he stepped out of the lift and all he could think about was locating Angie. He knew that something was very, very wrong, though, and a growing uneasiness washed over him especially when he spotted a female police officer openly crying. Jim recognised her as one of Angie's friends.

'What's happened?' he asked, a concerned edge to his voice.

'Angie,' was all she could say before breaking down, and then he knew.

He made his way over to where a crowd of police officers and paramedics stood, reached the open boot of the car and saw her lying there. The emotions he felt were so raw that he was unable to hide them. He had sent Angie to pick up the letter, wanting to save time so that they could go and have lunch together later, and now …

Everything became a blur after that. He was aware that his inspector had arrived. Vaguely noticed them remove her body from the trunk, place it in a body bag, but after that – he wasn't even sure who had taken him back to the police station, he was in such a state of shock. As much as Jim and Angie had thought they were keeping their relationship a secret, their colleagues in the

MIT had already guessed and they made sure Jim was supported, especially at the point when he broke down, unable to contain his grief any longer.

They wouldn't let him interview Eddie Carter. That job was handled by Inspector Goulding. Not that it did any good as the man refused to speak at all during interview. Jim would have liked five minutes alone with him. He had never hated anyone as much as he hated that man right now.

Then there were her parents. Who would tell them?

One of his colleagues reassured Jim that it had been taken care of; he then offered to take him home. The day had not turned out the way he had planned it. They had caught their killer but at what cost? The guilt was something Jim would live with for a long time.

Chapter Fifty-Three

He felt no remorse. Didn't feel much of anything really. His only regret was that he had finally been caught.

Following his arrest, Eddie Carter was taken to Steelhouse Lane police station in the centre of Birmingham, where he was held in one of the cells in the custody suite. They couldn't hold him at Aston Lane, as feelings were understandably running high amongst Angie's colleagues. Despite what he had done, Eddie's health and safety was paramount and emotions could not get in the way of that.

He didn't make it easy though.

Refusing to speak to the custody officer, Eddie wouldn't confirm his name or address. He ignored requests to hand over his clothes for forensic evidence, leaving officers with no choice but to remove them by force. He didn't fight them, just made it as difficult as possible to achieve by twisting and turning in awkward positions as they attempted to take them off him. Regulation grey sweatpants and top were left on the bed in the cell but Eddie wouldn't put them on. He just sat on the hard mattress staring straight ahead at the tiled wall of his cell, his face giving no indication of his emotions.

Any offers of food or drink were met with a stony silence.

Twice, during Eddie's time in the cells, Inspector Goulding had wanted to interview him but he would not go along to the interview room and still refused to speak, refused to offer any explanation or confess to his crimes. Not that it mattered anyway, as the following morning, draped only in a blanket since he was still in a state of undress, he was brought from his cell to face the custody sergeant who then charged him with five counts of murder, one attempted murder and three counts of sexual assault.

Despite his inner turmoil, Eddie didn't show any outward emotion as the charges were read out to him, he just stared past the officer at some unseen point on the wall.

Back in the cell, though, Eddie's anxiety was rising as the enormity of what he was facing hit him. Sitting on the bed, he brought his knees up to his chest, wrapped his arms around them, then slowly but methodically, began rocking back and forth in a slow monotonous motion.

Concerned by the behaviour Eddie had been displaying, the custody officer arranged for a medical assessment to be carried out. If Eddie Carter was going to rely on a defence of diminished responsibilities, he was starting to go about it the right way.

Despite refusing to speak with the appointed doctor, it was determined that he was competent enough to go before a judge and, later that same day, Eddie Carter, still wrapped in his coarse grey blanket, was taken from his cell down to the basement of the Victorian building, along an underground corridor and into the Magistrates' Court next door where he was remanded in custody until his trial at Crown Court. It only lasted a few minutes, after which Eddie was returned to his cell until transport was available to transfer him to Winson Green prison.

It wasn't a long drive to the prison, maybe twenty minutes or so, but it felt much longer. By now, Eddie was beginning to feel even more anxious than he had in the cell that morning. Not knowing what to expect once he arrived at the prison only served to heighten this feeling and, as he heard the heavy gates open then shut behind him, he began to feel physically sick. Beads of perspiration settled across his forehead, betraying his cold, controlled demeanour.

It took a while to be booked in to the system, not helped by Eddie's continual refusal to speak but, eventually, he had showered, was given fresh clothes – a claret t-shirt, grey sweat pants, socks and underwear – which he readily accepted without incident, before being shown to a cell on the induction wing.

As the door slammed shut behind him, Eddie could finally start to appreciate the enormity of his situation. He was angry at being locked up, blamed Alison for the fact that he was there, especially as that police officer had told him that she had given them the bag of underwear. She had told them what she had found in the garage. Feeling his anger rising, he wanted to lash out, scream at her, hating her for what she had done. She would have to live with this. It was all her fault.

It didn't matter anymore though.

He had a plan.

As he sat on the edge of the bed, he noticed a small hole in the t-shirt he had been given after his shower. He took it off and worked his finger into the hole to make it bigger, and then tore it into two pieces. He didn't have time to stop and think things through. Eddie tied the two ends together as tightly as he could, then tied one end of the shirt around his neck. He knelt on the floor and tied the other end around the top of the bed frame.

He could feel the tension in the fabric already.

He knew there was no other way out and, in a perverse way, this was his one final act of defiance, his final move in what had become a deadly game. Putting his hands in the pockets of his trousers, Eddie lunged himself forward, restricting the flow of oxygen to his brain. It didn't take long to lose consciousness. By the time the prison guards came to check on him and raised the alarm, it was too late.

Eddie Carter was dead.

Chapter Fifty-Four

Four weeks after Eddie Carter's death, Angie's funeral was held at her childhood church, St Thomas' in Stourbridge.

The mood was sombre on the morning of the funeral and this was reflected in the weather, as rain had been steadily falling since early morning. Despite the rain, hundreds of police officers followed the cortege as they slowly made their way through the streets of Stourbridge. Everyone wanted to pay their respects to a fellow police officer, killed in the line of duty.

As they neared the church, members of the public had lined the streets waiting to catch a glimpse of the hearse. Many bowed their heads as the cortege passed by. Despite not knowing Angie, some of those gathered openly cried, shocked at the officer's death and still trying to make sense of it all. Inside the church grounds there was a sea of flowers as more and more wreaths were delivered, such was the outpouring of grief over her death.

Six pall-bearers carried Angie's coffin, which had been draped with the force's crest, to the front of the church, where it was placed in front of a beautiful stained glass window. Either side of the coffin were two photographs of Angie. One in uniform, the other, a family photo; both showed her with that beaming smile that Jim would always remember. Taking his seat, he struggled to hold back tears as he thought about what could have been, how their relationship could have progressed, and now what they would never have.

The sun suddenly beamed through the stained glass, lighting up Angie's coffin, making the service even more poignant than it already was.

After the service, family, friends and immediate colleagues gathered at the graveside to say their final goodbyes.

Jim stood behind Angie's immediate family. Memories of the first time he had met her parents came flooding back. It had been a relaxed Sunday afternoon. They had enjoyed a pub lunch and Jim tried his best to make a good impression, which he thought he had achieved. Their relationship was beginning to move forward until fate had intervened. Still, although their time together was short, Jim would always cherish it.

He blamed himself. He knew it was irrational – no one could have expected things to turn out the way they did. Eddie Carter was so charming, so charismatic that many still could not believe he had been responsible. At least he was dead now, had saved the families the heartache of a trial.

'He was nothing but a coward,' Jim thought, bitterly.

As the coffin was lowered into the ground, Angie's mother let out an anguished cry, jolting Jim from his thoughts. Fearing she would collapse, her husband and son held on to her as the vicar spoke his final words.

'… as we commit her body to the ground. Earth to earth.'

The Reverend threw a handful of dust onto the coffin.

'Ashes to ashes.'

It started to rain again, which was only fitting as the rain mingled with tears.

'Dust to dust.'

With a heavy heart, Jim turned away and made his way back towards his car. He had decided not to attend the wake afterwards, even though he had been invited. Despite their blossoming relationship, Jim still didn't know Angie's family that well and felt it would be even more of an intrusion for them. Apart from that, he was still dealing with the guilt of that day and, although her parents had stressed they didn't blame him, he continued to blame himself, so he felt that it would be better if he left now.

He took one last look at the warm friendly face smiling back at him from the order of service and wiped a stray tear from the corner of his eye. He folded the service sheet and placed it in the inside pocket of his jacket. Angie had been a good police officer, a wonderful lover, but, above all, a great friend and he would never, ever forget her.

The End

A Note from Bloodhound Books

Thanks for reading A Deadly Game We hope you enjoyed it as much as we did. Please consider leaving a review on Amazon or Goodreads to help others find and enjoy this book too.

We make every effort to ensure that books are carefully edited and proofread, however occasionally mistakes do slip through. If you spot something, please do send details to info@bloodhoundbooks.com and we can amend it.

Bloodhound Books specialise in crime and thriller fiction. We regularly have special offers including free and discounted eBooks. To be the first to hear about these special offers, why not join our mailing list here? We won't send you more than two emails per month and we'll never pass your details on to anybody else.

Readers who enjoyed A Deadly Game will also enjoy

Undercurrent by JA Baker

Care To Die by Tana Collins.

Acknowledgements

I would like to say a heartfelt thank you to everyone at Bloodhound Books, first of all for taking a chance on an unknown author and secondly, for all the work done by everyone behind the scenes to make this book what it is. It is truly appreciated.

Lightning Source UK Ltd.
Milton Keynes UK
UKOW05f1529160617

303518UK00002B/54/P